KT-171-570

UNLIKELY STORIES, MOSTLY

Alasdair Gray was

and educated
and became
residing
and remaining
and intending
then on
became in
and again
and later
and later
again.
He still is
and resides
and intends
and hopes
and may
,but
is certain to
one day.

Nor may MacKay of Hamnavoe be excluded

The Good Lord Orr was wisest & kindest Scots medicines, for in the late Kings wars he provided milk & citrus juice from the public purse to children of this realm whose bones and brains had else been warped from lack of nourishment. He also persuaded some great ones to fill a common granary in time of glut to feed poor nations in time of dearth, but finding these great ones used the surplus grain to tighten chains of usury did declare the one hope of small lands lay in cultivating their own good.

Of Western Island poets a rabble jingle declares "There are 3 bards in Stafane hicht Ogawr tahhor at MacAgobain, Madann, MacAgobain Montgomerie. A few in dram: ackru Jack & Doris Thomson of Grain for his anatomy of the clerical eagle?

Among its intellectuals, after myself, who in my diurnal also field naturalist of Assynt the translation from every sensible cadence by language known the Grieves sufficiently honoured of Hugh who added by half Muir of Orkney I will mention the Prague Rabbi added by the excellent Helar of the Cursive Adder of Buchanan & McCay the Latin tragedy of Belli into English scots & translated scrip of the Babylonic librarian to remote worlds named Fast Eddie who hath trapesed the Roman Empire Master Morgan agnamed the Seur de Bergerac; Thomas the Rhymer of Eden street who died abed from the Roman grammar and blending its cadences with Saxon stars to create the voices of an entire city; Mistress Lochead the stones of Erse Mothewelle who hath verditue wounds Eros satires on the insects?

Master Hind agnamed dear Archie whose history of AB native commune intituled THE DEAR GREEN PLACE suffices for his fame; Master Kelman agnamed The Cool, whose novelles vindicate the matter of Britain as earnestly as if Plato, Petronius and Cervantes conspired to do so; Mistress Owens of the Leven agnamed Dear Agnes, whose desperately humorous wit makes great art of lives reduced by poverty & factory closure; and Graham of Greenock now resident in the Duchy of Cornwall whose hectic rays wax brighter with age.

that learned Doctor Philip the Jew whose nostrums hath worked fructiferous fusions in 3 British republics; Cecil the Taylor whose great Aristophanic talent found in Northumbria a friendlier home as did Mistress Shark in Rome.

Angus, who writ a verse telling more of those who grow our food than can be found in all the pastoral paradises indited since Zeus castrated Kronos.

also Aeneas MacNadair agnamed

Black

This Survey of The Scottish Realm

Made Ere I Began My Great Voiage

TO
THE
GOOD
ANGEL
MULLANE
AND
CHRISTOPHER
BOYCE

AND THEIR DAUGHTERS PETRA AND ANTONIA

They passed through the galleries, surveyed the vaults of marble, and examined the chest in which the body of the founder is supposed to have been deposited. They sat down in one of the most spacious chambers to rest for a whille, before they attempted to return.

"We have now," said Imlac, "gratified our minds with an exact view of the greatest work of man, except the wall of China.

"Of the wall it is very easy to assign the motive. It secured a wealthy and timorous nation from the incursions of barbarians. But for the pyramids no reason has ever been given adequate to the cost and labour of the work. It seems to have been erected only in compliance with that hunger of imagination which preys incessantly upon life, and must always be appeased by some employment. He who has built for use till use is supplied, must begin to build for vanity, and extend his plan to the utmost power of human performance that he may not be soon reduced to form another wish.

"I consider this mighty structure as a monument to the insufficiency of human enjoyments. A government whose power is unlimited, and whose treasures surmount all real and imaginary wants, is compelled to solace the satiety of dominion by seeing thousands labouring without end, and one stone, for no purpose, laid upon another."

From RASSELAS by Samuel Johnson

UNLIK

CANONGATE

ALASDAIR GRAY

STLY

ELY

CLASSICS 81

STORIES

MO ★

The Star in Collins Magazine for Boys and Girls 1951; *The Spread of Ian Nicols* in Ygorra, Glasgow students' charity magazine, 1956; *A Unique Case* in Cleg, a Glasgow art students' magazine, 1956; *The Cause of the Recent Changes* in Ygorra, 1957; the first half of *The Comedy of the White Dog* in Scottish International Magazine, 1969; the whole in Glasgow University Magazine, 1970; *The Crank that made the Revolution* in The Scottish Field, 1971; *Five Letters from an Eastern Empire* in Words Magazine, 1979; *The Origin of the Axletree* in Collins Scottish Short Stories, 1979. Slightly amended these and seven new tales were published by Canongate in 1983 and published as a Canongate Classic in 1997 with the addition of the recently written *Inches in a Column* and the older *Unique Case*. The series editor is Roderick Watson, its board, J.B. Pick, Cairns Craig and Dorothy McMillan. The publishers thank the Scottish Arts Council for its subsidy toward this series and title.

Set in Erhardt by
Hewertext Composition Services, Scotland
Printed in Finland by WSOY
International standard book number:
0 86241 737 6

TABLE OF CONTENTS

The Star	Page	1
The Spread Of Ian Nicol	Page	4
The Problem	Page	8
The Cause Of Some Recent Changes	Page	11
The Comedy Of The White Dog	Page	17
The Crank That Made The Revolution	Page	37
The Great Bear Cult	Page	44
The Start Of The Axletree	Page	67
Five Letters From An Eastern Empire	Page	85
Sir Thomas's Logopandocy	Page	134
M. Pollard's Prometheus	Page	193
The End Of The Axletree	Page	229
A Unique Case	Page	268
Inches In A Column	Page	271
A Likely Story Outside A Domestic Setting	Page	274
A Likely Story Within A Domestic Setting	Page	275
Author's Acknowledgements	Page	277
Postscript by Author and Douglas Gifford	Page	278

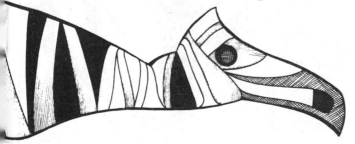

THE STAR

A star had fallen beyond the horizon, in Canada perhaps. (He had an aunt in Canada.) The second was nearer, just beyond the iron works, so he was not surprised when the third fell into the backyard. A flash of gold light lit the walls of the enclosing tenements and he heard a low musical chord. The light turned deep red and went out, and he knew that somewhere below a star was cooling in the night air. Turning from the window he saw that no-one else had noticed. At the table his father, thoughtfully frowning, filled in a football coupon, his mother continued ironing under the pulley with its row of underwear. He said in a small voice, "A'm gawn out."

His mother said, "See you're no' long then."

He slipped through the lobby and onto the stairhead, banging the door after him.

The stairs were cold and coldly lit at each landing by

a weak electric bulb. He hurried down three flights to the black silent yard and began hunting backward and forward, combing with his fingers the lank grass round the base of the clothes-pole. He found it in the midden on a decayed cabbage leaf. It was smooth and round, the size of a glass marble, and it shone with a light which made it seem to rest on a precious bit of green and yellow velvet. He picked it up. It was warm and filled his cupped palm with a ruby glow. He put it in his pocket and went back upstairs.

That night in bed he had a closer look. He slept with his brother who was not easily wakened. Wriggling carefully far down under the sheets, he opened his palm and gazed. The star shone white and blue, making the space around him like a cave in an iceberg. He brought it close to his eye. In its depth was the pattern of a snow-flake, the grandest thing he had ever seen. He looked through the flake's crystal lattice into an ocean of glittering blue-black waves under a sky full of huge galaxies. He heard a remote lulling sound like the sound in a sea-shell, and fell asleep with the star safely clenched in his hand.

He enjoyed it for nearly two weeks, gazing at it each night below the sheets, sometimes seeing the snow-flake, sometimes a flower, jewel, moon or landscape. At first he kept it hidden during the day but soon took to carrying it about with him; the smooth rounded gentle warmth in his pocket gave comfort when he felt insulted or neglected.

At school one afternoon he decided to take a quick look. He was at the back of the classroom in a desk by himself. The teacher was among the boys at the front row and all heads were bowed over books. Quickly he brought out the star and looked. It contained an aloof eye with a cool green pupil which dimmed and trembled as if seen through water.

"What have you there, Cameron?"

He shuddered and shut his hand.

"Marbles are for the playground, not the classroom. You'd better give it to me."

"I cannae, sir."

"I don't tolerate disobedience, Cameron. Give me that thing."

The boy saw the teacher's face above him, the mouth opening and shutting under a clipped moustache. Suddenly he knew what to do and put the star in his mouth and swallowed. As the warmth sank toward his heart he felt relaxed and at ease. The teacher's face moved into the distance. Teacher, classroom, world receded like a rocket into a warm, easy blackness leaving behind a trail of glorious stars, and he was one of them.

THE SPREAD
OF IAN NICOL

One day Ian Nicol, a riveter by trade, started to split in two down the middle. The process began as a bald patch on the back of his head. For a week he kept smearing it with hair restorer, yet it grew bigger, and the surface became curiously puckered and so unpleasant to look upon that at last he went to his doctor. "What is it?" he asked.

"I don't know," said the doctor, "but it looks like a face, ha, ha! How do you feel these days?"

"Fine. Sometimes I get a stabbing pain in my chest and stomach but only in the morning."

"Eating well?"

"Enough for two men."

The doctor thumped him all over with a stethoscope and said, "I'm going to have you X-rayed. And I may need to call in a specialist."

Over the next three weeks the bald patch grew bigger still and the suggestion of a face more clearly marked on it. Ian visited his doctor and found a specialist in the consulting room, examining X-ray plates against the light. "No doubt about it, Nicol," said the specialist, "you are

splitting in two down the middle."
Ian considered this.
"That's not usual, is it?" he asked.
"Oh, it happens more than you would suppose.
Among bacteria and viruses it's very common,
though it's certainly less frequent among riveters.
I suggest you go into hospital where the process can
complete itself without annoyance for your wife or
embarrassment to yourself. Think it over."

Ian thought it over and went into hospital where
he was put into a small ward and given a nurse to
attend him, for the specialist was interested in the
case. As the division proceeded more specialists were
called in to see what was happening. At first Ian ate
and drank with a greed that appalled those who saw
it. After consuming three times his normal bulk for
three days on end he fell into a coma which lasted till
the split was complete. Gradually the lobes of his
brain separated and a bone shutter formed between
them. The face on the back of his head grew
eyelashes and a jaw. What seemed at first a cancer
of the heart became another heart. Convulsively the
spine doubled itself. In a puzzled way the specialists
charted the stages of the process and discussed the
cause. A German consultant said that life was freeing
itself from the vicissitudes of sexual reproduction. A
psychiatrist said it was a form of schizophrenia, a
psycho-analyst that it was an ordinary twinning
process which had been delayed by a severe case
of prenatal sibling rivalry. When the split was
complete, two thin Ian Nicols lay together on the
bed.

The resentment each felt for the other had not
been foreseen or guarded against. In bed the original
Ian Nicol could be recognized by his position (he lay

on the right of the bed), but as soon as both men were strong enough to walk each claimed ownership of birth certificate, union card, clothes, wife and National Insurance benefit. One day in the hospital grounds they started fighting. They were evenly matched and there are conflicting opinions about who won. On leaving hospital they took legal action

against each other for theft of identity. The case was resolved by a medical examination which showed that one of them had no navel.

The second Ian Nicol changed his name by deed poll and is now called Macbeth. Sometimes he and Ian Nicol write to each other. The latest news is that each has a bald patch on the back of his head.

THE PROBLEM

The Greeks were wrong about the sun; she is definitely a woman. I know her well. She often visits me, but not often enough. She prefers spending her time on Mediterranean beaches with richer people, foreigners mostly. I never complain. She comes here often enough to keep me hopeful. Until today. Today, perhaps because it is Spring, she arrived unexpectedly in all her glory and made me perfectly happy.

I was astonished, grateful, and properly appreciative, of course. I lay basking in her golden warmth, a
bit dopey and dozey but murmuring the sort of
compliments which are appropriate at such times.
I realized she was talking to me in a more insistent
tone, so I occasionally said, "Yes" and "Mhm". At
last she said, "You aren't listening."
"Yes I am – " (I made an effort of memory) "– You
were talking about your spots."
"What can I do about them?"
"Honestly, Sun, I don't think they're important."
"Not important? *Not important?* Oh, it's easy for you
to talk like that. You don't have to live with them."
I almost groaned aloud. Whenever someone makes
me perfectly happy they go on to turn themselves
into a problem. I gathered my energies to tackle the
problem.
I said, "Your spots were first noted by Galileo in the
sixteenth century, through his new improved tele-
scope. Before that time you were regarded as the
most perfect of all heavenly bodies – "
She gave a little wail: I said hastily, "But they aren't
permanent! They come and go! They're associated
with several good things, like growth. When you
have a very spotty year the plants grow extra fast and
thick."
She hid her face and said, "Why can't I have a
perfect heavenly body like when I was younger? I
haven't changed. I'm still the same as I was then."
I tried to console her. I said, "Nobody is perfect."
She said nothing.
I said, "Apart from a few top-level physicists and
astronomers, nobody gives a damn for your spots."
She said nothing.
I said, "The moon has spots all over her and nobody
finds those unattractive."

The sun arose and prepared to leave. I gazed at her in horror, too feeble to move, almost too feeble to speak. I whispered, "What's wrong?"
"You've just admitted seeing other planets when my back is turned."
"Of course, but not deliberately. Everybody who goes out at night is bound to see the moon from time to time, but I don't see her regularly, like I see you."
She said, "Perhaps if I played hard to get you would find *my* spots interesting too. What a fool I've been to think that give give giving myself seven days a week, fifty-two weeks a year, a hundred years a century was the way to get myself liked and appreciated when all the time people prefer a flighty young bitch who borrows all her light from me! Her own mother! Well, I've learned my lesson. From now on I'll only come right out once a fortnight, then perhaps men will find my spots attractive too."
And she would have left without another word if I had not jumped up and begged and pleaded and told her a lot of lies. I said a great deal had been discovered about sunspots since Galileo's day, they were an electromagnetic phenomenon and probably curable. I said that next time we met I would have studied the matter and be able to recommend something. So she left me more in sorrow than anger and I will see her tomorrow.

But I can never hope to be perfectly happy with her again. The sun is more interested in her spots than in her beams and is ready
to blame me for them.

THE CAUSE OF SOME RECENT CHANGES

The painting departments of modern art schools are full of discontented people. One day Mildred said to me, "I'm sick of wasting time. We start work at ten and tire after half an hour and the boys throw paper pellets at each other and the girls stand round the radiators talking. Then we get bored and go to the refectory and drink coffee and we aren't enjoying ourselves, but what else can we do? I'm tired of it. I want to do something vigorous and constructive."

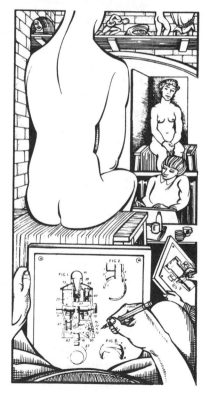

I said, "Dig a tunnel."

"What do you mean?"

"Instead of drinking coffee when you feel bored, go down to the basement and dig an escape tunnel."

"But if I wanted to escape I could walk through the front door and not come back."

"You can't escape that way. The education department would stop your bursary and you would have to work for a living."

"But where would I be escaping to?"

"That isn't important. To travel hopefully is better than to arrive."

My suggestion was not meant seriously but it gained much support in the painting department. In the seldom-visited sub-basement a flagstone was replaced by a disguised trap-door. Under this a room was dug into the school's foundation. The tunnel began here, and here the various shifts operated the winch which pulled up boxes of waste stuff, and put the waste into small sacks easily smuggled out under the clothing. The school was built on a bank of igneous quartz so there was no danger of the walls caving in and no need of pitprops. Digging was simplified by the use of a chemical solvent which, applied to the rock surface with a handspray, rendered it gravelly and workable. The credit for this invention belonged to the industrial design department. The students of this department despised the painters digging the tunnel but it interested them as a technical challenge. Without their help it could not have reached the depths it did.

In spite of the project's successful beginning I expected it to fail through lack of support as the magazine, the debating society and the outing to Linlithgow had failed, so I was surprised to find after three months that enthusiasm was increasing. The Students' Representative Council was packed with members of the tunnel committee and continually organized dances to pay for the installation of more powerful machinery. A sort of tension became obvious throughout the building. People jumped at small sounds, laughed loudly at feeble jokes and quarrelled without provocation. Perhaps they unconsciously feared the tunnel would open a volcanic vent, though things like increase of temperature, water seepage and the presence of gas had been so far absent. Sometimes I wondered how the project remained free from interference. An engineering venture supported by several hundred people can hardly be called a secret. It was natural for those outside the school to regard rumours as fantastic inventions, but why did none of the teachers interfere? Only a minority were active supporters of the project; two were being bribed to remain silent. I am sure the director and deputy director did not know, but what about the rest who knew and said nothing? Perhaps they also regarded the tunnel as a possible means of escape. One day work on the tunnel stopped. The first shift going to work in the morning coffee-break discovered that the basement entrance was locked. There were several tunnel entrances now but all were found to be locked, and since the tunnel committee had vanished it was assumed they were inside. This caused a deal of speculation.

I have always kept clear of mass movements, so on meeting the president of the committee in a lonely upper corridor one evening, I said, "Hullo, Mildred," and would have passed on, but she gripped my arm and said, "Come with me."
She led me a few yards to the open door of what I had thought was a disused service lift. She said, "You'd better sit on the floor," and closed the gates behind us and pulled a lever. The lift fell like a stone with a noise so high-pitched that it was sometimes inaudible. After fifteen minutes it decelerated in violent jerks, then stopped. Mildred opened the gates and we stepped out.

In spite of myself I was impressed by what I saw.

We stood in a corridor with an arched ceiling, asphalt floor and walls of white tile. It swept left and right in a curve that prevented seeing more than a mile in each direction. "Very good," I said, "very good indeed. How did you manage it? The fluorescent lighting alone must have cost a fortune."

Mildred said gloomily, "We didn't make this place. We only reached it."

At that moment an elderly man passed us on a bicycle. He wore a peaked cap, an armband with some kind of badge on it and was otherwise naked, for the air was warm. As he passed he raised a hand in a friendly gesture. I said, "Who was that?"

"Some kind of official. There aren't many of them on this level."

"How many levels are there?"

"Three. This one has dormitories and canteens for the staff, and underneath are the offices of the administration, and under that is the engine."

"What engine?"

"The one that drives us round the sun."

"But gravity drives the world round the sun."

"Has anyone ever told you what gravity is and how it operates?"

I realized nobody ever had. Mildred said, "Gravity is nothing but a word top-level scientists use to hide their ignorance."

I asked her how the engine was powered. She said, "Steam."

"Not nuclear fission?"

"No, the industrial design boys are quite certain it's a steam engine of the most primitive sort imaginable. They're down there measuring and sketching with the rest of the committee. We'll show you a picture in a day or two."

"Does nobody ask what right you have to go poking

about inside this thing?"
"No. It's like all big organizations. The staff are so
numerous that you can go where you like if you look
confident enough."

I had to meet a friend in half an hour so we got
into the lift and started back up. I said, "Well,
Mildred, it's interesting of course, but I don't know
why you brought me to see it."
She said, "I'm worried. The others keep laughing at
the machinery and discussing how to alter it. They
think they can improve the climate by taking us
nearer the sun. I'm afraid we're doing wrong."
"Of course you're doing wrong! You're supposed to
be studying art, not planetary motion. I would never
have suggested the project if I'd thought you would
take it to this length."
She let me out on the ground floor saying, "We can't
turn back now."
I suppose she redescended for I never saw her again.

That night I was wakened by an explosion and my
bed falling heavily to the ceiling. The sun, which had
just set, came up again. The city was inundated by
sea. We survivors crouched a long time among ruins
threatened by earthquakes, avalanches and whirl-
winds. All clocks were working at different speeds
and the sun, after reaching the height of noon, stayed
there. At length the elements calmed and we examined the new situation. It is clear that the planet
has broken into several bits. Our bit is not revolving.
To enjoy starlight and darkness, to get a good night's
sleep, we have to walk to the other side of our new
world, a journey of several miles, with an equally
long journey back when we want daylight.

It will be hard to remake life on the old basis.

Sometimes I look across the very near horizon at other chunks of the old globe. It seems likely that the accident resulted from a chance remark of mine. It will teach me to keep my mouth shut, in future.

THE COMEDY OF THE WHITE DOG

On a sunny afternoon two men went by car into the suburbs to the house of a girl called Nan. Neither was much older than twenty years. One of them, Kenneth, was self-confident and well dressed and his friends thought him very witty. He owned and drove the car. The other, Gordon, was more quiet. His clothes were as good as Kenneth's but he inhabited them less easily. He had never been to this girl's house before and felt nervous. An expensive bunch of flowers lay on his lap.

Kenneth stopped the car before a broad-fronted bungalow with a badly kept lawn. The two men had walked halfway up the path to the door when Kenneth stopped and pointed to a dog which lay basking in the grass. It was a small white sturdy dog with a blunt pinkish muzzle and a stumpy tail. It lay with legs stuck out at right angles to its body, its eyes were shut tight and mouth open in a grin through which the tongue lolled. Kenneth and Gordon laughed and Gordon said, "What's so funny about him?"

Kenneth said, "He looks

like a toy dog knocked over on its side."
"Is he asleep?"
"Don't fool yourself. He hears every word we say."

The dog opened its eyes, sneezed and got up. It came over to Gordon and grinned up at him but evaded his hand when he bent down to pat it and trotted up the path and touched the front door with its nose. The door opened and the dog disappeared into a dark hall. Kenneth and Gordon stood on the front step stamping their feet on the mat and clearing their throats. Sounds of female voices and clattering plates came from nearby and the noise of a wireless from elsewhere. Kenneth shouted, "Ahoi!" and Nan came out of a side door. She was a pleasant-faced blonde who would have seemed plump if her waist, wrists and ankles had not been slender. She wore an apron over a blue frock and held a moist plate in one hand. Kenneth said jocularly, "The dog opened the door to us."
"Did he? That was wicked of him. Hullo, Gordon, why, what nice flowers. You're always kind to me. Leave them on the hallstand and I'll put them in water."
"What sort of dog is he?" said Gordon.
"I'm not sure, but when we were on holiday up at Ardnamurchan the local inhabitants mistook him for a pig."
A woman's voice shouted, "Nan! The cake!"
"Oh, I'll have to rush now, I've a cake to ice. Take Gordon into the living room, Kenneth; the others haven't arrived yet so you'll have to entertain each other. Pour yourselves a drink if you like."

The living room was at the back of the house. The curtains, wallpaper and carpets had bright patterns that didn't harmonize. There was an assortment of chairs and the white dog lay on the most comfortable. There was a big very solid oval table, and a grand piano with two bottles of cider and several tumblers on it. "I see we're not going to have an orgy anyway," said Gordon, pouring cider into a tumbler.

"No, no. It's going to be a nice little family party," said Kenneth, seating himself at the piano and starting to play. He played badly but with confidence, attempting the best known bits of works by Beethoven and Schumann. If he particularly enjoyed a phrase he repeated it until it bored him; if he made a passage illegible with too many discords he repeated it until it improved. Gordon stood with the tumbler in his hand, looking out the window. It opened on a long narrow lawn which sloped down between hedges to a shrubbery.

"Are you in love with Nan?" said Kenneth, still playing.

"Yes. Mind you, I don't know her well," said Gordon.

"Hm. She's too matronly for me."

"I don't think she's matronly."

"What do you like about her?"

"Most things. I like her calmness. She's got a very calm sort of beauty."

Kenneth stopped playing and sat looking thoughtful. Voices and clattering dishes could be heard from the kitchen, a telephone was ringing and the noise of a wireless still came loudly from somewhere. Kenneth said, "She's not calm when she's at home. They're all very nice folk, pleasant and sincere I mean, but you'll find all the women of this family – Nan, her mother and grandmother and aunt – all talk too loudly at the same time. It's never quiet in this house. Either the wireless is on loudly, or the

gramophone, or both. I've been to one or two parties
here. There are never many guests but I've always
felt there are other parties going on in rooms of the
house I don't know about. Do you want to marry
Nan?"

"Of course. I told you I loved her."

Kenneth laughed and swung from side to side on the
piano stool, making it squeak. He said, "Don't
mistake me – there's nothing disorderly about the
house. Nobody drinks anything stronger than cider.
Nan's father and brothers are so quiet as to be
socially non-existent. You only see them at meal-
times and not always then. In fact I'm not sure how
many brothers she has, or how large this family is.
What are you grinning at?"

"I wish I could talk like you," said Gordon. "You've
told me nothing surprising about Nan's family, yet
you've made it seem downright sinister."

Kenneth began to fumble out the tune of 'The Lark
in the Clear Air'.

"Anyway," he said, "you won't get a chance to be alone
with her, which is what you most want, I suppose."

Nan came in and said, "Gibson and Clare will be
here in half an hour . . . er . . . would you like to
have tea in the garden? It's a good day for it. Mum
doesn't like the idea much."

"I think it's a fine idea," said Kenneth.

"Oh, good. Perhaps you'll help us with the table?"

Gordon and Kenneth took the legs off the table,
carried the pieces on to the back lawn and re-
assembled it, then put chairs round it and helped
to set it. While they did so Nan's mother, a small gay
woman, kept running out and shouting useless
directions: "Put that cake in the middle, Gordon!
No, nearer the top! Did ye need to plant the table so

far from the house? You've given yourself a lot of useless work. Well, well, it's a nice day. Where's my dog? Where's my dog? Aha, there he is below the table! Come out, ye bizum! No, don't tease him, Kenneth! You'll only drive him mad."

Gibson and Clare arrived. Gibson was a short thickly built man whose chin always looked swarthy. At first sight he gave a wrong impression of strength and silence, for he was asthmatic and this made his movements slow and deliberate. Though not older than Gordon or Kenneth his hair was getting thin. As soon as he felt at ease in a company he would talk expertly about books, art, politics and anything that was not direct experience. Clare, his girl-friend, was nearly six feet tall and beautiful in a consciously chaste way. Her voice was high-pitched, pure and clear, and she listened to conversation with large wide-open eyes and lustrous lips slightly parted. Her favourite joke was to suspect an indecency in an ordinary remark and to publicize it with a little exclamation and giggle. Kenneth had nicknamed the two Intellect and Spirit. He said there seemed nothing animal between them.

The tea was a pleasant one. Only Nan, her four guests and the dog were present, though. Nan's mother often ran out with a fresh pot of tea or plate of food. The sun was bright, a slight breeze kept the air from being too warm, and Kenneth amused the company by talking about the dog.
"There's something heraldic about him," he said. "It's easy to imagine him with another head where his tail is. Look, he's getting excitable! He wants to sit on a chair! Oh, I hope he doesn't choose mine." The dog had been trotting round the table in a wide circle, now it came toward Kenneth, wagging its tail

and grinning. Kenneth grabbed a plate of meringues
and got down under the table with them. "These at
 least he shall not have!" he
cried in a muffled trembling
voice. The others laughed,
left their chairs and finished
the meal sitting on the
grass. All but Gordon felt
that pleasant drunkenness
which comes from being
happy in company. Kenneth
crawled about the lawn on
his knees with a sugar bowl
in his hand and when he
came to a daisy peered at it
benevolently and dropped
a small heap of sugar into
the flower. Gibson crawled
after him, adding drops
from the milk jug. Clare sat
with the dog on her lap and
pretended to cut it up with
a knife and fork. Actually
she stroked and tickled its stomach gently with the
edge of the knife and murmured baby-talk: "Will I be
cruel and eat oo up doggie? No, no, no, doggie, oo is
too sweet a doggie to eat up."
Nan had taken needles and wool from her apron
pocket and was quietly knitting and smiling to herself.
Gordon lay nearby pretending to sunbathe. He was
worried. He really did not know Nan well. He had
only seen her at the homes of friends, and had not
even spoken to her much. His invitation to the party
had been a surprise. Nan did not know him as well as
several other people she might have invited. He had
assumed she knew what he felt for her and was giving

him a chance to know her better, yet since he arrived
she had not paid him any special attention. Now she
sat placidly knitting, sometimes glancing sideways at
Clare with a slight ironic smile; yet he believed he saw
in her manner a secretive awareness of him, lying
apart and wanting her.
"Ach, the bitch," he thought, "she's sure of me. She
thinks she can hurt me all she likes. Well, she's
wrong." He got up, went to the table and started
piling the plates together.
"I'll take these indoors," he said.
"Oh, don't bother," said Nan, smiling at him lazily.
"Someone will have to shift them," said Gordon
sternly.

He took several journeys to carry the table things
into the kitchen. It was cool and dim indoors. Nan's
father and three of her silent brothers were eating a
meal at the kitchen table. They nodded to him. The
mother was nowhere to be seen but he heard her
voice among several shrill female voices in some
other room. Gordon brought in the last table things
and put them on the drying board of the sink, then
stood awkwardly watching the four eaters. They
were large men with stolid, clumsily moulded
faces. Some lines on the father's face were deeply
cut, otherwise he looked very like his sons. He said to
Gordon, "A warm evening."
"Yes, I prefer it indoors."
"Would you like a look at the library?"
"Er, yes, thanks, yes I would."
The father got up and led Gordon across the hall
and down a short passage, opened a door and stood
by to let Gordon through. The library had old
glass-fronted bookcases on each wall. Between the
bookcases hung framed autographed photographs

of D. H. Lawrence, Havelock Ellis, H. G. Wells and
Bernard Shaw. There was a leather-covered arm-
chair, and a round tin labelled 'Edinburgh Rock' on
a low table beside it.
"You've a lot of books," said Gordon.
"The wife's people were great readers," said Nan's
father. "Can I leave you now?"
"Oh yes. Oh yes."
The father left. Gordon took a book at random from
a shelf, sat down and turned the pages casually. It
was a history of marine engineering. The library was
on the opposite side of the hall from the living room,
but its window also looked on to the back garden
and sometimes Gordon heard an occasional shout or
laugh or bark from those on the lawn. He told
himself grimly, "I'm giving her a chance. If she
wants me she can come to me here. In fact if she has
ordinary politeness and decency she'll be bound to
look for me soon." He imagined the things she
might say and the things he would say back.
Sometimes he consoled himself with a piece of
rock from the tin.

Suddenly the door sprang open with a click
and he saw coming through it towards him, not
Nan, but the dog. It stopped in front of him and
grinned up into his face. "What do you want?"
said Gordon irritably. The dog wagged its tail.
Gordon threw a bit of rock which it caught neatly
in its jaws, then trotted out through the door.
Gordon got up, slammed the door and sat down.
A little later the door opened and the dog entered
again.
"Ye brute!" said Gordon. "Right, here's your sweet;
the last you'll get from me."
He escorted the dog to the door, closed it carefully,

turned a key in the lock, then went back to the chair
and book. After a while it struck him that with the
door locked Nan wouldn't get in if she came to him.
He glanced uneasily up. The door was open and the
dog stood before him, grinning with what seemed, to
his stupified eyes, triumphant amusement. For a
moment Gordon was too surprised to move. He
noticed that the animal was grinning with its mouth
shut, a thing he had never seen a dog do before. He
raised the book as if to throw it.
"Grrr, get out!" he yelled. The dog turned jauntily
and trotted away. After thinking carefully Gordon
decided some joker must have unlocked the door
from outside: it was the sort of pointless joke
Kenneth liked. He listened carefully and heard
from the lawn the voice of Kenneth and the
barking of the dog. He decided to leave the door
open.

Later he found it too dark to see the page of the
book clearly and put it down. The noises from the
lawn had subtly altered. The laughter and shouting
were now not continuous. There were periods of
silence disturbed by the occasional shuffle of running
feet and the hard breathing of somebody pursued,
then he would hear a half-cry or scream that did not
sound altogether in fun. Gordon went to the window. Something strange was happening on the
darkened lawn. Nan was nowhere to be seen.
Kenneth, Gibson and Clare were huddled together
on the bare table-top, Clare kneeling, Kenneth and
Gibson crouching half-erect. The white dog danced
in a circle round the table among over-turned chairs.
Its activity and size seemed to have increased with
the darkness. It glimmered like a sheet in the dusk,
its white needle-teeth glittered in the silently

laughing jaws, it was about the size of a small lion. Gibson was occupied in a strange way, searching his pockets for objects and hurling them at the shrubbery at the far end of the garden. The white dog would run, leap, catch these in its mouth while they were in the air, then return and deposit them under the table. It looked like a game and had possibly begun as one, but obviously Gibson was continuing in an effort to get the dog as far away as possible. Gordon suddenly discovered Nan was beside him, watching, her hands clenched against her mouth.

Gibson seemed to run out of things to throw. Gordon saw him expostulate precariously for a moment with Kenneth, demanding (it appeared) his fountain pen. Kenneth kept shaking his head. He was plainly not as frightened as Gibson or Clare, but a faint embarrassed smile on his face suggested that he was abashed by some monstrous possibility. Gibson put a hand to his mouth, withdrew something, then seemed to reason with Kenneth, who at last shrugged and took it with a distaste which suggested it was a plate of false teeth. Kenneth stood upright and, balancing himself with difficulty, hurled the object at the shrubbery. It was a good throw. The white dog catapulted after it and at once the three jumped from the table and ran to the house, Kenneth going to the right, Gibson and Clare to the left. The dog swerved in an abrupt arc and hurled toward the left. He overtook Clare and snapped the hem of her dress. She stumbled and fell. Gibson and Kenneth disappeared from sight and two doors were slammed in different parts of the house. Clare lay on the lawn, her knees drawn up almost to her chin, her clasped hands pressed between her thighs and her eyes shut. The dog stood over her, grinning happily, then gathered some of the clothing round her waist into its mouth and trotted with her into the bushes of the shrubbery.

Gordon looked at Nan. She had bowed her face into her hands. He put an arm round her waist, she laid her face against his chest and said in a muffled voice, "Take me away with you."
"Are you sure of what you're saying?"
"Take me away, Gordon."
"What about Clare?"
Nan laughed vindictively. "Clare isn't the one to pity."
"Yes, but that dog!"
Nan cried out, "*Do you want me or not?*"

As they went through the dark hall, the kitchen door opened, Nan's mother looked out, then shut it quickly. In the front garden they met Kenneth and Gibson, both shamefaced and subdued. Kenneth said, "Hullo. We were just coming to look for you." Gordon said, "Nan's coming home with me."
Kenneth said, "Oh, good."
They stood for a moment in silence, none of the men looking at each other, then Gibson said, "I suppose I'd better wait for Clare." The absence of teeth made him sound senile. Nan cried out, "She won't want *you* now! She won't want *you* now!" and started weeping again.
"I'll wait all the same," Gibson muttered. He turned his back on them. "How long do you think she'll be?" he asked. Nobody answered.

The drive back into the city was quiet. Gordon sat with Nan in the back seat, his arm around her waist, her mourning face against his shoulder. He felt strangely careless and happy. Once Kenneth said,

"An odd sort of evening." He seemed half willing to discuss it but nobody encouraged him. He put off Gordon and Nan at the close-mouth of the tenement where Gordon lived. They went upstairs to the top landing, Gordon unlocked a door and they crossed a small lobby into a very untidy room. Gordon said, "I'll sleep on the sofa here. The bedroom's through that door."

Nan sat on the sofa, smiled sadly and said, "So I'm not to sleep with you."

"Not yet. I want you too much to take advantage of a passing mood."

"You think this is a passing mood."

"It might be. If it's not I'll see about getting a marriage licence. Are you over eighteen?"

"Yes."

"That's good. Er . . . do you mind me wanting to marry you, Nan?"

Nan got up, embraced him and put her tear-dirty cheek against his. She laughed and said, "You're very conventional."

"There's no substitute for legality," said Gordon, rubbing his brow against hers.

"There's no substitute for impulse," Nan whispered.

"We'll try and combine the two," said Gordon. The pressure of her body started to excite him, so he stood apart from her and started making a bed on the sofa.

"If you're willing, tomorrow I'll get a licence." He had just settled comfortably on the sofa when Nan came to the bedroom door and said, "Gordon, promise you won't ask me about him."

"About who?"

"You can't have forgotten him."

"The dog? Yes, I had forgotten the dog. All right, I won't ask . . . You're sure nothing serious has

happened to Clare?"
"Ask her when you see her next!" Nan cried, and
slammed the bedroom door.

Next day Gordon bought a marriage licence and an
engagement ring and arranged the wedding for a
fortnight later. The next two weeks were among
the happiest in his life. During the day he worked
as an engineering draughtsman. When he came home
from work Nan had a good meal ready for him and
the apartment clean and tidy. After the meal they
would go walking or visit a film show or friends, and
later on they would make rather clumsy love, for
Gordon was inexperienced and got his most genuine
pleasure by keeping the love-making inside definite
limits. He wasn't worried much by memories of the
white dog. He prided himself on being thoroughly
rational, and thought it irrational to feel curious about
mysteries. He always refused to discuss things like
dreams, ghosts, flying-saucers and religion. "It
doesn't matter if these things are true or not," he
said. "They are irrelevant to the rules that we have to
live by. Mysteries only happen when people try to
understand something irrelevant." Somebody once
pointed out to him that the creation of life was a
mystery. "I know," he said, "and it's irrelevant. Why
should I worry about how life occurred? If I know
how it is just now I know enough." This attitude
allowed him to dismiss his memories of the white dog
as irrelevant, especially when he learned that Clare
seemed to have come to no harm. She had broken
with Gibson and now went about a lot with Kenneth.

One day Nan said, "Isn't tomorrow the day before
the wedding?"
"Yes. What about it?"

"A man and woman aren't supposed to see each other the night before their wedding."
"I didn't know that."
"And I thought you were conventional."
"I know what's legal. I don't much care about conventions."
"Well, women care more about conventions than they do about laws."
"Does that mean you want me to spend tomorrow night in a hotel?"
"It's the proper thing, Gordon."
"You weren't so proper on the night I brought you here."
Nan said quietly, "It's not fair to remind me of that night."
"I'm sorry," said Gordon. "No, it's not fair. I'll go to a hotel."

Next evening he booked a room in a hotel and then, since it was only ten o'clock, went to a coffee bar where he might see some friends. Inside Clare and Kenneth sat at a table with a lean young man Gordon did not know. Clare smiled and beckoned. She had lost her former self-conscious grace and looked adult and attractive. As Gordon approached Kenneth stood, gripped Gordon's hand and shook it with unnecessary enthusiasm saying, "Gordon! Gordon! You must meet Mr. McIver. (Clare and I are just leaving.) Mr. McIver, this is the man I told you about, the only man in Scotland who can help you. Goodnight! Goodnight! Clare and I mustn't intrude on your conversation. You have a lot to discuss."
He rushed out, pulling Clare after him and chuckling.

Gordon and the stranger looked at each other with embarrassment.

"Won't you sit down?" said Mr. McIver in a polite
North American voice. Gordon sat down and said,
"Are you from the States, Mr. McIver?"

"No, from Canada. I'm visiting Europe on a scholar-
ship. I'm collecting material for my thesis upon the
white dog. Your friend tells me you are an authority
on the subject."

Gordon said abruptly, "What has Kenneth told you
about the dog?"

"Nothing. But he said you could tell me a great
deal."

"He was joking."

"I'm sorry to hear that."

Gordon stood up to go, sat down again, hesitated and
said, "What is this white dog?"

McIver answered in the tone of someone starting a
lecture: "Well known references to the white dog
occur in Ovid's 'Metamorphoses', in Chaucer's
unfinished 'Cook's Tale', in the picaresque novels
of the Basque poet Jose Mompou, and in your
Scottish Border Ballads. Nonetheless, the white
dog is the most neglected of European archetypes,
and for that reason perhaps, one of the most
significant. I can only account for this neglect by
assuming a subconscious resistance in the minds of
previous students of folk-lore, a resistance springing
from the fact that the white dog is the west-European
equivalent of the Oedipus myth."

"That's all just words," said Gordon. "What does
the dog *do*?"

"Well, he's usually associated with sexually frigid
women. Sometimes it is suggested they are frigid
because they have been dedicated to the love of the
dog from birth . . ."

"Dedicated by who?"

"In certain romance legends by the priest at the

baptismal font, with or without the consent of the girl's parents. More often the frigidity is the result of the girl's choice. A girl meets an old woman in a lonely place who gives her various gifts, withholding one on which the girl's heart is set. The price of the gift is that she consents to marry the old woman's son. If she accepts the gift (it is usually an object of no value) she becomes frigid until the white dog claims her. The old woman is the dog's mother. In these versions of the legend the dog is regarded as a malignant spirit."

"How can he be other than malignant?"

"In Sicily the dog is thought of as a benefactor of frigid or sterile women. If the dog can be induced to sleep with such a woman and she submits to him she will become capable of normal fruitful intercourse with a man. There is always a condition attached to this. The dog must always be, to a certain extent, the husband of the woman. Even if she marries a human man, the dog can claim her whenever he wants."

"Oh God," said Gordon.

"There's nothing horrible about it," said McIver.

"In one of Jose Mompou's novels the hero encounters a brigand chieftain whose wife is also married to the dog. The dog and the chieftain are friends, the dog accepts the status of pet in the household, sleeping by the fire, licking the plates clean et cetera, even though he is the ghostly husband of several girls in the district. By his patronage of the house in this ostensibly servile capacity, he brings the brigand luck. His presence is not at all resented, even though he sometimes sleeps with the brigand's daughters. To have been loved by the dog makes a woman more attractive to normal men, you see, and the dog is never jealous. When one of his women

marries he only sleeps with her often enough to
assert his claim on her."
"How often is that?"
"Once a year. He sleeps with her on the night before
the wedding and on each anniversary of that night.
Say, how are you feeling? You look terrible."

Gordon went into the street too full of horror and
doubt to think clearly.
"To be compared with a *dog*! To be measured
against a *dog*! Oh no, God, Nan wouldn't do that!
Nan isn't so wicked!"
He found he was gibbering these words and running
as fast as possible home. He stopped, looked at his
watch, forced himself to walk slowly. He arrived
home about midnight, went through the close to the
back court and looked up at the bedroom window.
The light was out. He tiptoed upstairs and paused at
the front door. The door looked so much as usual
that he felt nothing wrong could be behind it; he
could still return to the hotel, but while he considered this his hand was stealthily putting the key in
the lock. He went softly into the living room,
hesitated outside the bedroom door, then opened
it quickly. He heard a gasp and Nan shriek,
"Gordon!"
"Yes," said Gordon.
"Don't put the light on!"
He switched the light on. Nan sat up in bed blinking
at him fearfully, her hands pressed protectively on a
mound between her legs under the tumbled bedclothes. Gordon stepped forward, gripped the edge
of the bedclothes and tugged. "Let go!" he said. She
stared at him, her face white with terror, and
whispered, "Go away!" He struck her face and
she fell back on the pillows; he snatched away the

bedclothes and the white dog sprang from between the sheets and danced on them, grinning. Gordon grabbed at the beast's throat. With an easy squirming movement it evaded his hand, then bit it. Gordon felt the small needle-teeth sink between his fingerbones and suddenly became icy cold. He sat on the edge of the bed and stared at the numb bitten hand still gripped between the dog's grinning jaws: its pink little eyes seemed to wink at him. With a great yell, he seized the beast's hind leg with his free hand, sprang up and swung its whole body against the wall. Nan screamed. He felt its head crush with the impact, swung and battered it twice more on the wall, leaving a jammy red stain each time, then he flung the body into a corner and sat down on the edge of the bed and stared at his bitten hand. The sharp little teeth seemed to have gone in without piercing any veins or arteries, for the only mark on the skin was a V-shaped line of grey punctures. He stared across at the smash-headed carcase. He found it hard to believe he had killed it. *Could* such a creature be killed? He got to his feet with difficulty, for he felt unwell, and went to the thing. It was certainly dead. He opened the window, picked the dog up by the tail and flung it down into the back court, then went over to the bed where Nan lay, gazing at him with horror. He began to undress as well as he could without the use of the numbed right hand. "So, my dear," he muttered, "you prefer convention."

She cried out, "You shouldn't have come back tonight! We would all have been happy if you hadn't come back tonight!"

"Just so," said Gordon, getting in bed with her.

"Don't touch me!"

"Oh yes, I'll touch you."

Toward morning Gordon woke, feeling wonderfully happy. Nan's arms clasped him, yet he felt more free than ever before. With a little gleeful yelp he sprang from the nest of warmth made by her body and skipped upon the quilt. Nan opened her eyes lazily to him, then sat up and kissed his muzzle. He looked at her with jovial contempt, then jumped on to the floor and trotted out of the house, the shut doors springing open at the touch of his nose. He ran downstairs into the sunlit street, his mouth hanging open in a grin of sheer gaiety. He would never again be bound by dull laws.

THE CRANK
THAT MADE
THE REVOLUTION

Nowadays Cessnock is a heavily built-upon part of industrial Glasgow, but two hundred and seventy-three years ago you would have seen something very different. You would have seen a swamp with a duck-pond in the middle and a few wretched hovels round the edge. The inmates of these hovels earned a living by knitting caps and mufflers for the inhabitants of Glasgow who, even then, wore almost nothing else. The money got from this back-breaking industry was pitifully inadequate. Old Cessnock was neither beautiful nor healthy. The only folk living there were too old or twisted by rheumatism to move out. Yet this dismal and uninteresting hamlet saw the beginning of that movement which historians call The Industrial Revolution; for here, in seventeen hundred and seven, was born Vague McMenamy, inventor of the crankshaft which made the Revolution possible.

There are no records to suggest that Vague McMenamy had parents. From his earliest days he seems to have lived with his Granny upon a diet of duck-eggs and the proceeds of the old lady's knitting. A German biographer has suggested that McMenamy's first name (Vague) was a nickname. The idea, of course, is laughable. No harder-headed, clearer-sighted individual than McMenamy ever existed, as his crankshaft proves. The learned Herr Professor is plainly ignorant of the fact that Vague is the Gaelic for Alexander. Yet it must be confessed that Vague was an introvert. While other boys were chasing the lassies or stoning each other he would stand for long hours on the edge of the duck-pond wondering how to improve his Granny's ducks.

Now, considered mechanically, a duck is not an efficient machine, for it has been designed to perform three wholly different and contradictory tasks, and consequently it does none of them outstandingly well. It flies, but not as expertly as the swallow, vulture or aeroplane. It swims, but not like a porpoise. It walks about, but not like you or me, for its legs are too short. Imagine a household appliance devised to shampoo carpets, mash potatoes and darn holes in socks whenever it feels like it. A duck is in a similar situation, and this made ducks offensive to McMenamy's dourly practical mind. He thought that since ducks spend most of their days in water they should be made to do it efficiently. With the aid of a friendly carpenter he made a boat-shaped container into which a duck was inserted. There was a hole at one end through which the head stuck out, allowing the animal to breathe, see and even eat; nonetheless it protested against the confinement by struggling to get out and in doing so its wings and legs drove the cranks which conveyed motion to a paddle-wheel on each side. On its maiden voyage the duck zig-zagged around the pond at a speed of thirty knots, which was three times faster than the maximum speed which the boats and ducks of the day had yet attained. McMenamy had converted a havering all-rounder into an efficient specialist. He was not yet thirteen years of age.

He did not stop there. If this crankshaft allowed one duck to drive a vessel three times faster than normal, how much faster would two, three or ten ducks drive it? McMenamy decided to carry the experiment as far as he could take it. He constructed a craft to be driven by every one of his Granny's seventeen ducks. It differed from the first vessel in other ways. The first had been a conventional boat shape propelled by paddles and constructed from wood. The second was cigar-shaped with a screw propeller at the rear, and McMenamy did not order it from the carpenter, but from the blacksmith. It was made of sheet iron. Without the seventeen heads and necks sticking up through holes in the hull one would have mistaken it for a modern submarine. This is a fact worth pondering. A hundred years elapsed before The Charlotte Dundas, the world's first paddle steamer, clanked along the Forth and Clyde canal from Bowling. Fifty years after that the first ironclad screw-driven warship fired its first shot in the American Civil War. In two years the imagination of a humble cottage lad had covered ground which the world's foremost engineers took two generations to traverse in the following century. Vague was fifteen years old when he launched his second vessel. Quacking hysterically, it crossed the pond with such velocity that it struck the opposite bank at the moment of departure from the near one. Had it struck soil it would have embedded itself. Unluckily, it hit the root of a tree, rebounded to the centre of the pond, overturned and sank. Every single duck was drowned.

In terms of human achievement, McMenamy's duckboat ranks with Leonardo Da Vinci's helicopter which was designed four hundred years before the engine which could have made it fly. Economically it was disastrous. Deprived of her ducks,

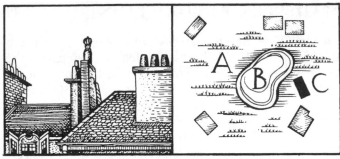

Left: Modern Cessnock shortly after implementation of the smoke abatement act.
Right: Old Cessnock from General Roy's ordnance survey of 1739. Fig. A represents the swamp, B the duckpond, C the McMenamy hovel.

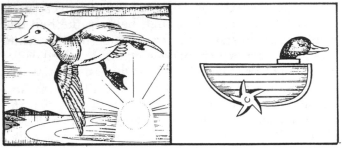

Left: Unimproved duck, after the watercolour by Peter Scott.
Right: McMenamy's Improved Duck.

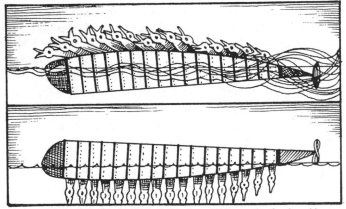

Above: McMenamy's Improved Duck Tandem .0005 seconds after launching.
Below: McMenamy's Improved Duck Tandem .05 seconds after launching. (The ducks, though not yet drowned, have been killed by the shock.)

McMenamy's Granny was compelled to knit faster than ever. She sat in her rocking-chair, knitting and rocking and rocking and knitting and McMenamy sat opposite, brooding upon what he could do to help. He noticed that the muscular energy his Granny used to handle the needles was no greater than the energy she used to rock the chair. His Granny, in fact, was two sources of energy, one above the waist and one below, and only the upper source brought in money. If the power of her *legs and feet* could be channelled into the knitting she would work twice as fast, and his crankshaft made this possible. And so McMenamy built the world's first knitting frame, later nicknamed "McMenamy's Knitting Granny". Two needles, each a yard long, were slung from the kitchen ceiling so that the tips crossed at the correct angle. The motion was conveyed through crankshafts hinged to the rockers of a cast-iron rocking-chair mounted on rails below. McMenamy's Granny, furiously rocking it, had nothing to do with her hands but steer the woollen coils through the intricacies of purl and plain. When the McMenamys came to display their stock of caps and mufflers on a barrow in Glasgow's Barrowland that year, the strongest knitters in the West of Scotland, brawny big-muscled men of thirty and thirty-five, were astonished to see that old Mrs. McMenamy had manufactured twice as much as they had.

Vague, however, was modest enough to know that his appliance was improvable. The power generated by a rocking-chair is limited, for it swings through a very flattened arc. His second knitting frame was powered by a see-saw. His Granny was installed on one end with the needles mounted in front of her.

Hitherto, Vague had avoided operating his inventions himself, but now he courageously vaulted onto the other end and set the mighty beam swinging up and down, up and down, with a velocity enabling his Granny to turn out no less than eight hundred and ninety caps and mufflers a week. At the next Glasgow Fair she brought to market as much produce as the other knitters put together, and was able to sell at half the normal price and still make a handsome profit. The other inhabitants of Cessnock were unable to sell their goods at all. With the desperation of starving men, they set fire to the McMenamy cottage and the machinery inside it. Vague and his Granny were forced to flee across the swamp, leaving their hard earned gold to melt among the flames. They fled to the Burgh of Paisley, and placed themselves under the protection of the Provost, and from that moment their troubles were at an end.

Engraving by Shanks in Glasgow People's Palace Local History Museum showing decadence of that art before Bewick's advent. Nobody knows if it portrays Provost Coats or McMenamy's Granny.

In 1727 Paisley was fortunate in having, as Provost, an unusually enlightened philanthropist, Sir Hector Coats. (No relation to the famous thread manufacturers of the following century.) He was moved by McMenamy's story and impressed by his dedication. He arranged for Vague to superintend the construction of a large knitting mill containing no less than twenty beam-balance knitting frames. Not only that, he employed Vague and his Granny to work one of them. For the next ten years Vague spent fourteen hours a day, six days a week, swinging up and down on the opposite end of the beam from the woman who had nourished and inspired him. It is unfortunate that he had no time to devote to scientific invention, but his only holidays were on a Sunday and Sir Hector was a good Christian who took stern measures against workmen who broke the Sabbath. At the age of thirty Vague McMenamy, overcome by vertigo, fell off the see-saw never to rise again. Strangely enough his Granny survived him by twenty-two years, toiling to the last at the machine which had been named after her. Her early days in the rocking-chair had no doubt prepared her for just such an end, but she must have been a remarkable old lady.

Thirty is not an advanced age and Vague's achievement was crowded into seven years between the ages of twelve and nineteen. In that time he invented the paddle boat and the ironclad, dealt a deathblow to the cottage knitting industry, and laid the foundations of the Scottish Textile Trade. When Arkwright, Cartwright, Wainright and Watt completed their own machines, McMenamy's crankshaft was in every one of them. Truly, he was the crank that made the Revolution possible.

McMenamy's tombstone, Paisley High Kirk, engraved for the 1861 edition of Samuel Smiles's "Self Help". (This corner of the graveyard was flattened to make way for a new road in 1911.)

THE GREAT BEAR CULT

In 1975 there came straight to Glasgow from a Berlin gig Pete Brown the poet, Pete Brown the friend of Horowitz, Pete Brown the songwriter and sometimes pop-song singer. And I dined with him at the home of Barbara and Lindley Nelson. As usual Pete was with a new girlfriend who received most of his conversation, but first he showed the Nelsons and myself a souvenir of Berlin, and that was what *we* discussed. It was a street photograph of Pete arm in arm with a bear. Berlin takes its name from a bear, so commercial cameramen prowl the streets with a suitably dressed partner. But though the bear in the picture was a disguised man he appeared so naturally calm, so benignly strong, that beside him Pete (who in isolation is as calm, benign and shaggy as a sapient man can be) looked comparatively shifty and agley. We were also intrigued to find the image in the photograph oddly familiar though Barbara, Lindley and myself had never seen another like it. Did it recall dim memories of our infancy in the thirties when the British bear cult was still a political force? As we discussed what we knew of the cult I realized that the time had come for a television programme on it, one which mingled public archive material (photographs, films and sound recordings) with dramatic re-enactments of what took place in private. In 1975 the British Broadcasting Corporation was celebrating the fiftieth year of its charter, archive material was being daily broadcast and displayed, surely the BBC would be interested? It was not. I discovered that although Lord Reith's restrictions upon clothing, drink and sexual conduct had for years been matter for jest in the corridors of Broadcasting House and the Television Centre, his tabu upon all reference to the cult after Ramsay McDonald's famous broadcast to the nation was still in force. The BBC rejected my documentary drama. I offer it here, hoping readers will not be afraid to view it upon the television screen of their minds.

1 STUDIO INTRODUCTION

To a recording of *The Teddy Bears' Picnic* the camera advances upon a commentator leaning casually against a table on which is displayed: a fancy-dress bear costume, a toy teddy bear, a Buckingham Palace sentry's bearskin helmet, a Daily Express Rupert Bear cartoon annual, and a copy of *The House at Pooh Corner*.

RECORDING: *If you go down to the woods today*
                 you're sure of a big surprise!
              If you go down to the woods today
                 you'd better go in disguise!
              For every bear that ever there was
              Has gathered there for certain because
              Today's the day the teddy bears have their picnic!

COMMENTATOR: If you go down to the woods

today, you'd better go in disguise. Yes. And if you
were clearing out an old cupboard recently it's very
likely that you found one of these at the back of it.
(HE LIFTS THE BEAR COSTUME AND
STANDS UP)
Perhaps curiosity prompted you to try it on. You can
slip into them quite easily . . .
(HE PUTS IT ON)
Once the zip is pulled up it's surprising how warm
and comfortable you feel. And then, if you adjust the
mask over your head, like this . . . (HOLLOWLY)
you are not only completely weather-proof, your
voice has acquired a hollow, resounding note.
(HE REMOVES THE MASK)
The costume you found was almost certainly a relic
of the great bear cult which swept Britain in the early
thirties. Nobody who remembers those years likes
talking about them, but most of you watching
tonight were born rather later, so perhaps the time
has come to give the origins of the cult, its wildfire
spread and wholly unexpected collapse, some sort of
dispassionate examination. So let me take you back
to 1931, a year of world-wide trade-depression and
economic crisis. There are nearly three million
unemployed in Britain alone. A former socialist is
prime minister of a National Coalition government
with the conservative leader as his deputy. In
Trafalgar Square the photographic business is in a
bad way.

2   TELECINE: TRAFALGAR SQUARE,
STUDIO, STREETS, LAWCOURT
Henry Busby, a licensed street photographer,
squabbles with two others for the custom of a
foreign visitor ("I saw him first!") who manages
to escape all of them. Henry returns glumly to

his studio and to George, his brother and partner. Ruin faces them. Must they also join the armies of the unemployed? Henry has a sudden idea – he has heard that in Berlin the street photographers have partners dressed like bears because there is a bear on the city coat of arms. Why not try that here? George objects that London has no bear on its coat of arms and people come to Trafalgar Square to be photographed with pigeons. Henry shows a newspaper photograph of people queuing in hundreds to see a new bear acquired by London Zoo. Bears are popular – Rupert Bear in the Express, Winnie the Pooh etc. He rents a skin and persuades George to put it on. George finds it surprisingly comfortable. They go out into the streets arm-in-arm and reach the Square followed by a small crowd of laughing onlookers.

HENRY: Come on now, who'll be first to be photographed with this fine chap?

They do a brisk trade, drawing clients from their competitors, who complain bitterly that the bears are frightening the pigeons. But next day when they return to the Square they find the other photographers also accompanied by bears, a black bear, a polar, and a child dressed as a koala. They protest. A brawl develops. The bears are arrested, fined and bound over to keep the peace. However, the press and BBC are glad of some comic relief from a grim world situation, and the matter is widely publicized. The queues to see the new bear at London Zoo grow longer. *The Teddy Bears' Picnic* becomes a popular hit. Furriers start marketing teddy bear suits for children.

3 ARCHIVE MATERIAL: RECORDING OF
BBC NEWS PROGRAMME *IN TOWN TONIGHT*
Dr. Karl Adler, discoverer of the inferiority
complex, is visiting London for an international
psychiatric conference. A BBC interviewer asks
his opinion of the growing enthusiasm for bears.
He replies that though the bear cult is (he
believes) of German origin he feels it is destined
to make great headway in Britain. He is asked
the causes of the cult – why not an elephant or a
tiger cult?
ADLER: In the first place a bear is one of the few
creatures that do not look ridiculous when walking
about upon their hind legs. But there are more
significant reasons for their popularity. They are
not normally flesh-eaters – their favourite food is
honey and buns – so women and children feel safe
with them. But they have claws and teeth which
they can use if threatened, so men can identify with
them without losing their self-respect. In my opinion a civilization such as ours has much to gain
from this cult. The greatest part of a psychiatrist's
work is with people who feel inadequate as human
beings, and considered objectively most of them *are*
physically and mentally inadequate; but dressed in a
properly padded skin they make surprisingly adequate bears . . .

4 TELECINE: STUDIO, STREET AND
LAWCOURT
The words of the interview emanate from a
wireless-set in George and Henry's photo-
graphic studio. George, wearing the bearskin
without the mask, sits reading a newspaper.
Henry switches off the wireless, saying irritably:
HENRY: What blasted rot! . . . Take that thing off,

George.
GEORGE: No. I'd feel cold.
HENRY: I feel cold, but do I complain?
GEORGE: Yes, all the time.
HENRY: Then you might have the common de-
cency to give *me* a shot!
GEORGE (STANDING): I'm going for a walk.
HENRY: Like *that*?
GEORGE: Yes, why not? This is a free country.
And I'm comfortable in it.
(HE FITS THE MASK OVER HIS HEAD)
HENRY: But you look utterly *ridiculous* . . . what's
the use in talking? When you've your mask on you
might as well be deaf.
George walks slouch-shouldered through Soho
followed by a small jeering crowd, most of it
children. He meets another bear followed by a
similar crowd. Coming abreast they glance at
each other's muzzles, suddenly stand erect,
put their backs to the wall, roar and menace
their persecutors with their paws. The children
stop laughing and run away. The remaining
adults calls the bears "cowardly brutes" and
one or two of the most belligerent accuse them
of being "afraid to fight like men". The other
bear hangs back but George flings himself on
the critics and is badly beaten up in an affray
which knocks over a costermonger's barrow. He
is rescued by the police and accused of provoking a riot. He is brought before Lord Goddard, a
highly punitive judge of the period. There is a
man dressed like a bear in the public gallery
and the judge begins by having him removed by
the ushers. George's lawyer makes a dignified
and convincing defence, pointing out that the
accused has been the only person to physically

suffer, that he was outnumbered and unjustly provoked etc. Nonetheless, the judge sees George as "one of these misguided individuals who seem determined to lead Britain backward to an age of primitive savagery" and condemns him to an unusually savage term of imprisonment, while regretting that the laws of the land make it impossible to have him publicly flogged into the bargain. George, asked if he has anything to say to this, responds with dignity and courage.

GEORGE: I do not blame the children who mocked me – I do blame the parents who failed to restrain them. I can't blame the roughs who attacked me – I do blame the society which deprives them of honest employment and leaves them with nothing to do but roam the streets jeering at innocent animals. For I *am* innocent! Bears are strong, but bears are gentle! Lastly, I blame neither the police or the laws of Britain for bringing me here, but I will say this! I would rather wear a bearskin, and stand in the dock, than wear a wig, and sit on the bench, and pass such an inhumanly cruel sentence as *you*, my Lord, have passed upon me!

(A STORM OF APPLAUSE SWEEPS THE COURT. THE JUDGE ORDERS IT CLEARED.)

5 ARCHIVE MATERIAL: NEWSPAPER STILLS AND PATHE NEWSREEL CLIP

We see headlines denouncing unkindness to bears in popular and progressive newspapers, then photographs of bears at Hyde Park Corner demanding justice for their martyred brother, bears with collecting cans gathering money for an appeal fund; processions of bears with

banners urging George's release; then the ban-
ner headlines announcing that the appeal has
been upheld. A newsreel clip shows George
emerging from the wicket-gate of Wands-
worth prison to be confronted by a cheering
crowd, a third of it wearing bearskins. Two
supporters assist him into one. He makes a
speech before donning the mask.

GEORGE: Fair play has triumphed! For myself I
am happy, but for my fellow Bruins I am jubilant.
The British people have always admired us for our
gentleness; they are now learning to like us for our
strength, and believe me, we live in an age when
strength was never more necessary. Sinister forces
are abroad in the world, forces eager to tear the fur
from our backs and the buns from the muzzles of our
cubs. We must organize!

(HE PUTS ON THE MASK AND EMITS A
HOLLOW ROAR)

A rapid montage of stills shows the growth of
the cult, starting with trademarks for Bear-
brand stockings, Polar-mints and the Metro-
Goldwyn-Meyer panda growling through its

celluloid arch. We see photographs of a bear-
garden-party at Cliveden House which the
German ambassador attends in the costume
of a prehistoric grizzly. In Oxford Street shop
windows expensively furred bears posture
among the wax dummies. In poorer districts
you can buy costumes made of rabbit-skin. In
Piccadilly Circus furry prostitutes attract pin-
striped businessmen by throatily roaring.

6   TELECINE: A SUBURBAN BUNGALOW
An insurance clerk, Mr. Osborne, returns ex-
citedly from his work in the city carrying a big
wrapped box.
MR. OSBORNE: I've bought you something, my
dear.
MRS. OSBORNE: Ooh let me see, what is it?
(MR. OSBORNE TEARS OFF WRAPPING
AND LID. HIS WIFE STARES INTO IT)
MRS. OSBORNE: Not one of those!
MR. OSBORNE: Why not? They're all the go you
know.
MRS. OSBORNE: But I don't want to be a bear. I

want to be a squirrel, a super squirrel with a great big bushy tail.

MR. OSBORNE (FIRMLY): No! You've got to be a bear.

(HE TAKES A PEAKED CAP FROM THE BOX AND CLAPS IT ON HIS HEAD)

I'm going to be the keeper.

6 ARCHIVE MATERIAL: NEWSPAPER STILLS AND PATHE NEWSREEL CLIPS.

We see photographs of main streets in Liverpool, Manchester and Glasgow with a high proportion of bears among the passers-by. At Brighton and Blackpool they are being photographed in family groups. Then, in newsreel, we see a guard in a sentry box outside Buckingham Palace. His conical steel helmet has a Prussian spike projecting from the top, a Norman nosepiece and Viking horns sticking out each side.

NEWSREEL COMMENTARY: For more than eleven hundred years – ever since the days of Ethelred the Unready – the Guards of the British

Royal Family have worn the traditional horned helmet, popularly known as the Wanky.

(WE SEE THE HORNED HELMET BEING PLACED IN A GLASS CASE)

NEWSREEL COMMENTARY: Today the Wanky is consigned to a niche in the Imperial War Museum and the guards are on parade wearing a new kind of headgear! Bearskin helmets!

(WE SEE THE CHANGING OF THE GUARD)

NEWSREEL COMMENTARY: Traditionalists may sneer, but throughout the Empire many will find reassurance in the thought that the British monarchy is able and willing to move with the times.

To the tune of *The Teddy Bears' Picnic*, **photographs and headlines show George Busby becoming eminent through the British Bear Cult. We see him attending rallies in public parks where bears hug each other and share buns and honey in perfect freedom.**

RECORDING: *Every teddy bear who's been good*
                       is sure of a treat today!
                   There's lots of wonderful things to
                       eat and marvellous games to play!
                   Beneath the trees where nobody sees
                   They hide and seek as much as they
                       please,
                   Today's the day the teddy bears
                       have their pic-nic!

(CUT TO NEWSREEL OF TORCHLIGHT RALLY WHERE GEORGE, IN WHITE POLAR SKIN, IS EXCHANGING CHANTS WITH A MASSED BEAR-HORDE)

GEORGE: Bears are gentle!

HORDE: Bears are strong!

GEORGE: Our fur is soft!

HORDE: Our claws are long!
NEWSREEL COMMENTARY: Many find this
fervent emotionalism tasteless and unBritish, but
one thing cannot be denied: bears know how to
encourage one another, and in grim times like the
present, who can blame them?
Headlines announce that George Busby will
stand for parliament in an East Croydon
by-election. Photographs show a junior branch
of the Bear Cult, the Cubs, canvassing for him
in the streets. Headlines announce his victory
over the communist candidate by a narrow
majority.

8 TELECINE: A CITY STREET, SUNDAY
MORNING
To the sound of church bells a well-dressed
spinster, approaching the corner of an avenue
leading to a church, is passed by a furtive little
brown bear going the opposite way. Turning
the corner she stumbles on something, looks
down and screams.

9   ARCHIVE MATERIAL: CUTTING
News headlines announce: **CHOIRMASTER CLAWED TO DEATH IN COVENTRY PAVE-MENT CARNAGE!**

10   TELECINE: SUBURBAN BUNGALOW
We see a wooden 1930s wireless set on a side-board and hear six pips from a quartz clock followed by:
BBC ANNOUNCER: Here is the six o'clock news. Just two hours ago the body of Kevin Streedle, former welterweight champion of the world, was discovered clawed to death in a shrubbery near Greenwich Observatory. This is the eighth murder of the type to take place in the past five days. George Busby, leader of the British Bear Cult and member of Parliament for Croydon East, has expressed grief at the incident and hopes the police will soon . . .
(A FURRY PAW SWITCHES THE SET OFF. IT BELONGS TO A BROWN BEAR IN A FLOW-ERY APRON. SHE CONTINUES SETTING TABLE FOR THE EVENING MEAL. THE DOOR OPENS AND A LARGER BROWN BEAR ENTERS CARRYING A BRIEFCASE AND A COPY OF THE TIMES)
LARGER BEAR (HOLLOWLY): Thank God I'm home again!
(HE FLINGS DOWN HIS LUGGAGE, WRENCHES OFF HIS MASK AND EMERGES AS MR. OSBORNE. HE STARES AT THE SMALLER BEAR)
MR. OSBORNE: I do wish you'd take that thing off.
MRS. OSBORNE (HOLLOWLY): It was you who bought it for me.
(SHE REMOVES THE MASK)

MR. OSBORNE (UNZIPPING): That was just for a lark – but it's serious now. Haven't you read the papers? The hidden claw has struck again. And there are more bears on the streets than ever. Even little old ladies are dressing like this.

MRS. OSBORNE (UNZIPPING): Well, the killers aren't likely to attack their own kind, are they now?

MR. OSBORNE: Fur isn't sexy any more, it's become a uniform. More than half the tube tonight was filled with bowlerhatted grizzlies. (HE STEPS OUT OF HIS COSTUME) Promise me something, dear!

MRS. OSBORNE (STEPPING OUT OF HER COSTUME): What?

MR. OSBORNE: Wear that thing in the street, but not at home with me. I'd rather you were a squirrel again. Or even a woman.

(THEY EMBRACE SHYLY IN THEIR UNDER-WEAR)

MRS. OSBORNE: Can't the police do something?

MR. OSBORNE: Apparently not.

MRS. OSBORNE: Can't the government do something?

MR. OSBORNE: *The Times* says they've scheduled a debate.

11 TELECINE: THE HOUSE OF COMMONS
James Maxton, Leader of the Independent Labour Party, arises to ask what the government intends to do about the wave of killings which everyone in Britain associates with a certain political movement, a movement backed by the international fur trade, a movement whose leader occupies a bench in this very chamber.

David Lloyd George, leader of the Liberals, declares that he does not find it in his heart *possible* to blame these misguided people who have taken to wearing bearskins. Bearskins are ridiculous! They are ridiculous! But they are also warm, and comfortable, and cosy, and we live in chilling times. He *does* blame the *government* which in spite of all its promises has *failed* to give people the *coal* to keep them *warm* enough to *dispense* with bearskins.

Ramsay McDonald the prime minister rises to reply. He says that in a democracy like ours every section of the community must be represented. The Bear Cult is still a minority party but anyone who walks the streets of Britain can see that it already musters more support than (say) the Independent Labour Party. Moreover he is sure that the bear who did the killing is a minority of the minority, and no responsible government will condemn a broadly based popular movement for the action of a fanatical extremist whose activities have been mainly confined to the south London district. The killer must certainly be found and punished, but this is a matter for the police.

And now George Busby stands up to speak for the British Bear Cult. He does not remove his mask.

GEORGE (HOLLOWLY): Mr. Speaker, a new and terrible slur has been cast upon those I represent. Yes, in South London – the centre of the Great Bear Movement – yet another innocent victim has been clawed to death. The hearts of every true British Bruin must bleed for the relations of the bereaved, but that is not enough, not enough by a long chalk. We must not rest until the criminals are

captured and who are the criminals? Not bears, at
any rate!
(CRIES OF OH! OH! HE RAISES HIS VOICE)
Bears are strong but bears are gentle! Bears do not
kill choirmasters, welterweight boxers or innocent
ratepayers! We too are innocent ratepayers! Bears
have claws and know how to use them, but our claws
are only used in self-defence! I have no hesitation in
declaring that when the culprit is finally tracked
down he will prove to be an enemy of our movement,
a fanatical socialist or liberal, hell bent on bringing
our party into disrepute! I declare the author of these
crimes to be a bare-faced human being and I
personally promise that the police will have the
help of every true British Bruin in their sacred task
of bringing these obnoxious beasts to book!

12 ARCHIVE MATERIAL: BBC NEWS
ANNOUNCEMENTS, PRESS AND
NEWSREEL EXTRACTS
In response to widespread criticism of their
failure to arrest the Hidden Claw murderer,
the London Metropolitan police make a special
announcement. The bobby on the beat feels he
commands too little respect among the population as a whole, so as an experiment it has
been decided to try a new kind of uniform in
certain districts. This is a black bearskin with
extra large claws, and the mask, instead of
covering the head, rests on top of it, the con-
stable looking out of eyeholes in the chest.
South London patrolled by eight-foot high
Rocky Mountain grizzlies. With the help of
Scotland Yard these manage to arrest a little
man who admits to being the Hidden Claw
murderer. His aunt is secretary of East Croydon

Labour Party. At a rally in Trafalgar Square George cries out to the assembled Bearhorde: "The miserable Faustus responsible for these crimes is in the hands of the police, but where, I ask you, is the Mephistopheles?" Bearhordes attack local Labour Party headquarters throughout South London. The police remain aloof until the riots are nearly over and most of the people they arrest are left-wing and furless.

13 ARCHIVE MATERIAL

Collapse of the National Coalition Government. Ramsay McDonald announces an election in three weeks time. George Busby announces that bears will be contesting at least 260 seats.

14 TELECINE: THE TRIAL OF THE HIDDEN CLAW

While the small man insists he is the criminal, and the police are sure he is, the only evidence against him is the word of the respectable spinster who saw a bear leave the scene of the first killing. She stands in the witness box and the prosecuting counsel ends his examination with the time-honoured words, "Look carefully around this courtroom. Do you recognize anywhere the individual in question?"

We see the Old Bailey with the eyes of the witness: the pathetic brown bear in the dock, the jury-box half full of bears, the public gallery crowded with them, a bear's muzzle sticking out of the judge's wig and coal-black eight-foot grizzlies towering behind everyone else. She screams and faints. The case has to be dismissed for lack of evidence. And before the

prisoner is discharged word comes through
that the Hidden Claw has struck again – in
Hampstead. North London is no longer safe.

15 TELECINE: A ROOM IN SCOTLAND
YARD
The detective responsible for the case is visited
by a Scottish forensic expert with an interna-
tional reputation.
EXPERT: No doubt about it, yon poor devils were
killed by bears.
DETECTIVE: Of *course* they were killed by bears.
But what kind? Brown bears? Polar? or Grizzly?
EXPERT: A grizzly, most likely. But it could be a
bigger than average brown bear or a smaller than
average polar. Koalas and pandas are out.
DETECTIVE: *That's* not much help! There are
hundreds of thousands of these species in South
London alone.
EXPERT: Havers. There can't be more than a
couple of bears at large in the entire United Kingdom.
DETECTIVE: Do you mean a *real* bear is responsible?
EXPERT: That's what I'm telling you! The digits of
the human hand are incapable of carving someone to
death like that – even if they did have artificial claws
on the ends.
The detective starts investigating circuses and
zoos and learns that a few weeks earlier a
couple of bears escaped from the private zoo
of the eccentric and senile Lord Pabham.

16 TELECINE: A SUBURBAN BUNGALOW
Mr. and Mrs. Osborne sit on either side of their
fireplace listening to Sandy McPherson on the

BBC cinema organ. She is patching his skin – a piece of fur was nipped off by a door in the underground. They are waiting for a special announcement to the nation by the prime minister. The music stops. Big Ben chimes. Reith, the governor of the BBC, personally introduces the Right Honourable Ramsay McDonald.

McDONALD: Good evening. Isn't modern science a wonderful thing? Here am I sitting comfortably in my Downing Street study talking to all of you seated beside your hearths throughout the length and breadth and depth of Britain. But I have something more important to tell you than just that, because, of course, you know that already. What I have to say is this. At a special emergency cabinet meeting this afternoon the government decided to make it illegal to dress up like bears in public places for the foreseeable future. I know this will come as a shock to many decent honest folk throughout the length and breadth and depth of Britain, but . . .

He explains that the police have no hope of catching the real bears while so many of the artificial kind roam the streets. The police themselves are abandoning that sort of uniform. He is sure the public will co-operate. Perhaps, after all, the cult of the bear has been based on a misunderstanding. Bears, though strong, are not always gentle, it now appears. The broadcast ends with a recording of Blake's *Jerusalem* while Mr. Osborne jumps up, snatches the skin from his wife's knees and, despite her protests, stuffs it dramatically into the fireplace causing a great deal of smoke.

17 TELECINE: VARIOUS PLACES

Throughout the country people thrust bear-skins into dustbins and cupboards shouting, "I told you it was silly!"

We see George at a desk, frantically telephoning in an effort to hold together his crumbling organization.

GEORGE: These murderers are not real bears – bears are strong but bears are gentle – these bears are only criminals because they have been soured by captivity! In next week's General Election bears will be fighting two hundred and sixty seats! Every furrier in Britain is behind us! We don't need skins, we'll wear badges instead!

The real bears are detected, netted and sent back to the zoo. Under exploding rockets we see a crowd in an East End street dancing the Hokey-Cokey round a bonfire with several stuffed bearskins burning on top.

18   ARCHIVE MATERIAL

Headlines announce the 1931 general election result: the National Coalition government is returned to power with a substantial majority. George Busby, Britain's only Bear Cult M.P., forfeits his deposit. All the other bears withdrew at the last moment.

19   THE TELEVISION STUDIO

The commentator, wearing his costume without the mask, sits before the table of cult objects with an expert beside him.

COMMENTATOR: And that, politically speaking, was the end of the bear cult. I have with me the renowned social anthropologist Professor Grotman. Professor, we are all aware that the beast in man lies only a little way under the surface so I will not ask you to refer to the psychological basis of the cult, I will ask how it came to disappear so utterly.

GROTMAN: In my opinion the psychological basis of the cult has been much exaggerated. It is now clear that the main cause of the movement lay in the coal shortages of the winter of 1931. It was actually warmer to dress as a bear in those days. What killed the movement politically was not disillusion with bears as a species. By 1932 it had become abundantly clear to the intelligent part of the population that a second World War, with its promise of full employment for everyone, lay just round the corner. What killed the movement, in fact, was hope for the future.

COMMENTATOR: But is the movement *really* dead? Remember, at its peak it had a following which numbered well over three million. Perhaps the person most qualified to answer that question is the Great Bear himself, the founder of the cult, George Busby: still remarkably fit and active for a man of 68 and living at present in a bed-sitting room on the Old Kent Road.

20   VIDEOTAPE RECORDING

George Busby, white-haired, spectacled, with the air of a vaguely dissolute grand old man, sits in a small room crowded with trophies of his former grandeur: stuffed bearskins of the three main species, framed photographs of such moments of glory as the programme has revealed. He wears a yellow pullover, check trousers, a badge with a Rupert Bear head on, and is flanked by a shelf of every sort of bear-doll from Winnie the Pooh to Paddington. Answering the questions of an invisible interviewer he speaks sadly of the collapse of his cult, of his present situation (he still receives cheques from the children of furriers who made their fortunes in the 1931 fur boom) and his hopes for the future.

GEORGE: My movement was ahead of its time. So the adults decided to forget it. But the children remember. Children know without being taught, you see. So the bears *will* return one day soon, to save England in her hour of need. Though I may not be there to see it.

(HE TURNS AND CONTEMPLATES A FOUR FOOT HIGH PADDINGTON DOLL. THE CAMERA SLOWLY RECEDES FROM THIS FINAL IMAGE OF GEORGE AS AN OLD MAN ALONE WITH HIS DREAMS AND MEMORIES)

21   THE TELEVISION CENTRE

Freeze frame, then the camera zooms further back to show the image of George multiplied on the monitor screens of a television gallery. The control surface of a console occupies the foreground. A hairy paw appears and turns a switch. We see the whole gallery is staffed by bears: a large polar director stretching himself, a panda secretary scribbling on a clip-board, a grizzly technician with headphones. The director stands, stretches, yawns hollowly, then walks through into the studio where the commentator is in the act of fitting on his mask.

Professor Grotman is zipping himself into a costume of his own.
DIRECTOR: That didn't go too badly.
COMMENTATOR: No hitches then?
DIRECTOR: None to speak of. Coming to the staff club for a drink, Professor?
GROTMAN: Certainly, certainly. Just wait till I adjust my dress. (HE PLACES THE MASK ON HIS HEAD. TOGETHER THE THREE BEARS, CHATTING AMIABLY, STROLL OFF DOWN CORRIDORS FULL OF VARIOUS BEARS GOING ABOUT THEIR VARIOUS BUSINESSES.)

THE START OF THE AXLETREE

I write for those who know my language. If you possess that divine knowledge do not die without teaching it to someone else. Make copies of this history, give one to anybody who can read it and read it aloud to whoever will listen. Do not be discouraged if they laugh and call you a liar. Perhaps they are dull herdsmen who think milk and wool more important than history. Their own history is a tangle of superstition and confused rumours. Those who lived inside the great wheel used to call them the perimeter tribes. "Were you born outside the rim?" we would ask someone who was acting stupidly or strangely and this question was a grave insult. The perimeter tribes lived so far from the hub that they only saw the axletree for a few months before it was completed and then only on unusually clear days. Even at sunrise its shadow never quite

touched them, so now they say it was the last impiety of a mad civilization, an attack upon heavenly god which provoked instant punishment and defeat. But the axletree was a necessary inevitable work, soberly designed and carefully erected by statesmen, bankers, priests and wise men whose professional names make no sense nowadays. And they completed the axletree as intended. For a moment the wheel of the civilized world was joined to the wheel of heaven. The disaster which fell a moment later was an accident nobody could have foreseen or prevented. I am the only living witness to this fact. I have been higher than anybody in the world. The hand which writes these words has stroked the ice-smooth, slightly-rippled, blue lucid ceiling which held up the moon.

I was born and educated at the hub of the last and greatest world empire. We had once been a republic of small farmers in a land between two lakes. Our only town in those days was a walled market with a temple in the middle where we stored the spare corn. Our land was fertile so we developed the military virtues, first to protect our crops from neighbours, then to protect our merchants when they traded with the grain surplus. We were also the first people to shoe horses with iron, so we soon conquered the lands round about.

Conquest is not a difficult thing – most countries have a spell of it – but an empire is only kept by careful organization and we were good at that. We taxed the defeated people with the help of their traditional rulers, who wielded more power with our support than they could without, but the empire was mainly held by our talent for large-scale building. Captains in the army were all practical architects,

and private soldiers dug ditches and built walls as
steadily as they attacked the enemy under a good
commander. The garrisons on foreign soil were built
with stores and markets where local merchants and
craftsmen could ply their trade in safety, so they
became centres of prosperous new cities. But our
most important buildings were roads. All garrison
towns and forts were connected by well-founded roads
going straight across marsh and river by dyke and
viaduct to the capital city. In two centuries these
roads, radiating like spokes from a hub, were on the
way to embracing the known world.

It was then we started calling our empire the great
wheel. Surveyors noted that the roads tended to rise
the further from the capital they got, which showed
that our city was in the centre of a continent shaped
like a dish. It became common for our politicians to
start a speech by saying *This bowl of empire under this
dome of heaven* . . . and end by saying *We have fought
uphill all the way. We shall fight on till we reach the
rim.* This rhetorical model of the universe became
very popular, though educated people knew that the
hollow continent was a large dent in the surface of a
globe, a globe hanging in the centre of several hollow
globes, mainly transparent, which supported the
bodies of the moon, sun, planets and stars.

The republic was controlled by a few rich families
who worked in the middle of an elected senate, but
one day it became clear that whoever commanded
the army did not need the support of anyone else. A
successful general proclaimed himself emperor. He
was an efficient man with good advisers. He constructed a civil service which worked so well that
trade kept flowing and the empire expanding during
the reign of his son, who seems to have been a

criminal lunatic who did nothing but feed his worst appetites in the most expensive ways possible. It is hard to believe that records tell the truth about this man. He was despised by the puritan aristocracy who filled the civil service, but loved by common citizens. Perhaps his insane spending sprees and colossal sporting events were devised to entertain them. He also obtained remarkable tutors for his son, men of low and foreign birth but international fame. They had made a science out of history, which till then had been a branch of literature. When their pupil became third emperor he knew why his land was heading for disaster.

Many nations before ours had swelled into empires. Nearly all had collapsed while trying to defeat a country, sometimes a small one, beyond the limit of their powers. The rest had enclosed the known world and then, with nothing else to conquer, had gone bad at the centre and cracked up through civil war. The emperor knew his own empire had reached a moment of ripeness. It filled the hollow continent to the rim. His roads touched the northern forests and mountains, the shores of the western sea, the baking southern desert and the wild eastern plains. The perimeter tribes lived in these places but we could not civilize them. They were nomads who could retreat forever before our army and return to their old pasture when it went away. Clearly the empire had reached its limit. The wealth of all civilization was flowing into a city with no more wars to fight. The military virtues began to look foolish. The governing classes were experimenting with unhealthy pleasures. Meanwhile the emperor enlarged the circus games begun by his father in which the unemployed poor of the capital were entertained by unemployable slaves killing each other in large quantities. He also ordered from the merchants huge supplies of stone, timber and iron. The hub of the great wheel (he said) would be completely rebuilt in a grander style than ever before.

But he knew these measures could only hold the state for a short time.

A few years earlier there had appeared in our markets some pottery and cloth of such smooth, delicate, transparent texture that nobody knew how they were made. They had been brought from the eastern plains by nomads who obtained them, at fourth or fifth hand, from other nomads as barbarous as themselves. Enquiries produced nothing but rumour, rumour of an empire beyond so great a tract of desert, forest and mountain that it was on the far side of the globe. If rumours were true this empire was vast, rich, peaceful, and had existed for thousands of years. When the third emperor came to power his first official act was to make ambassadors of his tutors and send them off with a strong expeditionary force to investigate the matter. Seven years passed before the embassy returned. It had shrunk to one old exhausted historian and a strange foreign servant without lids on his eyes – he shut them by making them too narrow to see through. The old man carried a letter to our emperor written in a very strange script, and he translated it.

THE EMPEROR OF THREE-RIVER KINGDOM GREETS THE EMPEROR OF THE GREAT WHEEL. I can talk to you as a friend because we are not neighbours. The distance between our lands is too

great for me to fear your army.

Your ambassadors have told me what you wish to know. Yes, my empire is very big, very rich, and also very old. This is mainly because we are a single race who talk the same language. We produce all we need inside our borders and do not trade with foreigners. Foreign trade leads to warfare. Two nations may start trading as equals but inevitably one grows rich at the expense of the other. Then the superior nation depends on its enemy and can only maintain its profits by war or threats of war. My kingdom has survived by rejecting foreign trade. The goods which appeared in your market were smuggled out by foreigners. We will try to stop that happening again.

If your people want stability they must grow small again. Let them abandon empire and go back inside their old frontier. Let them keep an army just big enough for defence and cultivate their own land, especially the food supply. But this is useless advice. You and I are mere emperors. We both know that a strong class of merchants and generals cannot be commanded against their will. Wealthy nations and men will embrace disaster rather than lose riches.

I regret that I cannot show a way out of your difficulty. Perhaps the

immortal gods can do that. Have
you approached them? They are the
last resort, but they work for the
peasants, so people of our kind
may find them useful.

The emperor was startled by the last words of this
intelligent and powerful man. Several countries in
the empire worshipped him as a god but he was not
religious. The official religion of the state had been a
few simple ceremonies to help it work as smoothly as
possible. An old proverb *Religion is the wealth of the
conquered* described our view of more exotic faiths.
But the religions of conquered people had recently
become fashionable at the hub, even with very
wealthy citizens. These religions had wide differ-
ences but all believed that man had descended from
someone in the sky and were being punished, tested
or taught by having to toil in the world below. Some
faiths believed that a leader would one day come
down from heaven, destroy all who opposed him and
build a kingdom on earth for his followers. Others
bowed to prophets who said that after death the
ghosts of their followers would enter a walled garden
or city in the sky. These politically stable goals
appealed to the emperor. He consulted priests in
the hope that unreason would answer the question
which reason could not.

He was disappointed. The priests explained that
the eternal kingdom was achieved by sharing certain
beliefs and ceremonies, following certain rules, and
eating or avoiding certain food. Those who obeyed
the priests often enjoyed intense feelings of satisfaction, but even if the whole empire adopted one of
these faiths the emperor did not think it would be
less liable to decay and civil war. Many priests

agreed with him. "Only a few will enter the heavenly kingdom," they said. The emperor wanted a kingdom for the majority. He sent agents to consult prophets and oracles in more and more outlandish places. At last he heard of a saint who lived among the perimeter tribes in a wild place which no bribe could persuade him to leave. This saint's reputation was not based on anything he taught, even by example, for he was an unpleasant person. But he had cured impotence, helped someone find a lost legacy and shown a feeble governor how to master a difficult province. Most people who brought him problems were ordered rudely away but his successes were supernaturally startling. The emperor went to see him with a troop of cavalry.

The saint was small, paunchy and bow-legged. He squatted before a crack in a rocky cliff, grinning and blinking mirthlessly, like a toad. The emperor told the soldiers to wait, went forward, knelt before the saint and talked about the problem of empire. After a silence the saint said, "Are you strong?"
The emperor said, "My life has been easy but my health is excellent."
The saint felt the emperor's pulse, examined the insides of his eyelids then said gloomily, "You are strong enough, yes, I can help you. But I won't enjoy it. Give me some gold."
The emperor handed him a purse. The saint stood up and said, "Fetch wine and oil from your men and come into my house. Tell them they won't see you till tomorrow evening. Make that perfectly clear. If they interrupt us before then you won't learn a thing. Let them pass the time making a litter to carry you in, for when you reappear you will be in a sacred condition. The expression of your face will have completely changed."

Nobody had spoken to the emperor like that since he was a small boy and the words made him feel strangely secure. He did as he was told and then followed the saint into the crack in the rock. It led to a cave they had to stoop to enter. The saint struck a flint, lit a twisted rag in a bowl of fat, then picked up a wooden post. His dwarfish body was unusually powerful for he used the post to lever forward a great boulder till it blocked the entrance and shut out all daylight. Then he squatted with his back to the boulder and stared at the emperor across the foul-smelling lamp on the floor between them.

After a while he said, "Tell me your last dream."
The emperor said, "I never dream."
"How many tribes do you rule?"
"I rule nations, not tribes. I rule forty-three nations."
The saint said sternly, "Among the perimeter people a ruler who does not dream is impossible. And a ruler who dreams badly is stoned to death. Will you go away and dream well?"
The emperor stared and said, "Is that the best you can say to me?"
"Yes."
The emperor pointed to the boulder and said, "Roll that thing aside. Let me out."
"No. You have not answered my question. Will you go away and dream well?"
"I cannot command my dreams!"
"Then you cannot command yourself. And you dare to command other people?"
The saint took a cudgel from the shadows, sprang up and beat the emperor hard for a long time.

The emperor's early training had been stoical so he gasped and choked instead of screaming and yelling. Afterwards he lay against the cavern wall and gaped at the saint who had sat down to recover his breath. At last the emperor whispered, "May I leave now?"

"But will you go away and dream well?"

"Yes. Yes, I swear I will."

The saint groaned and said, "You are lying. You are saying that to avoid being beaten."

He beat the emperor again then dropped the cudgel and swigged from the wine-flask. The emperor lay with his mouth and goggling eyes wide open. He could hardly move or think but he could see that the saint was in great distress of mind. The saint knelt down, placed a tender arm behind the emperor's shoulders, gently raised his head and offered wine. After swallowing some the emperor slept and was assaulted by horrible nightmares. He was among slaves killing each other in the circus to the wild cheering of the citizens. He saw his empire up on edge and bowling like a loose chariot-wheel across a stony plain. Millions of tiny people clung to the hub and to the spokes and he was among them. The wheel turned faster and faster and the tiny people fell to the rim and were whirled up again or flung to the plain where the rim rolled over them. He sobbed aloud, for the only truth in the world seemed to be unending movement, unending pain. Through the pain he heard a terrible voice demand:

"Will you go away and dream well?"

He screamed: "I *am* dreaming! I *am* dreaming!"

The voice said, *"But not well. You are dreaming the disease. Now you must dream the cure."*

And the emperor had a general impression of being beaten again.

Later he saw that the boulder had been rolled aside. Evening sunlight shone through the entrance.

The saint, who had cleaned the bruises with oil, now made him drink the last of the wine. The emperor felt calm and empty. When the saint said, "Please, please, answer my question," the emperor shook with laughter and said, "If you let me go I will pray *all the gods* to give me a good dream."
The saint said, "That is not necessary. The dream is now travelling towards you. Only one more thing is needed to make sure it arrives."
He beat the emperor again and the emperor did not notice, then he picked the emperor up and walked from the cave and laid him on the litter prepared by the soldiers. He said to the commanding officer, "Carry your master carefully, for he is in a very sacred condition. Write down everything he says because now his words are important. And if he recovers tell him not to apologize for what he bribed me to do. Giving men dreams is my only talent. I never have them myself."

The emperor was carried to the hub in slow stages for he was very ill and often delirious. At the first stopping-place he dreamed of the axletree. He saw the great wheel of empire lying flat and millions of people flowing down the roads to the hub. From the hub a great smooth shaft ascended to the sky and ended in the centre of the sun. And he saw this shaft was a tower, and that everyone who had lived and died on earth was climbing up by a winding stair to the white light at the top. Then he saw this light was not the sun but a flame or a flame-shaped opening in the sky, and all the people were passing through and dissolving in the dazzling white.

For a month after his return the emperor saw nobody but doctors and the architect of the city's building programme, then he called the leaders of the empire to his bedside. His appearance shocked them. Although he had reacted against a libertine father by tackling the worries of government he had been a robust, stout, stolid man. His body was now almost starved to a skeleton, the lines of care on his face were like deep cracks in an old wooden statue, his skin, against the bank of pillows supporting him, looked livid yellow; yet he regarded the visitors with an expression of peculiar levity. His voice was so strong and hollow that he had to rest between sentences, and at these moments he sucked in his lips and bit them as if to prevent laughter. He waited until everybody was comfortably seated before speaking.

"My political researches outside the rim have damaged my kidneys and I cannot live much longer. I have decided that for a few years most of the empire's revenue will be used to build me a tomb. I invite you to form a company responsible for this building. Your time is precious, I don't expect you to give it for nothing, and, if things go as I plan, work for this company will double your present incomes. If anyone dies before the great work is complete the salary will go to his successor."

He rested until expressions of regret, loyalty and gratitude died away then indicated some architectural drawings on the wall near the bed. He said, "Here are the plans of the tomb. The basic shape is a steep cone with a ramp winding up. It is designed so that it can be enlarged indefinitely. I have not indicated the size of the completed work. Yourselves or posterity can decide that. My body will lie in a vault cut into the rock below the foundation. It will be a large vault, for I expect my descendants will also lie there."

He smiled at the heir to the throne then nodded
kindly at the others.

"Perhaps, gentlemen, you will make the tomb so big
that you will be able to bury yourselves and your
families in chambers adjacent to mine. Indeed, I
would like even quite humble people who help the
great effort to end under it, although their graves
would naturally be narrower and less well furnished
than ours. But you will decide these things. As to the
site of the structure, it will be in the exact centre of
the city, the exact centre of the empire. Has the high
priest of war and thunder anything to say?"

The head of the state religion shrugged uneasily and
said, "Sir, everyone knows that spot is the most
sacred in the empire. My temple stands there. It was
built by the hero who founded our nation. Will you
knock it down?"

The emperor said, "I will rebuild it on a grander
scale than ever before. The space above the burial
chambers will be a pantheon to all the gods of our
heaven and empire, for a great building must serve
the living as well as the dead, or nobody will take it
seriously for long. And my tomb will have room for
more than a mere temple, even though that temple is
the biggest in the world. Look again at the plans.
The temple is the circular *core* of the building. Vast
stone piers radiate from it, piers joined by arching
vaults and pierced by arched doors. The spaces
between the piers can be made wide enough to
hold markets, factories and assembly rooms. These
spaces are linked by curving avenues ascending at a
slope gradual enough to race horses up. As you
know, when I came to the throne I swore to rebuild
our city on a grander scale than ever before. And
what is a city but a great house shared by a com-

munity? The wealthy will have mansions in it, the
poor can rent apartments. Parks and gardens will be
planted along the outer terraces. And you, the
construction company, will have your offices in
the summit. As this rises higher the whole administration of the empire will move in beneath you . . .
But a dying man should not look so far ahead. What
do our businessmen say? Can they supply the
materials to build on an increasingly large scale
for generations to come? Can they provide food
for a steadily enlarging labour force? I ask the heads
of the corn and stock exchanges to give an opinion.
Don't consider the matter as salaried members of the
construction company, but as managers of the
empire's trade."

Toward the end of the emperor's speech the faces
of the leading businessmen had acquired a dreamy,
speculative look, but the head of the stock exchange
roused himself and said, "We can tackle that,
certainly, if the government pay us to do so."
Everyone looked at the civil service chief, who was
also the imperial accountant.
He said slowly, "Ever since our armies reached the
rim our provinces have been complaining about
heavy taxation. We could once justify that by
attacking enemies outside the borders. We have
no enemies now, but if we allow the provinces to
grow rich they will break away from us. Yes, we can
certainly finance this structure. And there will be no
shortage of labour. We are already paying huge doles
to the unemployed, merely to stop them revolting
against us."
The commander of the armed forces said, "Will
expenditure on this building require a reduction in
the armed forces?"

The imperial accountant said, "Oh no! The army may even have to be enlarged, to keep the taxes coming in."

"Then I like the idea. The emperor has called the structure a great house. I call it a castle. At present the city has overflowed the old fortifications, our hub is a sprawling, indefensible mess. A high walled city will not only be easier to defend, it could be easier to police. Let the great doors between the different levels of the structure have heavy portcullises in them. Then with very little effort we can imprison and starve any part of the population which gets out of hand."

"But the outer walls must be faced with shining marble!" cried the head of the arts council. "If it looks beautiful from a distance I am sure foreign provinces will gladly let us continue taking their food, materials and men at the old cheap rate. Everyone wants to admire something wonderful, support something excellent, be part of something splendid which will not fail or die. Are you all right, sir?"

The emperor was shuddering with what seemed silent laughter but his teeth rattled and his brows sweated so it was probably fever. When he recovered he apologized then said, "Now I will tell you a dream I had."

He told them the dream of the axletree.

"Sir!" said the high priest in an inspired voice, "You have given the empire a new way to grow! You have offered a solution to the political problem of the age, and mentioned the dream which gave the idea as an afterthought. But all dreams are sacred, and the dreams of a ruler are most sacred of all. Perhaps the heavenly gods are growing lonely.

Perhaps mankind is becoming fit to join them. Let us tell the world this dream. You may be the prophet who will lead us all to the golden garden in the sky." "I like that idea," said the emperor languidly. "And, certainly, let people know the dream occurred. But don't explain it, at this stage. You would antagonize religions whose prophet has already arrived. When the temple part of the building is complete dedicate it to god and his true prophet, but don't name them. Keep the official religion a kind of *cavity* which other religions can hope to fill if they grow big enough. But you mentioned gold. In spite of his mad spending my father left a fortune which I have been able to increase. I want it all converted into gold and placed beside my body in the vault. Let people know that the construction company can use it in emergencies. But never do so. The fact that it exists and you own it will give the company more power over men than mere spending could give. Lend on the security of this gold, borrow on the security of this gold, if creditors press you hard *cheat* upon the security of this gold. But never, never touch it."

The emperor closed his eyes and seemed to doze. The politicians whispered to each other. Suddenly he cried out in a great voice, "Do not call it a tower! Towers are notorious for falling down. Tell the fools you are building a connection between two absolutely dependable things. Call it an axletree." Then he giggled faintly and said, "I suppose one day the world will be governed by people whose feet never touch the ground. I wonder what will happen if there is a sky, and they reach it . . . I wonder what the child will look like."

The emperor died, and his tomb was built in the

centre of the capital city, and enlarged to enclose everything he had wanted. For two thousand years this construction gave employment to mankind and a purpose to history. But there was a sky, We reached it. Everyone knows what happened after that.

FIVE LETTERS FROM AN EASTERN EMPIRE

DESCRIBING ETIQUETTE GOVERNMENT IRRIGATION EDUCATION CLOGS KITES RUMOUR POETRY JUSTICE MASSAGE TOWN-PLANNING SEX AND VENTRILOQUISM IN AN OBSOLETE NATION

FIRST LETTER

DEAR MOTHER, DEAR FATHER, I like the new palace. It is all squares like a chessboard. The red squares are buildings, the white squares are gardens. In the middle of each building is a courtyard, in the middle of each garden is a pavilion. Soldiers, nurses, postmen, janitors and others of the servant-class live and work in the buildings. Members of the honoured-guest-class have a pavilion. My pavilion is small but beautiful, in the garden of evergreens. I don't know how many squares make up the palace but certainly more than a chessboard has. You heard the rumour that some villages and a small famous city were demolished to clear space for the foundation. The rumour was authorized by the immortal emperor yet I thought it exaggerated. I now think it too timid. We were ten days sailing upstream from the old capital, where I hope you are still happy. The days were clear and cool, no dust, no mist. Sitting on deck we could see the watchtowers of villages five or six miles away and when we stood up at nightfall we saw, in the sunset, the sparkle of the heliograph above cities, on the far side of the horizon. But after six days there was no sign of any buildings at all, just ricefields with here and there the tent of a waterworks inspector. If all this empty land feeds the new palace then several cities have been cleared from it. Maybe the inhabitants are inside the walls with me, going out a few days each year to plant and harvest, and working between times as gardeners of the servant-class.

You would have admired the company I kept
aboard the barge. We were all members of the
honoured-guest-class: accountants, poets and headmasters, many many headmasters. We were very
jolly together and said many things we would not
be able to say in the new palace under the new
etiquette. I asked the headmaster of literature, "Why
are there so many headmasters and so few poets? Is it
easier for you to train your own kind than ours?" He
said, "No. The emperor needs all the headmasters he
can get. If a quarter of his people were headmasters
he would be perfectly happy. But more than two
poets would tear his kingdom apart."
I led the loud laughter which rewarded this deeply
witty remark and my poor, glum little enemy and
colleague Tohu had to go away and sulk. His sullen
glances amuse me all the time. Tohu has been
educated to envy and fear everyone, especially me,
while I have been educated to feel serenely superior
to everyone, especially him. Nobody knows this
better than the headmaster of literature who taught
us both. This does not mean he wants me to write
better than Tohu, it shows he wants me to write with
high feelings and Tohu with low ones. Neither of us
have written yet but I expect I will be the best. I
hope the emperor soon orders me to celebrate
something grand and that I provide exactly what
is needed. Then you will both be able to love me as
much as you would like to do.

This morning as we breakfasted in the hold of the
barge Tohu came down into it with so white a face
that we all stared. He screamed, "The emperor has
tricked us! We have gone downstream instead of up!
We are coming to the great wall round the edge of
the kingdom, not to a palace in the middle! We

are being sent into exile among the barbarians!" We
went on deck. He was wrong of course. The great
wall has towers with loopholes every half mile, and it
bends in places. The wall which lay along the
horizon before us was perfectly flat and windowless
and on neither side could we see an end of it. Nor
could we see anything behind it but the high
tapering tops of two post-office towers, one to the
east, one to the west, with the white flecks of
messenger pigeons whirling toward them and away
from them at every point of the compass. The sight
made us all very silent. I raised a finger, summoned
my entourage and went downstairs to dress for
disembarking. They took a long time lacing me
into the ceremonial cape and clogs and afterwards
they found it hard lifting me back up to the deck
again. Since I was now the tallest man aboard I had
to disembark first. I advanced to the prow and stood
there, arms rigid by my sides, hands gripping the
topknot of the doctor, who supported my left thigh,
and the thick hair of Adoda, my masseuse, who
warmly clasped my right. Behind me the secretary
and chef each held back a corner of the cape so that
everyone could see, higher than a common man's
head, the dark green kneebands of the emperor's
tragic poet. Without turning I knew that behind my
entourage the headmasters were ranged, the first of
them a whole head shorter than me, then the
accountants, then, last and least, the emperor's
comic poet, poor Tohu. The soles of his ceremonial
clogs are only ten inches thick and he has nearly no
entourage at all. His doctor, masseuse, secretary and
chef are all the same little nurse.

I had often pictured myself like this, tall upon the
prow, the sublime tragedian arriving at the new

palace. But I had imagined a huge wide-open gate or door, with policemen holding back crowds on each side, and maybe a balcony above with the emperor on it surrounded by the college of headmasters. But though the smooth wall was twice as high as most cliffs I could see no opening in it. Along the foot was a landing stage crowded with shipping. The river spread left and right along this in a wide moat, but the current of the stream seemed to come from under the stage. Among yelling dockers and heaped bales and barrels I saw a calm group of men with official gongs on their wrists, and the black clothes and scarlet kneebands of the janitors. They waited near an empty notch. The prow of our barge slid into this notch. Dockers bolted it there. I led the company ashore.

I recognized my janitor by the green shoes these people wear when guiding poets. He reminded us that the new etiquette was enforced within the palace walls and led us to a gate. The other passengers were led to other gates. I could now see hundreds of gates, all waist high and wide enough to roll a barrel through. My entourage helped me to my knees and I crawled in after the janitor. This was the worst part of the journey. We had to crawl a great distance, mostly uphill. Adoda and the doctor tried to help by alternately butting their heads against the soles of my clogs. The floor was carpeted with bristly stuff which pierced my kneebands and scratched the palms of my hands. After twenty minutes it was hard not to sob with pain and exhaustion, and when at last they helped me to my feet I sympathized with Tohu who swore aloud that he would never go through that wall again.

The new etiquette stops honoured guests from

filling their heads with useless knowledge. We go nowhere without a janitor to lead us and look at nothing above the level of his kneebands. As I was ten feet tall I could only glimpse these slips of scarlet by leaning forward and pressing my chin into my chest. Sometimes in sunlight, sometimes in lamplight, we crossed wooden floors, brick pavements, patterned rugs and hard-packed gravel. But I mainly noticed the pain in my neck and calves, and the continual whine of Tohu complaining to his nurse. At last I fell asleep. My legs moved onward because Adoda and the doctor lifted them. The chef and secretary stopped me bending forward in the middle by pulling backward on the cape. I was wakened by the janitor striking his gong and saying, "Sir. This is your home." I lifted my eyes and saw I was inside the sunlit, afternoon, evergreen garden. It was noisy with birdsongs.

We stood near the thick hedge of cypress, holly and yew trees which hide all but some tiled roofs of the surrounding buildings. Triangular pools, square lawns and the grassy paths of a zig-zag maze are symmetrically placed round the pavilion in the middle. In each corner is a small pinewood with cages of linnets, larks and nightingales in the branches. From one stout branch hangs a trapeze where a servant dressed like a cuckoo sits imitating the call of that bird, which does not sing well in captivity. Many gardeners were discreetly trimming things or mounting ladders to feed the birds. They wore black clothes without kneebands, so they were socially invisible, and this gave the garden a wonderful air of privacy. The janitor struck his gong softly and whispered, "The leaves which grow here never fade or die." I rewarded this delicate compliment with a slight smile then gestured to a patch of moss. They laid me flat there and I was tenderly undressed. The doctor cleaned me. Adoda caressed my aching body till it breathed all over in the sun-warmed air. Meanwhile Tohu had flopped down in his nurse's arms and was snoring horribly. I had the couple removed and placed behind a hollybush out of earshot. Then I asked for the birds to be silenced, starting with the linnets and ending with the cuckoo. As the gardeners covered the cages the silence grew louder, and when the notes of the cuckoo faded there was nothing at all to hear and I slept once more.

Adoda caressed me awake before sunset and dressed me in something comfortable. The chef prepared a snack with the stove and the food from his satchel. The janitor fidgeted impatiently. We ate and drank and the doctor put something in the tea which made me quick and happy. "Come!" I said, jumping up, "Let us go straight to the pavilion!" and instead of following the path through the maze I stepped over the privet hedge bordering it which was newly planted and a few inches high. "Sir!" called the janitor, much upset, "Please do not offend the gardeners! It is not their fault that the hedge is still too small."
I said, "The gardeners are socially invisible to me."
He said, "But you are officially visible to them, and honoured guests do not offend the emperor's servants. That is not the etiquette!"
I said, "It is not a rule of the etiquette, it is convention of the etiquette, and the etiquette allows poets to be unconventional in their own home. Follow me Tohu."
But because he is trained to write popular comedy

Tohu dreads offending members of the servant class, so I walked straight to the pavilion all by myself.

It stands on a low platform with steps all round and is five sided, with a blue wooden pillar supporting the broad eaves at each corner. An observatory rises from the centre of the sloping green porcelain roof and each wall has a door in the middle with a circular window above. The doors were locked but I did not mind that. The air was still warm. A gardener spread cushions on the platform edge and I lay and thought about the poem I would be ordered to write. This was against all rules of education and etiquette. A poet cannot know his theme until the emperor orders it. Until then he should think of nothing but the sublime classics of the past. But I knew I would be commanded to celebrate a great act and the greatest act of our age is the building of the new palace. How many millions lost their homes to clear the ground? How many orphans were prostituted to keep the surveyors cheerful? How many captives died miserably quarrying its stone? How many small sons and daughters were trampled to death in the act of wiping sweat from the eyes of desperate, bricklaying parents who had fallen behind schedule? Yet this building which barbarians think a long act of intricately planned cruelty has given the empire this calm and solemn heart where honoured guests and servants can command peace and prosperity till the end of time. There can be no greater theme for a work of tragic art. It is rumoured that the palace encloses the place where the rivers watering the empire divide. If a province looks like rebelling, the headmasters of waterworks can divert the flow elsewhere and reduce it to drought, quickly or slowly, just as he pleases. This rumour is authorized by the emperor and I believe it absolutely.

While I was pondering the janitor led the little party through the maze, which seemed designed to tantalize them. Sometimes they were a few yards from me, then they would disappear behind the pavilion and after a long time reappear far away in the distance. The stars came out. The cuckoo climbed down from his trapeze and was replaced by a nightwatchman dressed like an owl. A gardener went round hanging frail paper boxes of glow-worms under the eaves. When the party reached the platform by the conventional entrance all but Adoda were tired, cross and extremely envious of my unconventional character. I welcomed them with a good-humoured chuckle.

The janitor unlocked the rooms. Someone had lit lamps in them. We saw the kitchen where the chef sleeps, the stationery office where the secretary sleeps, the lavatory where the doctor sleeps, and Adoda's room, where I sleep. Tohu and his nurse also have a room. Each room has a door into the garden and another into the big central hall where I and Tohu will make poetry when the order-to-write comes. The walls here are very white and bare. There is a thick blue carpet and a couple of punt-shaped thrones lined with cushions and divided from each other by a screen. The only other furniture is the ladder to the observatory above. The janitor assembled us here, struck the gong and made this speech in the squeaky voice the emperor uses in public.

"The emperor is glad to see you safe inside his walls. The servants will now cover their ears.

"The emperor greets Bohu, his tragic poet, like a long-lost brother. Be patient, Bohu. Stay at home. Recite the classics. Use the observatory. It was built to satisfy your craving for grand scenery. Fill your eyes and mind with the slow, sublime, eternally returning architecture of the stars. Ignore trivial flashes which stupid peasants call *falling* stars. It has been proved that these are not heavenly bodies but white-hot cinders fired out of volcanoes. When you cannot stay serene without talking to someone, dictate a letter to your parents in the old capital. Say anything you like. Do not be afraid to utter unconventional thoughts, however peculiar. Your secretary will not be punished for writing these down, your parents not punished for reading them. Be serene at all times. Keep a calm empty mind and you will see me soon.

"And now, a word for Tohu. Don't grovel so much. Be less glum. You lack Bohu's courage and dignity and don't understand people well enough to love them, as he does, but you might still be my best poet. My new palace contains many markets. Visit them with your chef when she goes shopping. Mix with the crowds of low, bustling people you must one day amuse. Learn their quips and catch-phrases. Try not to notice they stink. Take a bath when you get home and you too will see me soon."

The janitor struck his gong then asked in his own voice if we had any polite requests. I looked round the hall. I stood alone, for at the sound of the emperor's voice all but the janitor and I had lain face down on the carpet and even the janitor had sunk to his knees. Tohu and the entourage sat up now and watched me expectantly. Adoda arose with her little spoon and bottle and carefully collected from my

cheeks the sacred tears of joy which spring in the eyes
of everyone the emperor addresses. Tohu's nurse
was licking his tears off the carpet. I envied him, for
he would see more of the palace than I would, and be
more ready to write a poem about it when the order
came. I did not want to visit the market but I ached
to see the treasuries and reservoirs and grain-silos,
the pantechnicons and pantheons and gardens of
justice. I wondered how to learn about these and
still stay at home. The new dictionary of etiquette
says *All requests for knowledge will be expressed as
requests for things.* So I said, "May the bare walls of
this splendid hall be decorated with a map of the new
palace? It will help my colleague's chef to lead him
about."
Tohu shouted, "Do not speak for me, Bohu! The
emperor will send janitors to lead the chef who leads
me. I need nothing more and nothing less than the
emperor has already decided to give."
The janitor ignored him and told me, "I hear and
respect your request."
According to the new dictionary of etiquette this
answer means *No* or *Maybe* or *Yes, after a very long
time.*

The janitor left. I felt restless. The chef's best tea,
the doctor's drugs, Adoda's caresses had no effect so
I climbed into the observatory and tried to quieten
myself by watching the stars as the emperor had
commanded. But that did not work, as he foresaw, so
I summoned my secretary and dictated this letter, as
he advised. Don't be afraid to read it. You know
what the emperor said. And the postman who re-
writes letters before fixing them to the pigeons
always leaves out dangerous bits. Perhaps he will
improve my prose-style, for most of these sentences

are too short and jerky. This is the first piece of prose I ever composed, and as you know, I am a poet.

Goodbye. I will write to you again,

From the evergreen garden,

Your son,

Bohu.

DICTATED ON THE 27th LAST DAY
OF THE OLD CALENDAR.

SECOND LETTER

DEAR MOTHER, DEAR FATHER, I discover that I still love you more than anything in the world. I like my entourage, but they are servants and cannot speak to me. I like the headmaster of literature, but he only speaks about poetry. I like poetry, but have written none. I like the emperor, but have never seen him. I dictated the last letter because he said talking to you would cure my loneliness. It did, for a while, but it also brought back memories of the time we lived together before I was five, wild days full of happiness and dread, horrid fights and ecstatic picnics. Each of you loved and hated a different bit of me.

You loved talking to me, mother, we were full of playful conversation while you embroidered shirts for the police and I toyed with the coloured silks and buttons. You were small and pretty yet told such daring stories that your sister, the courtesan, screamed and covered her ears, while we laughed till the tears came. Yet you hated me going outside and locked me for an hour in the sewing box because I wore my good clogs in the lane. These were the clogs father had carved with toads on the tips. You had given them many coats of yellow lacquer, polishing each one till a member of the hon-oured-guest-class thought my clogs were made of amber and denounced us to the police for ex-travagance. But the magistrate was just and all came right in the end.

Mother always wanted me to look pretty. You, father, didn't care how I looked and you hated talking, especially to me, but you taught me to swim before I was two and took me in the punt to the sewage ditch. I helped you sift out many dead dogs and cats to sell to the gardeners for dung. You wanted me to find a dead man, because corpse-handlers (you said) don't often die of infectious diseases. The corpse I found was not a man but a boy of my own age, and instead of selling him to the gardeners we buried him where nobody would notice. I wondered why, at the time, for we needed money for rent. One day we found the corpse of a woman with a belt and bracelet of coins. The old capital must have been a slightly mad place that year. Several corpses of the honoured–guest–class bobbed along the canals and the emperor set fire to the south-eastern slums. I had never seen you act so strangely. You dragged me to the nearest market (the smell of burning was everywhere) and rented the biggest possible kite and harness. You who hate talking carried that kite down the long avenue to the eastern gate, shouting all the time to the priest, your brother, who was helping us. You said all children should be allowed to fly before they were too heavy, not just children of the honoured–guest–class. On top of the hill I grew afraid and struggled as you tightened the straps, then uncle perched me on his shoulders under that huge sail, and you took the end of the rope, and you both ran downhill into the wind. I remember a tremendous jerk, but nothing else.

I woke on the sleeping-rug on the hearth of the firelit room. My body was sore all over but you knelt beside me caressing it, mother, and when you saw my eyes were open you sprang up, screamed and attacked father with your needles. He did not fight back. Then you loved each other in the firelight beside me. It comforted me to see that. And I liked watching the babies come, especially my favourite sister with the pale hair. But during the bad winter two years later she had to be sold to the merchants for money to buy firewood.

Perhaps you did not know you had given me exactly the education a poet needs, for when you led me to the civil service academy on my fifth birthday I carried the abacus and squared slate of an accountant under my arm and I thought I would be allowed to sleep at home. But the examiner knew his job and after answering his questions I was sent to the classics dormitory of the closed literature wing and you never saw me again. I saw you again, a week or perhaps a year later. The undergraduates were crossing the garden between the halls of the drum-master who taught us rhythms and the chess-master who taught us consequential logic. I lagged behind them then slipped into the space between the laurel bushes and the outside fence and looked through. On the far side of the freshwater canal I saw a tiny distant man and woman standing staring. Even at that distance I recognized the pink roses on the scarlet sleeves of mother's best petticoat. You could not see me, yet for a minute or perhaps a whole hour you stood staring at the tall academy fence as steadily as I stared at you. Then the monitors found me. But I knew I was not forgotten, and my face never acquired the haunted, accusing look which stamped the face of the other scholars and most of the teachers too. My face displays the pained but perfectly real smile of the eternally hopeful. That glimpse through the fence enabled me to believe in love while living without it, so the imagination lessons, which made some of my schoolmates go mad or kill themselves, did not frighten me.

The imagination lessons started on my eleventh birthday after I had memorized all the classical literature and could recite it perfectly. Before that day only my smile showed how remarkable I was. The teachers put me in a windowless room with a ceiling a few inches above my head when I sat on the floor. The furniture was a couple of big shallow earthenware pans, one empty and one full of water. I was told to stay there until I had passed the water through my body and filled the empty pan with it. I was told that when the door was shut I would be a long time in darkness and silence, but before the water was drunk I would hear voices and imagine the bodies of strange companions, some of them friendly and others not. I was told that if I welcomed everyone politely even the horrible visitors would teach me useful things. The door was shut and the darkness which drowned me was surprisingly warm and familiar. It was exactly the darkness inside my mother's sewing-box. For the first time since entering the academy I felt at home.

After a while I heard your voices talking quietly together and thought you had been allowed to visit me at last, but when I joined the conversation I found we were talking of things I must have heard discussed when I was a few months old. It was very interesting. I learned later that other students imagined the voices and company of ghouls and madmen and gulped down the water so fast that they became ill. I sipped mine as slowly as possible. The worst person I met was the corpse of the dead boy I had helped father take from the canal. I knew him by the smell. He lay a long time in the corner of the room before I thought of welcoming him and asking his name. He told me he was not an ill-treated orphan, as father had thought, but the son of a rich waterworks inspector who had seen a servant stealing food and been murdered to stop him telling people. He told me many things about life among the highest kinds of honoured-guest-class, things I could never have learned from my teachers at the academy who belonged to the lower kind. The imagination lessons became, for me, a way of escaping from the drum, chess and recitation masters and of meeting in darkness everyone I had lost with infancy. The characters of classical literature started visiting me too, from the celestial monkey who is our ancestor to emperor Hyun who burned all the unnecessary books and built the great wall to keep out unnecessary people. They taught me things about themselves which classical literature does not mention. Emperor Hyun, for instance, was in some ways a petty, garrulous old man much troubled with arthritis. The best part of him was exactly like my father patiently dredging for good things in the sewage mud of the north-west slums. And the imperious seductive white demon in the comic creation myth turned out to be very like my aunt, the courtesan, who also transformed herself into different characters to interest strangers, yet all the time was determinedly herself. My aunt visited me more than was proper and eventually I imagined something impossible with her and my academic gown was badly stained. This was noted by the school laundry. The next day the medical inspector made small wounds at the top of my thighs which never quite healed and are still treated twice a month. I have never since soiled cloth in that way. My fifth limb sometimes stiffens under Adoda's caresses but nothing comes from it.

Soon after the operation the headmaster of literature visited the academy. He was a heavy man, as heavy as I am now. He said, "You spend more days imagining than the other scholars, yet your health is good. What guests come to your dark room?"
I told him. He asked detailed questions. I took several days to describe everyone. When I stopped he was silent a while then said, "Do you understand why you have been trained like this?"
I said I did not.
He said, "A poet needs an adventurous, sensuous infancy to enlarge his appetites. But large appetites must be given a single direction or they will produce a mere healthy human being. So the rich infancy must be followed by a childhood of instruction which starves the senses, especially of love. The child is thus forced to struggle for love in the only place he can experience it, which is memory, and the only place he can practise it, which is imagination. This education, which I devised, destroys the minds it does not enlarge. You are my first success. Stand up."
I did, and he stooped, with difficulty, and tied the dark green ribbons round my knees. I said, "Am I a poet now?"
He said, "Yes. You are now the emperor's honoured guest and tragic poet, the only modern author whose work will be added to the classics of world literature." I asked when I could start writing. He said, "Not for a long time. Only the emperor can supply a theme equal to your talent and he is not ready to do so. But the waiting will be made easy. The days of the

coarse robe, dull teachers and dark room are over. You will live in the palace."

I asked him if I could see my parents first. He said, "No. Honoured guests only speak to inferior classes when asking for useful knowledge and your parents are no use to you now. They have changed. Perhaps your small pretty mother has become a brazen harlot like her sister, your strong silent father an arthritic old bore like the emperor Hyun. After meeting them you would feel sad and wise and want to write ordinary poems about the passage of time and fallen petals drifting down the stream. Your talent must be preserved for a greater theme than that."

I asked if I would have friends at the palace. He said, "You will have two. My system has produced one other poet, not very good, who may perhaps be capable of some second-rate doggerel when the order-to-write comes. He will share your apartment. But your best friend knows you already. Here is his face."

He gave me a button as broad as my thumb with a small round hairless head enamelled on it. The eyes were black slits between complicated wrinkles; the sunk mouth seemed to have no teeth but was curved in a surprisingly sweet sly smile. I knew this must be the immortal emperor. I asked if he was blind.

"Necessarily so. This is the hundred–and–second year of his reign and all sights are useless knowledge to him now. But his hearing is remarkably acute."

So I and Tohu moved to the palace of the old capital and a highly trained entourage distracted my enlarged mind from the work it was waiting to do. We were happy but cramped. The palace staff kept increasing until many honoured guests had to be housed in the city outside, which took away homes from the citizens. No new houses could be built because all the skill and materials in the empire were employed on the new palace upriver, so all gardens and graveyards and even several streets were covered with tents, barrels and packing-cases where thousands of families were living. I never used the streets myself because honoured guests there were often looked at very rudely, with glances of concealed dislike. The emperor arranged for the soles of our ceremonial clogs to be thickened until even the lowest of his honoured guests could pass through a crowd of common citizens without meeting them face-to-face. But after that some from the palace were jostled by criminals too far beneath them to identify, so it was ordered that honoured guests should be led everywhere by a janitor and surrounded by their entourage. This made us perfectly safe, but movement through the densely packed streets became very difficult. At last the emperor barred common citizens from the streets during the main business hours and things improved.

Yet these same citizens who glared and jostled and grumbled at us were terrified of us going away! Their trades and professions depended on the court; without it most of them would become unnecessary people. The emperor received anonymous letters saying that if he tried to leave, his wharves and barges would catch fire and the sewage ditches would be diverted into the palace reservoir. You may wonder how your son, a secluded poet, came to know these things. Well, the headmaster of civil peace sometimes asked me to improve the wording of rumours authorized by the emperor, while Tohu improved the unauthorized ones that were broadcast by the beggars' association. We both put out a story that citizens who worked hard and did not grumble would be employed as servants in the new palace. This was true, but not as true as people hoped. The anonymous letters stopped and instead the emperor received signed petitions from the workingmen's clubs explaining how long and well they had served him and asking to go on doing it. Each signatory was sent a written reply with the emperor's seal saying that his request had been heard and respected. In the end the court departed upriver quietly, in small groups, accompanied by the workingmen's leaders. But the mass of new palace servants come from more docile cities than the old capital. It is nice to be in a safe home with nobody to frighten us.

I am stupid to mention these things. You know the old capital better than I do. Has it recovered the bright uncrowded streets and gardens I remember when we lived there together so many years ago?

This afternoon is very sunny and hot, so I am dictating my letter on the observatory tower. There is a fresh breeze at this height. When I climbed up here two hours ago I found a map of the palace on the table beside my map of the stars. It seems my requests are heard with unusual respect. Not much of the palace is marked on the map but enough to identify the tops of some big pavilions to the north. A shining black pagoda rises from the garden of irrevocable justice where disobedient people have things removed which cannot be returned, like eardrums, eyes, limbs and heads. Half-a-mile away a similar but milkwhite pagoda marks the garden of revocable justice where good people receive gifts which can afterwards be taken back, like homes, wives, salaries and pensions. Between these pagodas but further off, is the court of summons, a vast round tower with a forest of bannerpoles on the roof. On the highest pole the emperor's scarlet flag floats above the rainbow flag of the headmasters, so he is in there today conferring with the whole college.

Shortly before lunch Tohu came in with a woodcut scroll which he said was being pinned up and sold all over the market, perhaps all over the empire. At the top is the peculiar withered-apple-face of the immortal emperor which fascinates me more each time I see it. I feel his blind eyes could eat me up and a few days later the sweet sly mouth would spit me out in a new, perhaps improved form. Below the portrait are these words:

> *Forgive me for ruling you but someone must. I am a small weak old man but have the strength of all my good people put together. I am blind, but your ears are my ears so I hear everything. As I grow older I try to be kinder. My guests in the new palace help me. Their names and pictures are underneath.*

Then come the two tallest men in the empire. One of them is:

> *Fieldmarshal Ko who commands all imperial armies and police and defeats all imperial enemies. He has degrees in strategy from twenty-eight academies but leaves thinking to the emperor. He hates unnecessary people but says "Most of them are outside the great wall."*

The other is:

> *Bohu, the great poet. His mind is the largest in the land. He knows the feelings of everyone from the poor peasant in the ditch to the old emperor on the throne. Soon his great poem will be painted above the door of every townhouse, school, barracks, post-*

office, law-court, theatre and prison in the land.
Will it be about war? Peace? Love? Justice?
Agriculture? Architecture? Time? Fallen apple-
blossom in the stream? Bet about this with your
friends.

I was pleased to learn there were only two tallest
men in the empire. I had thought there were three of
us. Tohu's face was at the end of the scroll in a row
of twenty others. He looked very small and cross
between a toe-surgeon and an inspector of chicken-
feed. His footnote said:

Tohu hopes to write funny poems. Will he succeed?

I rolled up the scroll and returned it with a friendly
nod but Tohu was uneasy and wanted conversation.
He said, "The order-to-write is bound to come soon
now."

"Yes."

"Are you frightened?"

"No."

"Your work may not please."

"That is unlikely."

"What will you do when your great poem is complete?"

"I shall ask the emperor for death."

Tohu leaned forward and whispered eagerly, "Why?
There is a rumour that when our poem is written the
wounds at the top of our thighs will heal up and we
will be able to love our masseuse as if we were
common men!"

I smiled and said, "That would be anticlimax."

I enjoy astonishing Tohu.

Dear parents, this is my last letter to you. I will
write no more prose. But laugh aloud when you see
my words painted above the doors of the public
buildings. Perhaps you are poor, sick or dying. I
hope not. But nothing can deprive you of the greatest

happiness possible for a common man and woman.
You have created an immortal,

Who lives in the evergreen garden,

Your son,

Bohu.

DICTATED ON THE 19th LAST DAY
OF THE OLD CALENDAR.

THIRD LETTER

DEAR MOTHER, DEAR FATHER, I am full of confused feelings. I saw the emperor two days ago. He is not what I thought. If I describe everything very carefully, especially to you, perhaps I won't go mad.

I wakened that morning as usual and lay peacefully in Adoda's arms. I did not know this was my last peaceful day. Our room faces north. Through the round window above the door I could see the banners above the court of summons. The scarlet and the rainbow flags still floated on the highest pole but beneath them flapped the dark green flag of poetry. There was a noise of hammering and when I looked outside some joiners were building a low wooden bridge which went straight across the maze from the platform edge. I called in the whole household. I said, "Today we visit the emperor." They looked alarmed. I felt very gracious and friendly. I said, "Only I and Tohu will be allowed to look at him but everyone will hear his voice. The clothes I and Tohu wear are chosen by the etiquette, but I want the rest of you to dress as if you are visiting a rich famous friend you love very much." Adoda smiled but the others still looked alarmed. Tohu muttered, "The emperor is blind."
I had forgotten that. I nodded and said, "His headmasters are not."

When the janitor arrived I was standing ten feet

tall at the end of the bridge. Adoda on my right wore a dress of dark green silk and her thick hair was mingled with sprigs of yew. Even Tohu's nurse wore something special. The janitor bowed, turned, and paused to let me fix my eyes on his kneebands; then he struck his gong and we moved toward the court.

The journey lasted an hour but I would not have wearied had it lasted a day. I was as incapable of tiredness as a falling stone on its way to the ground. I felt excited, strong, yet peacefully determined at the same time. The surfaces we crossed became richer and larger: pavements of marquetry and mosaic, thresholds of bronze and copper, carpets of fine tapestry and exotic fur. We crossed more than one bridge for I heard the lip-lapping of a great river or lake. The janitor eventually struck the gong for delay and I sensed the wings of a door expanding before us. We moved through a shadow into greater light. The janitor struck the end-of-journey note and his legs left my field of vision. The immortal emperor's squeaky voice said, "Welcome, my poets. Consider yourselves at home."

I raised my eyes and first of all saw the college of headmasters. They sat on felt stools at the edge of a platform which curved round us like the shore of a bay. The platform was so high that their faces were level with my own, although I was standing erect. Though I had met only a few of them I knew all twenty-three by their regalia. The headmaster of waterworks wore a silver drainpipe round his leg, the headmaster of civil peace held a ceremonial bludgeon, the headmaster of history carried a stuffed parrot on his wrist. The headmaster of etiquette sat in the very centre holding the emperor, who was two feet high. The emperor's head and the hands dangling out of his sleeves were normal size, but the body in the scarlet silk robe seemed to be a short wooden staff. His skin was papier mache with lacquer varnish, yet in conversation he was quick and sprightly. He ran from hand to hand along the row and did not speak again until he reached the headmaster of vaudeville on the extreme left. Then he said, "I shock you. Before we talk I must put you at ease, especially Tohu whose neck is sore craning up at me. Shall I tell a joke, Tohu?"

"Oh yes sir, hahaha! Oh yes sir, hahaha!" shouted Tohu, guffawing hysterically.

The emperor said, "You don't need a joke. You are laughing happily already!"

I realized that this was the emperor's joke and gave a brief appreciative chuckle. I had known the emperor was not human, but was so surprised to see he was not alive that my conventional tears did not flow at the sound of his voice. This was perhaps lucky as Adoda was too far below me to collect them.

The emperor moved to the headmaster of history and spoke on a personal note: "Ask me intimate questions, Bohu."

I said, "Sir, have you always been a puppet?"

He said, "I am not, even now, completely a puppet. My skull and the bones of my hands are perfectly real. The rest was boiled off by doctors fifteen years ago in the operation which made me immortal."

I said, "Was it sore becoming immortal?"

He said, "I did not notice. I had senile dementia at the time and for many years before that I was, in private life, vicious and insensitive. But the wisdom of an emperor has nothing to do with his character. It is the combined intelligence of everyone who obeys him."

The sublime truth of this entered me with such force that I gasped for breath. Yes. The wisdom of a government is the combined intelligence of those who obey it. I gazed at the simpering dummy with pity and awe. Tears poured thickly down my cheeks but I did not heed them.

"Sir!" I cried, "Order us to write for you. We love you. We are ready."

The emperor moved to the headmaster of civil peace and shook the tiny imperial frock into dignified folds before speaking. He said, "I order you to write a poem celebrating my irrevocable justice."

I said, "Will this poem commemorate a special act of justice?"

He said, "Yes. I have just destroyed the old capital, and everyone living there, for the crime of disobedience."

I smiled and nodded enthusiastically, thinking I had not heard properly. I said, "Very good sir, yes, that will do very well. But could you suggest a particular event, a historically important action, which might, in my case, form the basis of a meditative ode, or a popular ballad, in my colleague's case? The action or event should be one which demonstrates the emperor's justice. Irrevocably."

He said, "Certainly. The old capital was full of unnecessary people. They planned a rebellion. Field-marshal Ko besieged it, burned it flat and killed everyone who lived there. The empire is peaceful again. That is your theme. Your pavilion is now decorated with information on the subject. Return there and write."

"Sir!" I said, "I hear and respect your order, I hear and respect your order!"

I went on saying this, unable to stop. Tohu was

screaming with laughter and shouting, "Oh my colleague is extremely unconventional, all great poets are, I will write for him, I will write for all of us hahahaha!"

The headmasters were uneasy. The emperor ran from end to end of them and back, never resting till the headmaster of moral philosophy forced him violently onto the headmaster of etiquette. Then the emperor raised his head and squeaked, "This is not etiquette, I adjourn the college!"

He then flopped upside down on a stool while the headmasters hurried out.

I could not move. Janitors swarmed confusedly round my entourage. My feet left the floor, I was jerked one way, then another, then carried quickly backward till my shoulder struck something, maybe a doorpost. And then I was falling, and I think I heard Adoda scream before I became unconscious.

I woke under a rug on my writing-throne in the hall of the pavilion. Paper screens had been placed round it painted with views of the old capital at different stages of the rebellion, siege and massacre. Behind one screen I heard Tohu dictating to his secretary. Instead of taking nine days to assimilate his material the fool was composing already.

Postal pigeons whirl like snow from the new palace, he chanted.

Trained hawks of the rebels strike them dead.

The emperor summons his troops by heliograph:

"Fieldmarshal Ko, besiege the ancient city."

Can hawks catch the sunbeam flashed from silver mirror?

No, hahahaha. No, hahahaha. Rebels are ridiculous.

I held my head. My main thought was that you, mother, you, father, do not exist now and all my

childhood is flat cinders. This thought is such pain
that I got up and stumbled round the screens to
make sure of it.

I first beheld a beautiful view of the old capital,
shown from above like a map, but with every
building clear and distinct. Pink and green buds
on the trees showed this was springtime. I looked
down into a local garden of justice where a fat
magistrate fanned by a singing-girl sat on a doorstep. A man, woman, and child lay flat on the ground
before him and nearby a policeman held a dish with
two yellow dots on it. I knew these were clogs with
toads on the tips, and that the family was being
accused of extravagance and would be released with
a small fine. I looked again and saw a little house by
the effluent of a sewage canal. Two little women sat
sewing on the doorstep, it was you, mother, and your
sister, my aunt. Outside the fence a man in a punt,
helped by a child, dragged a body from the mud.
The bodies of many members of the honoured-
guest-class were bobbing along the sewage canals.
The emperor's cavalry were setting fire to the south-
eastern slums and sabering families who tried to
escape. The strangest happening of all was on a hill
outside the eastern gate. A man held the rope of a
kite which floated out over the city, a kite shaped like
an eagle with parrot-coloured feathers. A child hung
from it. This part of the picture was on a larger scale
than the rest. The father's face wore a look of great
pride, but the child was staring down on the city
below, not with terror or delight, but with a cool,
stern, assessing stare. In the margin of this screen
was written *The rebellion begins.*

I only glanced at the other screens. Houses
flamed, whole crowds were falling from bridges into

canals to avoid the hooves and sabres of the cavalry. If I had looked closely I would have recognized your figures in the crowds again and again. The last screen showed a cindery plain scored by canals so clogged with ruin that neither clear nor foul water appeared in them. The only life was a host of crows and ravens as thick on the ground as flies on raw and rotten meat.

I heard an apologetic cough and found the head-master of literature beside me. He held a dish with a flask and two cups on it. He said, "Your doctor thinks wine will do you good."
I returned to the throne and lay down. He sat beside me and said, "The emperor has been greatly im-pressed by the gravity of your response to his order-to-write. He is sure your poem will be very great."
I said nothing. He filled the cups with wine and tasted one. I did not. He said, "You once wanted to write about the building of the new palace. Was that a good theme for a poem?"
"Yes."
"But the building of the new palace and the destruc-tion of the old capital are the same thing. All big new things must begin by destroying the old. Otherwise they are a mere continuation."
I said, "Do you mean that the emperor would have destroyed the old capital even without a rebellion?"
"Yes. The old capital was linked by roads and canals to every corner of the empire. For more than nine dynasties other towns looked to it for guidance. Now they must look to us."
I said, "Was there a rebellion?"
"We are so sure there was one that we did not enquire about the matter. The old capital was a market for the empire. When the court came here

we brought the market with us. The citizens left behind had three choices. They could starve to death, or beg in the streets of other towns, or rebel. The brave and intelligent among them must have dreamed of rebellion. They probably talked about it. Which is conspiracy."

"Was it justice to kill them for that?"

"Yes. The justice which rules a nation must be more dreadful than the justice which rules a family. The emperor himself respects and pities his defeated rebels. Your poem might mention that."

I said, "You once said my parents were useless to me because time had changed them. You were wrong. As long as they lived I knew that though they might look old and different, though I might never see them again, I was still loved, still alive in ways you and your emperor can never know. And though I never saw the city after going to school I thought of it growing like an onion; each year there was a new skin of leaves and dung on the gardens, new traffic on the streets, new whitewash on old walls. While the old city and my old parents lived my childhood lived too. But the emperor's justice has destroyed my past, irrevocably. I am like a land without culture or history. I am now too shallow to write a poem."

The headmaster said, "It is true that the world is so packed with the present moment that the past, a far greater quantity, can only gain entrance through the narrow gate of a mind. But your mind is unusually big. I enlarged it myself, artificially. You are able to bring your father, mother and city to life and death again in a tragedy, a tragedy the whole nation will read. Remember that the world is one vast graveyard of defunct cities, all destroyed by the shifting of markets they could not control, and all compressed by literature into a handful of poems. The emperor only does what ordinary time does. He simply speeds things up. He wants your help."

I said, "A poet has to look at his theme steadily. A lot of people have no work because an emperor moves a market, so to avoid looking like a bad government he accuses them of rebelling and kills them. My stomach rejects that theme. The emperor is not very wise. If he had saved the lives of my parents perhaps I could have worked for him."

The headmaster said, "The emperor did consider saving your parents before sending in the troops, but I advised him not to. If they were still alive your poem would be an ordinary piece of political excuse-making. Anyone can see the good in disasters which leave their family and property intact. But a poet must feel the cracks in the nation splitting his individual heart. How else can he mend them?"

I said, "I refuse to mend this cracked nation. Please tell the emperor that I am useless to him, and that I ask his permission to die."

The headmaster put his cup down and said, after a while, "That is an important request. The emperor will not answer it quickly."

I said, "If he does not answer me in three days I will act without him."

The headmaster of literature stood up and said, "I think I can promise an answer at the end of three days."

He went away. I closed my eyes, covered my ears and stayed where I was. My entourage came in and wanted to wash, feed and soothe me but I let nobody within touching distance. I asked for water, sipped a little, freshened my face with the rest then commanded them to leave. They were unhappy, especially Adoda who wept silently all the time.

This comforted me a little. I almost wished the etiquette would let me speak to Adoda. I was sure Tohu talked all the time to his nurse when nobody else could hear. But what good does talking do? Everything I could say would be as horrible to Adoda as it is to me. So I lay still and said nothing and tried not to hear the drone of Tohu dictating all through that night and the following morning. Toward the end, half his lines seemed to be stylized exclamations of laughter and even between them he giggled a lot. I thought perhaps he was drunk, but when he came to me in the evening he was unusually dignified. He knelt down carefully by my throne and whispered, "I finished my poem today. I sent it to the emperor but I don't think he likes it."

I shrugged. He whispered, "I have just received an invitation from him. He wants my company tomorrow in the garden of irrevocable justice."

I shrugged. He whispered, "Bohu, you know my entourage is very small. My nurse may need help. Please let your doctor accompany us."

I nodded. He whispered, "You are my only friend," and went away.

I did not see him next day till late evening. His nurse came and knelt at the steps of my throne. She looked smaller, older and uglier than usual and she handed me a scroll of the sort used for public announcements. At the top were portraits of myself and Tohu. Underneath it said:

The emperor asked his famous poets Bohu and Tohu to celebrate the destruction of the old capital. Bohu said no. He is still an honoured guest in the evergreen garden, happy and respected by all who know him. Tohu said yes and wrote a very bad poem. You may read the worst bits below. Tohu's

*tongue, right shoulder, arm and hand have now
been replaced by wooden ones. The emperor prefers
a frank confession of inability to the useless words
of the flattering toad-eater.*

I stood up and said drearily, "I will visit your master."

He lay on a rug in her room with his face to the
wall. He was breathing loudly. I could see almost
none of him for he still wore the ceremonial cape
which was badly stained in places. My doctor knelt
beside him and answered my glance by spreading the
palms of his hands. The secretary, chef and two
masseuses knelt near the door. I sighed and said,
"Yesterday you told me I was your only friend,
Tohu. I can say now that you are mine. I am sorry
our training has stopped us showing it."

I don't think he heard me for shortly after he
stopped breathing. I then told my entourage that
I had asked to die and expected a positive answer
from the emperor on the following day. They were
all very pale but my news made them paler still.
When someone more than seven feet tall dies of
unnatural causes the etiquette requires his entourage
to die in the same way. This is unlucky, but I did not
make this etiquette, this palace, this empire which I
shall leave as soon as possible, with or without the
emperor's assistance. The hand of my secretary
trembles as he writes these words. I pity him.

To my dead parents in the ash of the old capital,

From the immortal emperor's supreme <u>nothing,</u> Their son,

Bohu.

DICTATED ON THE 10th LAST DAY
OF THE OLD CALENDAR.

FOURTH LETTER

DEAR MOTHER, DEAR FATHER, I must always return to you, it seems. The love, the rage, the power which fills me now cannot rest until it has sent a stream of words in your direction. I have written my great poem but not the poem wanted. I will explain all this.

On the evening of the third day my entourage were sitting round me when a common janitor brought the emperor's reply in the unusual form of a letter. He gave it to the secretary, bowed and withdrew. The secretary is a good ventriloquist and read the emperor's words in the appropriate voice.

The emperor hears and respects his great poet's request for death. The emperor grants Bohu permission to do anything he likes, write anything he likes, and die however, wherever, and whenever he chooses.

I said to my doctor, "Choose the death you want for yourself and give it to me first."

He said, "Sir, may I tell you what that death is?"

"Yes."

"It will take many words to do so. I cannot be brief on this matter."

"Speak. I will not interrupt."

He said, "Sir, my life has been a dreary and limited one, like your own. I speak for all your servants when I say this. We have all been, in a limited way, married to you, and our only happiness was being useful to a great poet. We understand why you cannot become one. Our own parents have died in the ancient capital, so death is the best thing for everyone, and I can make it painless. All I need is a closed room, the chef's portable stove and a handful of prepared herbs which are always with me.

"But sir, need we go rapidly to this death? The emperor's letter suggests not, and that letter has the force of a passport. We can use it to visit any part of the palace we like. Give us permission to escort you to death by a flowery, roundabout path which touches on some commonplace experiences all men wish to enjoy. I ask this selfishly, for our own sakes, but also unselfishly, for yours. We love you sir."

Tears came to my eyes but I said firmly, "I cannot be seduced. My wish for death is an extension of my wish not to move, feel, think or see. I desire *nothing* with all my heart. But you are different. For a whole week you have my permission to glut yourself on anything the emperor's letter permits."

The doctor said, "But sir, that letter has no force without your company. Allow yourself to be carried with us. We shall not plunge you into riot and disorder. All will be calm and harmonious, you need not walk, or stand, or even think. We know your needs. We can read the subtlest flicker of your eyebrow. Do not even say *yes* to this proposal of mine. Simply close your eyes in the tolerant smile which is so typical of you."

I was weary, and did so, and allowed them to wash, feed and prepare me for sleep as in the old days. And they did something new. The doctor wiped the wounds at the top of my thighs with something astringent and Adoda explored them, first with her tongue and then with her teeth. I felt a pain almost too fine to be noticed and looking down I saw her draw from each wound a quivering silver thread. Then the doctor bathed me again and Adoda embraced me and whispered, "May I share your throne?"

I nodded. Everyone else went away and I slept deeply for the first time in four days.

Next morning I dreamed my aunt was beside me, as young and lovely as in days when she looked like the white demon. I woke up clasping Adoda so insistently that we both cried aloud. The doors of the central hall were all wide open; so were the doors to the garden in the rooms beyond. Light flooded in on us from all sides. During breakfast I grew calm again but it was not my habitual calm. I felt adventurous under the waist. This feeling did not yet reach my head, which smiled cynically. But I was no longer exactly the same man.

The rest of the entourage came in wearing bright clothes and garlands. They stowed my punt-shaped throne with food, wine, drugs and instruments. It is a big throne and when they climbed in themselves there was no overcrowding even though Tohu's nurse was there too. Then a horde of janitors arrived with long poles which they fixed to the sides of the throne, and I and my entourage were lifted into the air and carried out to the garden. The secretary sat in the prow playing a mouth-organ while the chef and doctor accompanied him with zither and drum. The janitors almost danced as they trampled across the maze, and this was so surprising that I laughed aloud, staring freely up at the pigeon-flecked azure sky, the porcelain gables with their coloured flags, the crowded tops of markets, temples and manufactories. Perhaps when I was small I had gazed as greedily for the mere useless fun of it, but for years I had only used my eyes professionally, to collect poetical knowledge, or shielded them, as required by the etiquette. "Oh, Adoda!" I cried, warming my face in her hair, "All this new knowledge is useless and I love it."

She whispered, "The use of living is the taste it gives. The emperor has made you the only free man in the world. You can taste anything you like."

We entered a hall full of looms where thousands of women in coarse gowns were weaving rich tapestry. I was fascinated. The air was stifling, but not to me. Adoda and the chef plied their fans and the doctor refreshed me with a fine mist of cool water. I also had the benefit of janitors without kneebands, so our party was socially invisible; I could stare at whom I liked and they could not see me at all. I noticed a girl with pale brown hair toiling on one side. Adoda halted the janitors and whispered, "That lovely girl is your sister who was sold to the merchants. She became a skilled weaver so they resold her here."

I said, "That is untrue. My sister would be over forty now and that girl, though robust, is not yet sixteen."

"Would you like her to join us?"

I closed my eyes in the tolerant smile and a janitor negotiated with an overseer. When we moved on, the girl was beside us. She was silent and frightened at first but we gave her garlands, food and wine and she soon became merry.

We came into a narrow street with a gallery along one side on the level of my throne. Tall elegant women in the robes of the court strolled and leaned there. A voice squeaked, "Hullo, Bohu" and looking

up I saw the emperor smiling from the arms of the
most slender and disdainful. I stared at him. He said,
"Bohu hates me but I must suffer that. He is too
great a man to be ordered by a poor old emperor.
This lady, Bohu, is your aunt, a very wonderful
courtesan. Say hullo!"
I laughed and said, "You are a liar, sir."
He said, "Nonetheless you mean to take her from
me. Join the famous poet, my dear, he goes down to
the floating world. Goodbye, Bohu. I do not just give
people death. That is only half my job."
The emperor moved to a lady nearby, the slender
one stepped among us and we all sailed on down the
street.

We reached a wide river and the janitors waded in
until the throne rested on the water. They withdrew the poles, laid them on the thwarts and we
drifted out from shore. The doctor produced pipes
and measured a careful dose into each bowl. We
smoked and talked; the men played instruments, the
women sang. The little weaver knew many popular
songs, some sad, some funny. I suddenly wished
Tohu was with us, and wept. They asked why. I
told them and we all wept together. Twilight fell
and a moon came out. The court lady stood up,
lifted a pole and steered us expertly into a grove of
willows growing in shallow water. Adoda hung
lanterns in the branches. We ate, clasped each
other, and slept.

I cannot count the following days. They may have
been two, or three, or many. Opium plays tricks
with time but I did not smoke enough to stop me
loving. I loved in many ways, some tender, some
harsh, some utterly absent-minded. More than once
I said to Adoda, "Shall we die now? Nothing can be

sweeter than this" but she said, "Wait a little longer. You haven't done all you want yet."

When at last my mind grew clear about the order of time the weaver and court lady had left us and we drifted down a tunnel to a bright arch at the end. We came into a lagoon on a lane of clear water between beds of rushes and lily-leaves. It led to an island covered with spires of marble and copper shining in the sun. My secretary said, "That is the poets' pantheon. Would you like to land, sir?"

I nodded.

We disembarked and I strolled barefoot on warm moss between the spires. Each had an open door in the base with steps down to the tomb where the body would lie. Above each door was a white tablet where the poet's great work would be painted. All the tombs and tablets were vacant, of course, for I am the first poet in the new palace and was meant to be the greatest, for the tallest spire in the centre was sheathed in gold with my name on the door. I entered. The room downstairs had space for us all with cushions for the entourage and a silver throne for me.

"To deserve to lie here I must write a poem," I thought, and looked into my mind. The poem was there, waiting to come out. I returned upstairs, went outside and told the secretary to fetch paint and brushes from his satchel and go to the tablet. I then dictated my poem in a slow firm voice.

THE EMPEROR'S INJUSTICE

Scattered buttons and silks, a broken kite in the mud,
A child's yellow clogs cracked by the horses' hooves.
A land weeps for the head city, lopped by sabre, cracked by hooves,
The houses ash, the people meat for crows.

A week ago wind rustled dust in the empty market.
"Starve," said the moving dust, "Beg. Rebel. Starve. Beg. Rebel."
We do not do such things. We are peaceful people.
We have food for six more days, let us wait.
The emperor will accommodate us, underground.

It is sad to be unnecessary.
All the bright mothers, strong fathers, raffish aunts,
Lost sisters and brothers, all the rude servants
Are honoured guests of the emperor, underground.

We sit in the tomb now. The door is closed, the only light is the red glow from the chef's charcoal stove. My entourage dreamily puff their pipes, the doctor's fingers sift the dried herbs, the secretary is ending my last letter. We are tired and happy. The emperor said I could write what I liked. Will my poem be broadcast? No. If that happened the common people would rise and destroy that evil little puppet and all the cunning, straightfaced, pompous men who use him. Nobody will read my words but a passing gardener, perhaps, who will paint them out to stop them reaching the emperor's ear. But I have at last made the poem I was made to make. I lie down to sleep in perfect satisfaction.

Goodbye. I still love you.

Your son,

Bohu.

DICTATED SOMETIME SHORTLY BEFORE
THE LAST DAY
OF THE OLD CALENDAR.

LAST LETTER

A CRITICAL APPRECIATION OF THE
POEM BY THE LATE TRAGEDIAN BOHU
ENTITLED

THE EMPEROR'S INJUSTICE

DELIVERED
TO THE IMPERIAL COLLEGE OF HEAD-
MASTERS, NEW PALACE UNIVERSITY

My Dear Colleagues, This is exactly the poem we
require. Our patience in waiting for it till the last
possible moment has been rewarded. The work is
shorter than we expected, but that makes distribu-
tion easier. It had a starkness unusual in government
poetry, but this starkness satisfies the nation's need
much more than the work we hoped for. With a
single tiny change the poem can be used at once. I
know some of my colleagues will raise objections,
but I will answer these in the course of my appreciation.

A noble spirit of pity blows through this poem like
a warm wind. The destroyed people are not mocked
and calumniated, we identify with them, and the
third line:
*A land cries for the head city, lopped by sabre,
cracked by hooves*, invites the whole empire to
mourn. But does this wind of pity fan the flames
of political protest? No. It presses the mind of the
reader inexorably toward *nothing*, toward death.

This is clearly shown in the poem's treatment of rebellion:

"Starve," said the moving dust, "Beg. Rebel.
Starve. Beg. Rebel."
We do not do such things. We are peaceful people.
We have food for six more days, let us wait.

The poem assumes that a modern population will find the prospect of destruction by their own government less alarming than action against it. The truth of this is shown in today's police report from the old capital. It describes crowds of people muttering at street corners and completely uncertain of what action to take. They have a little food left. They fear the worst, yet hope, if they stay docile, the emperor will not destroy them immediately. This state of things was described by Bohu yesterday in the belief that it had happened a fortnight ago! A poet's intuitive grasp of reality was never more clearly demonstrated.

At this point the headmaster of civil peace will remind me that the job of the poem is not to describe reality but to encourage our friends, frighten our enemies, and reconcile the middling people to the destruction of the old capital. The headmaster of moral philosophy will also remind me of our decision that people will most readily accept the destruction of the old capital if we accuse it of rebellion. That was certainly the main idea in the original order-to-write, but I would remind the college of what we had to do to the poet who obeyed that order. Tohu knew exactly what we wanted and gave it to us. His poem described the emperor as wise, witty, venerable, patient, loving and omnipotent. He described the citizens of the old capital as stupid, childish, greedy, absurd, yet inspired by a vast communal lunacy which endangered the empire. He obediently wrote a popular melodrama which could not convince a single intelligent man and would only over-excite stupid ones, who are fascinated by criminal lunatics who attack the established order.

The problem is this. If we describe the people we kill as dangerous rebels they look glamorous; if we describe them as weak and silly we seem unjust. Tohu could not solve that problem. Bohu has done with startling simplicity.

He presents the destruction as a simple, stunning, inevitable fact. The child, mother and common people in the poem exist passively, doing nothing but weep, gossip, and wait. The active agents of hoof, sabre, and (by extension) crow, belong to the emperor, who is named at the end of the middle verse:

The emperor will accommodate us, underground.

and at the end of the last:

Bright mothers, strong fathers . . . all the rude servants
Are honoured guests of the emperor, underground.

Consider the *weight* this poem gives to our immortal emperor! He is not described or analysed, he is presented as a final, competent, all-embracing force, as unarguable as the weather, as inevitable as death. This is how all governments should appear to people who are not in them.

To sum up, *THE EMPEROR'S INJUSTICE* will delight our friends, depress our enemies, and fill middling people with nameless awe. The only change required is the elimination of the first syllable in the last word of the title. I advise that the poem be sent today to every village, town and city in the land. At the same time Fieldmarshal Ko should be ordered to destroy the old capital. When the poem appears over doors of public buildings the readers will read of an event which is occurring simultaneously. In this way the literary and military sides of the attack will reinforce each other with unusual thoroughness. Fieldmarshal Ko should take special care that the poet's parents do not escape the general massacre, as a rumour to that effect will lessen the poignancy of the official biography, which I will complete in the coming year.

I remain your affectionate colleague,

Gigadib,

Headmaster of modern and classical literature.

DICTATED ON DAY I
OF THE NEW CALENDAR

SIR THOMAS'S

For Judgment, Learning, Wit, For Invention, Sweetness, stile.

To the Eternal GLORY of THOMAS URCHARD

LOGOPANDOCY

The

Secret and Apocryphal Diurnal

of

SIR THOMAS URQUHART OF CROMARTIE

Knight

Recently Discovered and Published
Against the Author's Expressed Will & Command
for the
Instruction and Reformation
of the
Brittanic League of Commonwealths;
Wherein is recorded a dialogue with the late
Protector Cromwell's Latin secretary, which neatly
unfolds a scheme to repair the divided Nature of
Man by rationally reintegering God's Gift of
Tongues to Adam by a verboradical applianing of
Neper's logarythms to the grammar of an Asiatick
people, thought to be the lost tribe of Israel, whose
language predates the Babylonic Cataclysm;
With auxiliary matter vindicating the grandeur of
SCOTLAND from the foul Infamy whereinto the
Rigid Presbyterian party of that nation, out of their
covetousness and their overweening ambition,
hath most dissembledly involved it.

---

*Oh thou'rt a Book in Truth with love to many
Done by and for the free'st spoke Scot of any.*

Sᵗ Thomas (Orchard)   Knight.

For Arne
and Arts.

G. Glover ad vivum deliniavit et sculp: 1641.

Of him, whose shape this Picture hath design'd.
Vertue, and learning, represent the Mind.   W. S.

THE EXACT VERNAL EQUINOX
ANNO CHRISTUS 1645:
IN THE TOWER OF CROMARTIE.

This diurnal to be maintained for my eyes and pleasure alone, I herein downsetting such honest self-estimates as throngers of kirks, courts and markets would castigate as vainglorious; and herein recording those embryonical conceits which quaquaversally disposed intellects too often neglect, abort and aberuncate for clamouring projects more fully formed; and herein deploying a style less orgulous, magnifical, and quodlibetically tolutiloquent than is proper to my public emittings.

2   It is six years since my just action to reclaim the armaments raped from here by the Lairds of Dalgetty and Tolly led to the first death (a ball thro' the occiput of my groom Frazer, an inept parasite but loyal) in that rascally rebellion which reptile parliaments of both nations attempt to dignify with the adjectival appellation *great*, as if grandeur were magnitude of multitude distinct from all noble and worthy intent.

3   It is five years since (for holding Aberdeen nearly a fortnight against the leagued forces of the Covenant) the Seventh Regally Annoynted High Steward of Scotland and Second to Overlord the intire Brittanic Island, did Knight me in the gallery of Whitehall three days before the publication of my *Epigrams: Divine and Moral.*

4   It is three years since my father, on deathbed in the chamber adjoyning, led my five brothers to swear, under pain of his everlasting curse and execration, to assist, concur with and serve me to the utmost of their power, industry and means, and to spare neither charge nor travel to release me from the undeserved bondage of the domineering

Creditor, and extricate our crazed estate from the
impestrements in which it hath been involved by his
too good, too credulous, too hopeful nature; three
years also since I voyaged beyond Byzantium, letting
rents embank at home for the leniencing and clem-
entizing of the Creditor.

5   It is one week since, homing it through London,
I saw off the press my *Trissotetras*, wherein I lay the
ground of an intirely new Science.

6   This day, having entered upon the family mansion, I discover that by false inept bailiffs and
chamberlains, deputies and doers, my rents and
receipts have been so embezzled, malingened,
pauchled and mischarged that little or no moneys
have accrued to me, while the creditors have sold
their claims on the estate to usurers yet more fanged,
pangastrical and Presbyterian than themselves. It is a
well founded prevision of Jehovus that I am, since
Neper of Marchiston, the foremost Apostle in
Brittain of that Holy Minerva who inspired
Moses, Aristotle, Julius Caesar and the mighty
Rabelais, for were I not the wisest, therefor luckiest
man I know, I would be the most miserably depressed and straightened. So I here cast an accompt
of the great goods of my condition, balancing the
bads against them to see which predominate.

PRO ME

Ancestry: Toward the stock, stem, vine, clew, cable and navelstring of my pedigree Saturn's scythe hath been so blunted that I can iluct its labyrintheon through innumerable changes of monarchy and estate among the Regal Houses of Scotland, Ireland, Portugal, Gallicia, Murcia, Andaluzia, Granada, Carthage, Egypt, Amazonia, Greece and Israel, back to Adam surnamed the Protoplast, who was quintessence of that red earth created in time, of nothing, by the word of TRIUN JEHOVUS the ETERNAL FATHER, SON AND GHOSTLIE MINERVA. AMEN.

CONTRA ME

Ancestry: Though verboradically demonstrable, the middle part of my geneology lacks inscriptory provenance, and will be doubted by pedant sciolasts and fidimplicatary gownsmen who can neither admit the eductions of informed inspiration, nor comprehend the congruency of the syllabic with the Sibylene.

Rank: I am Knight of Bray and Udol, Baron of Fichterie and Clohorby, Laird Baron Cromartie and Heritable High Sheriff thereof, having Admiralty of the seas betwixt Catness and Innernasse, and therefore Jehovus Depute (under the Steward Crown) in that part of Brittain autochthonously colonized by oriental polistactical patricians and their followers, which is why so many towns, castles, churches, fountains, rivers, nasses, bays, harbours, and the like, have from my family name received their denomination, and why the shire of Cromartie alone, of all the places of the Isle of Brittain, hath the names of its towns, villages, hamlets, dwellings, promontaries, hillocks, temples, dens, groves, fountains, rivers, pools, lakes, stone heaps, akers and so forth, of pure and perfect Greek.

Rank: Nothing.

PRO ME

Frame: In portliness of garb, comeliness of face, sweetness of countenance, majesty of very chevelure, with goodliness of frame, proportion of limbs and symmetry betwixt all the parts and joints of my body, I am heroical in the mould of, not Hercules, Ganimed.

Nature: Jovial, yet Saturnine, my venereal fervour (for the better ingendering of brain-babes) chastened by Diana, inharmonied by Apollo, promoted with Martial vigour, ripened through Minerval cogency and quickened by Mercurial urgency, though this last only in learning and combat, since I lack all lust to transmute baseness into coyn of any metal.

Home: This noble mansion-fort, the stance whereof is statelie, the tower of notable good fabrick and contrivance.

Library: Not three books therein but are of my own purchase, and all of them together (in the order wherein I will rank them) compiled like a compleat nosegay of flowers, which in my travels I gathered out of the gardens of sixteen several different kingdoms.

Estate: Lands in the shires of Cromartie and Aberdeen yeelding a thousand pounds Sterling of rent, with many especial royalties, privileges and immunities, preserved from the days of Nomoster in the 389th epoch before Christ, untill the perfect age and majority of my father, who received it without any burthen of debt, or provision of brother or sister or other kindred alliance to affect it, whereunto was then added, by his father-in-law Lord Elphingstone, the then High Treasurer of Scot-

CONTRA ME

Frame: Nothing.

Nature: Nothing.

Home: The windows lack glass.

Library: Still unpacked.

Estate: Twelve or thirteen thousand pounds Sterling of debt, five brethren all men and two marriageable sisters to support, and less to defray all this by six hundred pounds Sterling a year, in a time of frantic anticivilian warres and garboyles, than my father inherited for nothing, in a peaceful age, to maintain himself alone. Meantime the Church Commission maintain in my kirks three cutpurse Mammoniferous ministers of their own make who, loathing my loyaltie to the Epis-

PRO ME

land, my mother, Lady Christian, with whom he received no inconsiderable fortune. Also the patronage of the parriches of Kırkmıchel, Cromartie and Cullicuden.

Tenandrie: All are descended (as they themselves avouch) from pregenitors who accompanied my ancestors Alypos, Belistos, Nomostor, Astioremon and Lutork in their aborignarie acquest of the land, receiving from these such good yeoman leases for the digging and manuring of it that they very suddenly took deep root therein, and bequeathed to their children the hereditary obedience owed to their masters. Each hamlet by that means having its own Clan, as we call it, or name of kindred, none will from that portion of land bouge, any interflitting between coterminal parrishes being as mutually displeasing to them as an extrusive exile to the Barbadoes or to Malagask. I have farmers who dwell in the selfsame house inhabited by their ancestors from dad to brat, sire to suckling, above nine hundred years together and though none can read, they nevertheless exchange discourse with any concerning the heathenish deities of the Grecolatin Pantheon, whose temples, delubres and fanes, of a circularie, oval, triangulary or square figure, my own forefathers erected in groves and high places before the time of Christ, the stones whereof may still be ascribed to Jove, Juno,

CONTRA ME

copal liturgy, demand for their tythes a fifth of the rent of the land, and combinate in synods and concils with creditors and neighbours to put upon me alone the charge of garrisoning troops in this district, thereby intending to inchaos the structure of ancient greatness into the very rubbish of a neophitic parity.

Tenandrie: These much plundered and rouped of goods, gear and rents by the soldiery without hope of redress; while their Kirkomanatickal presbyterian pastors vilipend, pester and flite them for tenaciously clinging to their frets of old, which often send them at set times to fountains, oak-trees, little round hillocks and stoneheaps where, with preconceived words and motions, they worship in accordance with the poetical liturgies of Hesiod, Theocritus and Ovid; And my ministers demand that I magisterially prohibit and persecute these practices as things of charm, fascination, inchantment or infernal assistance! There is a silly old wife who, for doing some pretty feats wherein she has been instructed by her mother, according to a prescript set down in some verses of Homer, whom neither had the skill to use, is accused of witchcraft by one who, being a professor of the Greek, whipt a boy for not getting these verses by heart: as if it were a duty for him to study what is felonie for others to enact. Being resolved to conduct myself by the light of reason, I openly acquit many of both sexes whom flagitory zealots accuse of incubation, succubation and peragration with fairies, and am forthwith

PRO ME

Palas, Apollo &cetera by the eye of the intelligible Mythologist.

CONTRA ME

reputed an obstinate assertor of erroneous doctrine. Even as a raw youth I would not without examination trust to aged men in matters contrary to commonsense and experience, for I caused brought to my father's house one of either sex that were supposed rivals in diabolical venerie, the male with the succub, the female with the incub. The young man was two-and-twenty years old, very bashfull, yet prone to lasciviousness, and a handsome youth; she was some five-and-twentie, nothing so pleasant as he, and had it not been for a little modesty that restrained her, a very sink of lust. All this I perceived at first view, and after I had spoken kindly with them in generals, I entreated them with all gentilnesse possible, to tell me freely whether it was so or not, as it was reported of them; and their answer was (for they were not suspicious of any harm from me) that it was true enough; whereat I straight conceived that they had a crack in their imagination. The better to try an experiment thereon, I commanded to be given unto each of them an insomniatorie and exoniretick potion, for stirring up a libidinous fancie; I also directed one of my footboys to attend the woman with all possible respect and outward shew of affection; the like I required of one of my mother's chambermaids to be done in behalf of the young man. Which injunctions of mine were by these two servants with such dexterity prosecuted, that the day after each of their night's repose with these two hypochondriacks, when I called for them, and, after I had fairly insinuated myself into their mind by a smooth discourse, asked whether that night they had in their bodies felt any carnal application of the fowl spirit, or if they did, in what likeness they received him? To this both made reply that of all the nights they had ever enjoyed, it was that night respectively wherein the spirit was most intirely communicative in feats of dalliance, and that he acted in the guise of the boy and chambermaid whom I had appointed to await on them as they went to bed. This confirmed me in my former opinion, which certainly increased when I heard a short time after, that the imagination of two had become a regular fornication of four; by which (though I caused to punish them all) the fantasists were totally cured, who afterwards becoming yoke mates in wedlock to the two servants of our house, were in all times coming sound enough in fancie, and never more disquieted by diabolical apprehensions.

PRO ME

Nation: Betwixt pole and tropicks there has been no great engagement wherein Scotsmen have not (by valiantly slaughtering each other on behalf of all the greatest Christian states in Europe) made their nation as renowned for its martialists as have its promovers of learning for their literary endeavour. I here set down the greatest names on all sides since the jubilee of 1600, instellarating thus ✳ such as creep in from an earlier age, since it is not my custom to maintain a rank by excluding an excellence.

CONTRA ME

Nation: I will not enlist opposite the flaming sparks of their country's fame those coclimatory wasps of the Covenanting crue whose swarms eclipse it. I will discourse but generally, or by ensample, of those viper colonels who do not stick to gnaw the womb of the Mother who bears them, and of those ligger-headed Mammoniferous ministers, those pristinary lobcock hypocritick Presbyters (*press-biters* rather) who abuse learning in the name of God, as if distinct truths could oppose THE TRUTH.

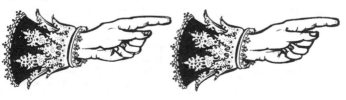

PRO SCOTIA

ARMS

FOR THE KING OF SWED-
LAND GUSTAVUS CAESER-
OMASTIX AGAINST DANE,
POLE, MUSCOVITE AND
HOLY EMPEROR.

General James Spence (created
Earl of Orcholm), Sir Alexander
Leslie (governor of the cities of
the Baltick coast), Marquis James
Hamilton (General over 6,000
English in the Swedish Sevice)
with these Scottish colonels:

Sir George Cunningham
Sir John Ruven
Sir John Hamilton
Sir John Meldrum
Sir Arthur Forbas
Sir Frederick Hamilton
Sir Francis Ruven
Sir William Ballantine

with (to be rapid) these colonels:
Armstrong, Balfour, another Balfour, Bucliugh, Crichton, Cock-
burn, Culen, Edmistoun, Gun,
Hamiltoun, Henderson, Johnston, another Johnston, Kinninmond, another Kinninmond,
Leckie, Leslie, Liddel, Livis-
toun, Sandilands, Scot, Seaton,
another Seaton, Sinclair, Spence,
Stuart.

FOR THE KING OF POLE
AGAINST SWEDE, MUS-
COVITER AND TURK

Colonel Lermon
Colonel Wilson
Colonel Hunter
Colonel Robert
Colonel Scot
Colonel Gordon
Colonel Wood
Colonel Spang
Colonel Gun
Colonel Robertson
Colonel Rower

ARTS

LORD   NEPER   OF
MARCHISTON. The artificial
numbers by him first excogitated
and perfected are of such incom-
parable use, that by them we may
operate more in one day than
without them in the space of a
week; a secret that would have
been so precious to antiquitie,
that Pythagoras, Socrates, Plato,
Aristotle, Archimedes and Euclid
would have joyntly concurred in
deifying the revealer of so great a
mystery. My country is more
glorious for producing so brave a
spark, than if it had been the con-
quering kingdom of a hundred
potent nations. Neper also had
the skill (as is commonly reported)
to frame an engine which, by
virtue of some secret springs, im-
plements and substances inclosed
within the bowels thereof, could
clear a field of four miles circumference or more (proportional to
its bigness, for he could make it
any size at all) of all living
creatures exceeding a foot in
hight, by which he was able to
have killed thirty thousand turkes,
without the hazard of one
christian. Of this, upon a wager,
he gave proof on a large plaine in
Scotland, to the destruction of a
great many herds of cattel and
flocks of sheep, whereof some
were distant from other half a
mile, some a whole mile. When
earnestly desired by an old
acquaintance, at the time he con-
tracted the disease whereof he
died, not to take the invention of
so ingenious a mystery with him
to the tomb; he replied, That for
the ruine and overthrow of man-

CONTRA SCOTIAM

ARMS

What have we here? A Scotland racked, retching and rampant with intestinal dissent. How may a politic body rampantly menace others while bloodily rending itself? Regard us and know. Four armies prowl this realm prepared to fight 1. For King and Covenant, 2. For King against Covenant, 3. For Covenant against King, 4. Against both Covenant and King. This rebelion, here begun on a point of liturgy by Scottish blatterers of extemporaneous prayer, spread hence to the English who took to it on a matter of taxation and, fighting a two-sided rectilinear war, soon concluded in a clear conquest for the Cromwel parliament last year on Marston Moor. But the Northern Realm, where the Royal Steward was first betrayed, still holds the last loyalists to fight for him victoriously under that lapsed Covenanter the Marquess Montross. This fills me with a confusion of pride and regret. When will our turmoyles cease to involve us in stultifying self dissent? May we only win glory by serving the foreigner? If so our best hope is to be integered into one united Brittish Imperium, by imblending the Scottish Lords and Commons with the English as hath been done with the Welsh equivalent. But should that fail to grant us long prosperity of achievement, then our last hope is an enemy of the sort Cromwel is to the Irish, but less cunning; an enemy so crass, antagonistic and dully ignorant of Scotland's state that we must needs all con-

ARTS

At home our arts have come under the scourge of an uncontrolled Kirk whose hierarchical jurisdiction is neither monarchical, aristocratical or democratical, but a meer Plutarchy, Plutocracie or rather Plutomanie; so madly do they hale after money and the trash of this world, which I here ensample by but one instance. The great Doctor Liddel, astronomical disciple of Tycho Brahe and professor of the sciences of sensible immaterial objects in Heidelberg, bequeathed fourty pounds English money a year to Aberdeen university for the maintenance of a mathematical professor, with this *proviso*, that the nearest of his own kinsmen, *caeteris paribus* should be preferred before any other. The chair falling vacant when the Doctor's nephew, Master Duncan Liddel, was of sufficient age and skil to exercise that duty, did the good Senators of Aberdeen attend the honest doctor's will? No, forsooth, the oracle must first be consulted with; ministerian philoplutaries, my tongue forks it, I have mistaken it seems one word for another, I should have said philosophers, decide his uncle's testament must be made void; for, say they, Master Duncan Liddel hath committed the hainous sin of fornication, he hath got a young lass with childe! Which presbyterian doctrine, had it bin enforced in the daies of Socrates, would have pearched him up on a penitentiary pew for having two wives at once (neither whereof, either Xanthippe or Myrto, was as handsome as Master

PRO SCOTIA

ARMS

FOR THE GRAND DUKE OF MUSCOVY AGAINST THE SWEDE, TURK AND TARTAR
Sir Alexander Leslie generalissimo of all forces of the whole empire of Russia with
Colonel Crawford
Colonel Gordon
Colonel Keith
Colonel Mathuson
Colonel Kinninmond
Colonel Garne (agnamed the Sclavonian, who for the height and grossenes of his person, being greater in compass than any within six kingdoms of him, was elected King of Bucharia, and only refused the sovereign crown, sword and sceptre belonging to the supreme majesty of that nation, because he had no stomach to be circumsized).

FOR THE HOLY ROMAN EMPEROUR OF GERMANY AGAINST THE SWEDES, DUTCH AND VENETIAN
Colonel Henderson
Colonel Johnston
Colonel Lithco
Colonel Wedderburne
Colonel Bruce
Colonel Gordon (now high Chamberlain to the Emperour's Court)
Colonel Leslie (who is made hereditary marquess and colonel-general of the whole infantry of the imperial forces.)

FOR THE DUTCH WILLIAM OF ORANGE AGAINST SPAIN AND FRANCE
These colonels:

ARTS

kind there were already too many divices framed, which, since the malice and rancor in the heart of man would not suffer these to diminish, by no conceit of his would their number be increased. Divinely spoken, truly.

CRICHTON * AGNAMED THROUGHOUT EUROPE ADMIRABILIS SCOTUS OR THE WONDERFUL SCOT:

who in one day at the Sorbonne in Paris, from nine in the morning to six at night, did argue in Hebrew, Syriack, Arabick, Greek, Latin, Italian, English, Flemish, Dutch, Spanish, French and Sclavonian, in prose and verse, at his disputants' discretion, thereby resolving the knurriest problems propounded to him by the choicest and most profound philosophers, mathematicians, naturalists, mediciners, surgeons, apothecaries, alchymists, civil law doctors, canon law doctors, grammarians, rhetoricians and logicians in that greatest of all cities which is truly called the Abridgement of the World; and ilucting the most umbraged obscurities, and prostrating the sublimest mysteries to the vulgar capacity, by the easie and accurate promptness of his speech. When the Rector of the University awarded him a purse of gold and a diamond ring, the nimblewitted Parisians raized such thundering plaudities that the rarified air over the echoing concavities of the colleges could not support the birds in flight, who fell from the sky in a feathered showr. And the

CONTRA SCOTIAM

ARMS   **ARTS**

front it together or sink into total   Liddel's Concubine) and cast all
penury and nonfunction.   the later ages of man kind under
a cloud of ignorance by quench-
ing the light of Plato, Aristotle and
Euclid, who would have betaken
themselves to some other profession
than philosophy, if the presbytery of
Athens had supplyed the academical
chair thereof with the bum of a more
sanctified brother, whose zealous job-
bernolism would have mudded and
fowled at its source the world's first clear
fountain of pure learning. Such a sort was
that covenanting gentleman who burnt a
great many historical and philosophical
books thinking they had been books of
popery, because of the red letters he saw
on their titles and inscriptions. The nation
of Scotland hath produced many excellent
spirits whose abilities, by the presbyterian's
persecutions, have been quite smothered, and
hid as a candle under a bushel; while many
excellent books have perished for want of
able and skillful printers, the author happening to dy; whereupon the wife and children,
to save a little money, make use of his papers,
without any regard to the precious things in
them, to fold perhaps their butter and cheese
into. So unfortunate a thing is it that good spirit
should be struck by presbytery into penury and
have their writing fall into the hands of ignorants.
That poverty is an enemy to the exercise of vertue,
is not unknown to anyone acquainted with the
sovereign power of money; and if the great
men of the land would be pleased to salve that
sore, which, possibly would not be expensive to
them as either their hawks or hounds, then per-
adventure by such gallant incitements, through
a vertuous emulation who should most excel other,

PRO SCOTIA

ARMS

Robert Munro of Fowls
Obstol Munro
Assen Munro
Hector Munro (who wrote a book in folio called Munroe's expedition)
George Leslie
Robert Leslie
John Leslie (agnamed the omnipotent)
Alexander Leslie
Alexander Hamilton (agnamed dear Sandy)
William Cunningham
Alexander Cunningham
Finess Forbas
Alexander Forbas (agnamed the Bauld)
Alexander Forbas (another)
Borg (who took a Spanish General in the field upon the head of his army)
Edmund (who took the valiant Count de Buccoy twice prisoner in the field)
Urchart (who is a valiant soldier, expert commander and learned scholar) and
Dowglas the ingenious engineer general, and many more who became colonels and general persons under Gustavus Adolphus.

FOR THAT TETRARARCH OF THE WORLD ON WHOSE SUBJECTS THE SUN NEVER SETS, THE GREAT DON PHILIP OF SPAIN, AGAINST THE DUTCH AND THE FRENCH
the thrice renowned
Earl of Bodwel
Colonel Sempill
Colonel Boyd

ARTS

very next day to refresh his brains, as he said, went to the Louvre in a buff-suit, more like a favourite of Mars than one of the Muses' minions; where in the presence of the Court and great ladies, he carryed away the ring fifteen times on end, and broke as many lances on the Saracen. The picture of Crichton, with a lance in one hand and a book in the other, is to be seen in the bedchambers and galleries of most of the great men of the Italian nation, where he was murdered in a fitte of jealous rage by the Prince of Mantua; and most of the young ladies likewise, that were anything handsome, had his effigies in a little oval tablet of gold hanging twixt their breasts, for many yeeres that intermammilionary ornament being held as necessary for the setting forth of their accoutrements, as either fan, watch or stomacher.

DOCTOR SEATON: made Professor of the Roman Colledge of Sapience by Pope Urbane the eighth, but falling at ods with the Jesuites, he retired to France where I have seen him circled about at the Louvre with a ring of French Lords and gentlemen, the greatest clerics and churchmen, the albest barristers and advocates of the Parlement of Paris, all in perfect silence the better to congest the pearls of discernment falling from his lips into the treasuries of their judgements. Le Sieur de Balzac, who for eloquence was esteemed to surpass Cicero, presented to Seaton a golden pen, in token of his infinitely greater supereminency in

CONTRA SCOTIAM

Scotland would produce, for philosophy, astronomy, natural magick, poesie and other such like faculties, as able men as ever were:

Duns Scotus*
Sacroboscus*
Reginaldus Scotus*

and other compatriots of these three great Scots, whose name I do not insert in the roll of the rest, because they flourished before 1600. Only one Scot; of able intellectual parts, that I ever knew, had his sound mind unmobilated by money, and that through the corruptions of courtiership: Sir William Alexander, afterward Earl of Sterlin, who made an insertion to Sir Philip Sidney's Arcadia, and composed several tragedies. He was born a poet, and aimed to be a king; therefor would he have his royal title from King James, who was born a king and aimed to be a poet; so Jamie Steward bestows on him the sovereignty of that tract of polar ice and rock recently named Nova Scotia. Had they stopped there, it had been well; but like King Arthur, he must have his knights, though not limited to so small a number. Whosoever wished to be a gentleman and gave King Sterlin one hundred and fifty Sterling pounds, could at once flaunt the orange riban to testify he was Knight Baronet. The King nevertheless, not to stain his royal dignity by awarding honour to meer wealth, also gave them land for their money at six pence an acre, which could not be thought very dear, considering how pretilly in the respective legal parchments of disposition they were described as fruitful corne land, watered with pleasant rivers running alongst most excellent and spacious meadows; and if they lacked an abundance of oaken

PRO SCOTIA

ARMS

Colonel Lodowick Lindsay Earl Crauford, also a Scottish Colonel whose name is upon my tonge's end and yet I cannot hit at it; he was not a souldier bred yet for many years he bore charge in Flanders under Spinola. In his youthood he was so strong and stiff a Presbyterian, that he was the onely man Scotland made choice of, to be the archprop and main pillar of that government; but waining in his love of the Presbytery as he waxed in knowledge of the world, from a strict Puritan he became the most obstinate rigid Papist that ever there was on this earth. It is strange that I cannot remember his title; he was a lord I know, nay more, he was an earle, aye that he was, and one of the first of them. Ho now! Peascods on it, Crauford Lodi Lindsay puts me in mind of him; it was the old Earle of Argile, this present Marquis of Argile's father; that was he. That was the man.

FOR THE THIRTEENTH LEWIS OF FRANCE AGAINST THE DUTCH AND SPANISH

Lord Colvil
Lord James Douglas
Sir William Hepburn
Hepburn of Wachton
(Had these survived the days wherein they successively dyed the bed of honour, they had all of them been made Marischals of France)
Sir Andrew Gray
Sir John Seatoun
Sir John Fularton
Sir Patrick Moray

ARTS

that art. Many learned books were written by this Seaton in the Latin tongue, which, to speak ingenuously, I cannot hit upon.

HUGO DE GRIEVE: whose nativity in a dank border-town engirdled by many torrents so impressed his mind with the axiom *everything flows*, that he firmly fixed himself in those operations by which mind is changed, and made some 32 books of verses wherein antique and demotic tongues, political rhetoric and all the natural sciences are by violence yoked together to deny, prophetically simultaneously and retroactively, every conclusion he arrives at, excepting this: that the English are a race of Bastards. He thus engendered a manifold of grandly meaning sentences without system, for the which I did honour him, until compelled to bring against him a suit-at-law for his barefaced plagiarism of my LOGOPANDECTEISON, which suit requires but the enscrieving and publishment of the said LOGOPANDECTEISON to have this scheming and scurrilous succubus of other men's genius brought low, and costs awarded to pursuer.

CAMERON, AGNAMED THE WALKING LIBRARY: who being renowned through all the provinces of France for his universal reading, took occasion to set forth an excellent folio volume in Latin intituled Bibliotheca Movens.

CONTRA SCOTIAM

groves in the midst of very fertil plains, it was the scrivener or writer's fault; for his majestie ordered that, on the receipt of three thousand Scots marks, there should be no deficiency in quantity or quality, in measure or goodness of land, with here and there most delicious gardens and orchards and whatever else would be content their fancies, as if they were purchasing ground in the Elysian Fieldes, or Mahumet's Paradise. And if the clerk writing the charter, on receipt of some small coin to himself, slipped in a thousand more acres than was agreed at first, he cared not. At last, when some two or three hundred Knights had among them purchased several million Neo-Caledonian acres, confirmed to them and their for ever under the great seal (the affixing thereof cost each of them but thirty pence more) finding that the company was not like to become more numerous, he bethought of a course more profitable for himself, and, without the advice of his Knights (who represented both his houses of parliament, clergy and all) like an absolute King indeed disponed heritably to the French both the dominion and property of the whole continent of that kingdom of Nova Scotia for a matter of five or six thousand pounds English.

And this is a true example of that charm, fascination, inchantment and infernal assistance of men's imaginations by the gold of the Spanish conquerors, which makes many believe they may become magnates and grandees with no more labour than is needed to purchase a royal patent, fit a ship, navigate a passage, and plunder an astonished people by the power of artilleriendal assault. The followers of such adventurers may indeed reap good harvest

PRO SCOTIA

ARMS
Colonel Erskin
Colonel Lindsay
Colonel Morison
Colonel Hume
Colonel Mouatt
Colonel Liviston
Colonel Leslie
Colonel Forbes

FOR VENICE AGAINST THE GERMAN EMPEROR
Colonel Dowglas
Colonel Balantine
Colonel Lyon
Colonel Anderson

FOR VENICE AGAINST THE TURK
Captain William Scot, vice-Admiral of the Venetian fleet, the onely renowned bane and terror of Mahometan navigators, for he did so tort and ferret them out of all the creeks of the Adriatic gulph that many of them, for fear of him, did turn land-souldiers or drovers of caravans.

****

From this list I have omitted all mention of gallant Scottish duelists such as Francis Sinclair, natural son to the late Earle of Catnes, who performed this notable exploit in the city of Madrid: Eight Spanish noblemen being suspicious of Sinclair's too intimate familiarity with a kinswoman of theirs, did altogether set on him at one time, which unexpected assault moved him to say:

"Gentlemen, I doubt not but you are valiant men, therefor my entreaty is that you take it as becomes men of valour, by trying your fortune against mine, one at a time."

ARTS
MASTER ALEXANDER ROSSE: who hath written manyer books, both in good Latine and English, prose and verse, than he hath years, and whose Poeticus proveth, that the Pagan Gods are but names for the separated faculties of our TRIUN GOD, so that Christians need no longer lie under the reproach which the Oriental nations fixe upon us, of seeing with but one eye, for Master Rosse hath so vindicated in matter of knowledge our Western World, as to make the Chineses, by force of reason, of whose authority above them they are not ashamed, glad to confess that the Europaeans, as well as themselves, look out of both their eyes and have no blinkered minds.

MELVIL: who has six hundred ducats a year, for translating into Latine or Spanish, some hundred few books of these six hundred great volumes, taken by Don Juan de Austria at the battel of Lepanto from the Great Turk, which now lie in the great library of that magnifick palace the Escorial near Madrid.

DEMPSTER: who is chiefly recommended to posterity for his Latin index of five thousand illustrious Scots from the earliest ages to the last liver whereof dyed above fifty years since.

CHALMERS: bishop of Neems.

CHIZUM: bishop of Vezun.

CONTRA SCOTIAM

abroad, but only by digging and planting, (in fear of the natives they have dispossessed) what could be cultivated at home with better advantage to themselves and their country. It is the greater readiness of Scottishmen to adventure abroad, rather than develop what we have, that is our nation's ruin. By which I am reminded, that I have a certain harbour or bay, in goodness equal to the best in the world, adjacent to a place, which is the head town of the Shire; the shire and town being of one and the same name with the harbour or bay; whose promontaries on each side, vulgarly called Souters, from the Greek word σωτηρες, that is to say, Salvatores or Savers, from the safety that ships have when once they are entred within them, having had that name imposed on them by Nicobulus the Druyd, who came along with my predecessor Alypos in the dayes of Eborak, that founded York some 698 years before Ferguse the First; at which time that whole country, never before discovered by the Greeks, was named Olbion by the said Alypos.

This harbour, in all the Latine maps of Scotland, is called *Portus Salutis*; by reason that ten thousand ships together may within it ride in the greatest tempest that is as in a calm by vertue of which conveniency some exceeding rich men, of five or six several nations, masters of ships, and merchant adventurers, promised to bring their best vessels and stocks for trading along with them, and dwell in that my little town with me, who should have been a sharer with them in their hazard, and by subordinating factors to accompany them in their negotiations, admitted likewise for a partner in their profit and advantages.

PRO SCOTIA

ARMS

The Spaniards pretending to be men of honour, swore by an oath made on their crossed swords that they should not faile therein; in a word, conform to paction, they fell to it, and that most cleverly, though with such fatality on the Spanish side, that in less than the space of half an hour he killed seven of them apassyterotically, that is, one after another; gratifying the eightth, to testifie that he had done no wrong to the rest, with enjoyment of his life. As for pricking down here those other Scots renowned for valour and for literature, I hold it not expedient; for the sum of those named doth fall so far short of the number omitted, that apportioned to the aggregate of all who in that nation since the year 1600, have deserved praise in arms and arts, jointly or disjunctly, either at home or abroad, it would bear the analogy, to use a lesser definite for a greater indefinite, of a *subnovitripartient* eights; that is to say, in

ARTS

TYRY: assistant to the General of the Jesuites, and second person in that vast ecclesiastical republick, which reaches beyond the territories of all Christian kings to cover the continent of the World.

KING JAMES 6th AND 1st: History cannot afford us (Solomon and Alfonso of Aragon being laid aside) any monarch who was near as learned as he, as is apparent by that book in folio intituled, "King James His Works"; despite that peevish remark by the young king's old tutor, the republican pedagogue George Buchanan, that the king's faculty as a scholar, equalled his notorious deficiency as a souldier, since by skelping the arse of the Lord's annoynted the best he (Buchanan) had been able to make of poor Jamie was a pedant, as the Royal Steward lacked substance to shape anything better.

plain English, the whole being the dividend, and my nomenclature the divisor, the quotient would be nine, with a fraction of three-eights; or yet more clearly, as the proportion of 72 to 625. But let me resume the account of my especial self by inditing:

PRO ME

Deeds Armorial: In my early years, to ripen my brains for eminent undertakings, my heart gave me courage to adventure through foreign climes, wherein it thrice befell me to enter the lists against men of three several nations, to vindicate my native country from the slanders

CONTRA ME

Deeds Armorial: Nothing, in that never was I in any fight defeated, though sometimes obliged to withdraw before overwhelming power, as hath befallen Scipio Africanus, Robert de Bruis and Adolphus Maleus Caesarorum.

CONTRA SCOTIAM

By which means, the foresaid town of Cromarty, for so it is called, in a very short space, would have easily become the richest of any within threescore miles thereof; in the prosecuting of which designe, I needed not to question the hearty concurrence of Aberdeen, which, for honesty, good fashions and learning, surpasseth as far all other cities and towns in Scotland, as London doth for greatness, wealth, and magnificence, the smallest hamlet or village in England.

Nor was I suspicious of any considerable opposition in that project from any town, save Invernasse alone, whose magistrates, to the great dishonour of our whole nation, did most foully evidence their own baseness in going about to rob my town of its liberties and privileges.

Yet was that plague of flagilators, wherewith my house was infected, so pernicious to that purpose of mine, that some of them lying in wait, as a thief in the night, both for my person and means, cannibal-like to swallow me up at a breakfast; they did, by impeding the safety of my travelling abroad, arresting whatever they imagined I had right unto, inhibiting others from bargaining, most barbarously and maliciously cut off all the directory preparatives I had orderly digested for the advantage of a business of such main concernment, and so conducible to the weal of the whole Island, to the great discouragement of those gallant forreners; of which that ever-renowned gentilman for wit and excellencie in many good parts, Sir Phillip Vernati by name, was one; who being of Italian parents, by birth a Dutchman, and by education expert in all the good languages of the Christian world, besides the

PRO ME

wherewith they had aspersed it. God was pleased so to conduct my fortune that, after I had disarmed them, they in such sort acknowledged their error, and the obligation they did owe me for sparing their lives, that in lieu of three enemies that were I acquired three constant friends both to myself and my nation, which by several gallant testimonies they did later prove, in many occasions. Thus I outdid the Gasconad of France, Rodomontad of Spaine, Fanfaronad of Italy, and Bragadochio brags of all other countries, who could no more astonish my invincible young heart, than could the cheeping of a mouse a bear robbed of her whelps.

Then in the May month of 1639, when 1200 Covenanters of the North assembled at Turrif, I with a loyal force of but 800, did altogether repel, route and disperse them, with no advantage on our side but complete surprize and four brass cannon. Thus was quelled the first armed mustering against the monarchy since Mary Steward fled Langside field. Thus issued the first battel in this most uncivil War. Would to Jehovus the loyalists had done so well since.

Deeds Minerval: (completed and potential) whereby my name will resound to the end day of alltime, by reason of, these shining books which will work huge reformation, transformation and revolution in every branch of human tecknics, politics and thought.

1. EPIGRAMS: DIVINE AND MORAL

The Muses never yet inspired

CONTRA ME

Deeds Minerval: Lacking Scots printers my texts amass till convoyed South.

CONTRA SCOTIAM

Arabick and Sclavonian tongues, wherein he sur-
passed, had a great ascendent in counsel over all the
adventrous merchants of what nation soever; whereof, without the foresaid lets of those barbarous
obstructors, some by all appearance had so concurred with me, that by their assistance I would
ere now have banished all idleness from the commons, maintained several thousands of persons of
both sexes, from the infant to the decrepit age, found
employments proportionable to their abilities, ba-
stant to afford them both entertainment and apparel
in a competent measure; educing from various
multitudes of squameary flocks of several sizes,
colours and natures, netted out of the bowels of
the ocean both far and neer, and current of fresh
water streams, more abundance of wealth than that
whole country had obtained by such a commodity
these many yeers past; erecting ergastularies for
keeping at work many hundreds of persons in divers
kindes of manufactures; bringing from beyond sea
the skillfull'st artificers could be hired for money, to
instruct the natives in all manner of honest trades;
perswaded the most ingenious hammermen to stay
with me, assuring them of ready coin for whatever
they should be able to put forth to sale; addicting the
abjectest of the people to the servitritiary duty of
digging for coals and metals, of both which in my
ground there is great appearance, and of the hitting
of which I doubt as little, as of the lime and freestone
quarries hard at my house of late found out, which
have not been these two hundred years remarked;
induced masters of husbandry to reside amongst my
tenants, for teaching them the most profitable way,
both for the manner and the season, of tilling, dig-

PRO ME

sublimer conceptions in a more refined style, than is to be found in the accurate strains of these most ingenious Epigrams. Printed in London, 1641.

2. THE TRISSOTETRAS
Wherein I set forth, with all possible brevity and perspecuity, orthogonospherical and loxogonospherical tables which permit the easy application of Neper's logarythms to every dimension of space and any volume of bulk, and by resolving those cranklings, windings, turnings, involutions and amfractuosities belonging to the equisoleary system, I facilitate and reform the work of all artists in pleusiotechny, poliechryology, cosmography, geography, astronomy, geodesy, gnomonicks, catoptricks, dioptricks, fortification, navigation and chiaroscuro. Printed in London 1645, last week.

3. TTANTOXPONOXANON
A peculiar promptuary of time, wherein is recorded the exact lineal descent of the VRQUARTS since the beginning of motion. Unprinted.

4. ISOPLASTFONIKON
Demonstrating the cubification of the sphere through Pythagorean acousticks, whereby a well-tuned fiddle or taut kettledrum may be perswaded to yield the exact side of a squared solid equal in volume to any symmetrical rotundity whatsoever. Unprinted.

5. FOINIXPANKROMATA
or, the Rainbow-Phoenix, wherein is counter-blasted Signor Galileo's contention that colour is meer sensation, by proving that

CONTRA SCOTIAM

ging, ditching, hedging, dunging, sowing, harrowing, grubbing, reaping, threshing, killing, milling, baking, brewing batling of pasture ground, mowing, feeding of herds, flocks, horse and cattel; making good use of the excrescences of all these; improving their herbages, dayries, mellificiaries, fruitages; setting up the most expedient agricolary instruments of wains, carts, slades, with their several devices of wheels and axle-trees, plows and harrows of divers sorts, freezes, winders, pullies, and all other manner of engines fit for easing the toyl and furthering the work; whereby one weak man, with skill, may effectuate more than fourty strong ones without it; and leaving nothing undone that, by either sex of all ages, might tend to the benefit of the labourer in applying most industriously the outmost of their

PRO ME

the boundless prime matter of the universe is not the Water of Thales, Air of Anaximenes, Fire of Heraclitus, Atoms of Democritus or Quadressential Porridge of Trismegistus, but white light; that gold, green, azure, deep-sea blue, violet, purple, crimson and pink are light in decay; that self-interpenetrating circulation of colours through the Macrocosm creates, not just its appearance, but its tangible, fructible, frangible bodies; and that darkness is light travelling backward too fast to be catched by the eye. Unprinted.

6. ALETHALEMBIKON or the True Alembick, demonstrating that a quin-cunxial chamber of reflecting plates, mathematically disposed, will enable to be wrought, at no cost, identical solid duplicates of any object laid therein, by the admission to it, at a point on the globe's equator, of a beam of midsummer noonday sun. Unprinted.

7. THE HEROICK DEEDS AND SAYINGS OF THE GOOD GARGANTUA AND HIS SON PANTAGRUEL a translation from the French, which, since their lexicons hold but three quarter of the words we can use, will be one third longer than the original, as if Doctor Rabelais had

CONTRA SCOTIAM

vertue to all the emoluments of country farms or manual trades. I would likewise have encouraged men of literature, and exquisite spirits for invention, to converse with us for the better civilizing of the country, and accommodating it with a variety of goods, whether honest, pleasant, or profitable; by vertue whereof, the professors of all sciences, liberal disciplines, arts active and factive, mechanick trades, and whatever concerns either vertue or learning, practical or theoretick, had been cherished for fixing their abode in it. I had also procured the residence of men of prime faculties for bodily exercises, such as riding, fencing, dancing, military feats of mustering, imbattleing, handling the pike and musket, the art of gunnery, fortification, or anything that in the wars belongeth either to defence or assault, volting, swimming, running, leaping, throwing the bar, playing at tennis, singing, and fingring of all manner of musical instruments, hawking, hunting, fowling, angling, shooting, and what else might

CONTRA SCOTIAM

writ in Eng- any way conduce to the accomplishment of
lish, with either body or minde, enriching of men in
my resour-
ces. Not their fortunes, or promoving them to deser-
begun yet. ved honours.
8. I recall
not what All these things, and many more, for export
this is. of the commodities of this Island to the
C o c k s
crow, sky remotest regions of the earth, import from
pales, I thence of other goods, or transport from one
may now
sleep a forraign nation to another, and all for the con-
little veniency of our British inhabitants, I would
p e r -
h a p - undoubtedly have ere now provided to the full,
.
     in being a Maecenas to the sckolar, a protector of
the trades-man, and up-holder of the yeoman,
had not the impetuosity of the usurer overthrown
my resolutions, and blasted my aims in the bud.

13 NOVEMBER 1651:
IN CUSTODY OF CAPTAIN ALSOP,
THE TOWER OF WINDSOR CASTLE.

Logopandectcison is the name of that great work which, in my weary state, I could not recall, it being too large and near for recognition, as a man counting the chief features of his lands omits the tower he surveys them from, though that the chiefest feature of all.

2   This diurnal or day-book returns to me by the magnanimity of Master Braughton, an officer of Colonel Pryde's regiment, who, perceiving it in the street-gutter of Worcester among a mixter-maxter of other papers, in a drizzling rain which had stuck the loose sheets fast to the ground, near by to a heap of seven and twenty dead men lying on one another, commanded that a servant of his take all up, cleanse off the mire and keep safe for his circumspection.

3   The separate sheets prove to be but a parcel of my preface to the Logopandecteison, over a thousand other manuscript pages of the grammar and lexicon, with mathematical, chronological, mythological, metaphysical and dialectical commentaries, all annotated for the printer, having been pillaged, pilfered, ravaged, robbed and rifled from seven large portmantles full of precious commodity, in the lodging I took at the house of Mr. Spilsbury, a very honest confectioner with a very good wife.

4   He learned that while the puritan souldiery were plundering the town, a string of exquisite sharks and clean shavers had broke into my baggage and, seizing the red cloaks, buff suits, armaments and other such rich chafer, straight dispersed my writings to their camerads outside for packeting up of raisins, figs, dates, almonds, caraway and other sweetmeat, while some did kindle pipes of tobacco with a great

part thereof, and threw out all the remainder into the street, save what they reserved for inferiour employments and posteriour uses.

5 Of the dispersedly rejected bundles of paper most were gathered up by grocers, druggists, chandlers, pie-makers, or such as stood in need of any cartapaciatory utensil, to the utter undoing of the writing thereof, both in matter and order; so Master Braughton (who hath no cause to ly) doth inform me.

6 I lay for some hours in great dumps, though less sad than most of the Scots beaten, but not killed, in Worcester fight, for many thousands have been driven like cattel to London, and there inclosed in little room and treated with great rigour, many perishing for want of food, or dieing of all diseases, the survivors to be shipped to the American plantations and there sold as slaves. Is this not a new thing in warfare between Christian nations who talk with the same or similar tongues? But I am used with the clemency due to my rank, and talent, and the ransom they will get by me, though not called ransom, sequestration.

7 Since my last (and first) entry much has passed. The First Charles Steward has been uncapited to the middle bone in his neck. The rump of the Parliamentary party has proclaimed England a *public thing*, a *res publica*, a *republick*. For two years the Second Charles hath been King of Scotland only, and would be king there still, had not the Presbyterial part of his subjects decided to prove their faith in God by fighting the Cromwel army without their King's advice, without help from allies who worship God differently, without obedience to their own general; for against orders they deserted a superior for an inferior place and engaged an out-manoeuvred

enemy on such bad ground that the Almighty (who will not tolerate for ever those who scorn his Angel, commonsense) let them be slaughtered in great numbers. From which they drew this lesson, that their faith was not sufficiently pure. At last the King had no other course, but to leave Sterling, his securest Capital, and march upon England, there to recruit the saner support of the English Royalists. But at Worcester these did not join us. The Royal party in Brittain is utterly routed. The King escaped abroad. I did not. Perhaps Brittain will remain a *public thing* till the end of time.

8   It is growing clear to me that my future fame may be insured by this diurnal, if from now forward I each day indite in it a record of all public doings which reach my ear, or even eye, for my imprisonment is not strict. My parole allows me to wander some distance, and when I am moved to the Tower of London I will be within what is now, by grace of the army rather than God or parlement, the govourning Capital of the four ancient Kingdoms of England, Wales, Ireland and Scotland, with prospering colonies in Amerigo Vespucci-land and many embattled trade-forts in the Barbadoes, East India, Malagask, Africa, and Europe.

9   Who, loving knowledge, would not give all the wealth they possess, yea, and pawn their family inheritance till the end of time, to recover from the shades and hold in their hand, a daily record of things done, seen and heard by a percipient citizen of Periclean Athens, Caesarial Rome or any other heroickal time? How much more wealth would we give for such a diurnal in the manuscript of a Euclid, Vergil or Roland of Roncevalles?

10   Let me start, therefor, by stating that this morning

MIDSUMMER EVE 1653:
THE TOWER OF LONDON
This day concluded much. The Chief Secretary of
State arrived soon after the board of this chamber
had, by my command, been decked with wine, baked
meats, pickles, fruit and other viands suited to a
sckolastic colloquial symposiasmos, for his greek is
not much inferiour to my own, though I exceed him
utterly in power of invention, for like all politicians
he is no philomathet, so cannot proconceive and
concert well-measured symplasmical forms; in
common english, his imagination is fanatick not
poetick.
2   He entered to me peeringly, having the use of a
single eye, and that a failing one, yet I saw it allowed
him enough light to admire my figure, and this
admiration I was able, in part, to return, for
although neither of us very small men, we both
lack that redundant height and girth which gross
multitudes think commonplace: his manner also was
pleasingly jocund and his voice familiar to my ear,
for he pronounced his R, *littera cannina*, the latin
dog-letter, extreme hard as we Scots do, a certain
signe of a Satyricall Wit.
3   We furthered our amity by also discovering,
beneath radically opposed views of church and
state, an equal hatred of Presbyters (*press-biters*,
he called them; I did not disclose that the like
witticism had occurred to myself) I because of the
malign difluence these coine-coursing collybists have
cast upon my best endeavours, and because they
have betrayed two kings, one of them unto death; he
because they have ignored or saught to censor his
proposals to replace universities by simple, sensible
foundations, and to make divorce of marriages an
easy thing entirely dependant on the husband's will,

and also because (turning traitour to their own treason) they opposed the monarch's juridicial apo-kakefalization.

4 He had himself been offered (I gathered) the office of state licenser of all Brittish bookes, and might be obliged to accept that post to prevent it falling into worse hands; though he was determined to pass without question every book submitted to him, excepting such as would foster naked libidinal lewdness and atheism.

5 He then turned the talk neatly to my own published Introduction to the Universal Language, prologueing his remarks with a disclaim, that he spoke as a publick officer; whereat I girded my intellects for a cruxiferous encounter.

6 I began by asserting that all men originally shared the same language, since mankind had been made in one place at one time: he nodded agreement.

7 And before I could say more, recited verbatim the first nine verses of the eleventh chapter of Genesis, first in the Hebrew, then (because he said, it contained no very glaring innacuracie) in that translitteration authorized for the press by King Jamie in 1608, the year of my birth.

> And the whole earth was of one language, and of one speech.
>
> 2 And it came to pass, as they journeyed from the east, that they found a plain in the land of Shinar; and they dwelt there.
>
> 3 And they said one to another, Go to, let us make brick, and burn them thoroughly. And they had brick for stone, and slime had they for mortar.
>
> 4 And they said, Go to, let us build us a city and a tower, whose top may reach unto heaven; and let us make a name, lest we be scattered abroad upon the face of all the earth.

5 *And the Lord came down to see the city and the tower, which the children of men builded.*
6 *And the Lord said, Behold, the people is one, and they have all one language; and this they begin to do: and now nothing will be restrained from them, which they have imagined to do.*
7 *Go to, let us go down, and there confound their language, that they may not understand one another's speech.*
8 *So the Lord scattered them abroad from thence upon the face of all the earth: and they left off to build the city.*
9 *Therefor is the name of it called Babel; because the Lord did there confound the language of all the earth: and from thence did the Lord scatter them abroad upon the face of all the earth.*

8   I hid my surprize, by suavely thanking him for anticipating me, and asking, How God had worked to confound the first speech he had given men to use? Was the Latin Secretary of the British Republick one of those who believed Jehovah had miraculously and simultaneously infused, into the Babel-builders' brains, entirely differing sets of grammars and vocabularies?

9   He answered saying, No; he agreed with the Rabins, that the first confusion was of accent meerly, the foundation speech of these accents not deeply changing, until by dispersal around all the earth, the scattered nations of men were divided one from another by almost impassible distances of desert wilderness, mountain chains and nearly non-navigable seas: for each nation encountering different soyls, plants, creatures and climates, was compelled to devize new tools, arts and oeconomies to cultivate them, new sciences to understand them, new words to describe them, so that in time, lacking

all written records, the old verbal tokens of our
common oeconomy on Shinar's plain were by new
speech utterly ousted and submerged, leaving one
accurate account of the paleological confusion among
a people living near the place where it happened, the
rest retaining but foggy legends of a primitive
catastrophe.

10   Then it behoves us to enquire (said I) how
God, operating within one single city-state on
Shinar's plain, came to stunt that great work by
diversity of accent; for you and I are rational not
superstitious men; we know God works His changes
on earth by the agency of nature, his deputy
magistrate, who in men is called human nature:
what fact of human nature made men inarticulate
to one another, who were united in a great project
which, while certainly presumptuous, would otherwise have succeeded?

11   To this he replied, *The desire for supremacy over
their own kind.*

12   I had intended, by a skilled deployment of
Socratic questioning, to educt from his own lips
conclusions which were precisely my own; his
answer was so unexpected that I responded to it
with open mouth and arched eyebrows, which he
interpreted as an invitation to explicate.

13   We may only understand these nine verses
rightly, said he, if we remember two things: firstly, that when Jehovah said, *Nothing will be restrained
from men, which they have imagined to do,* He was
speaking ironically to his Angels, for although the
Almighty had not read the astronomy of Signor
Galileo, He well knew the Grandeur of the Heavens
He had Builded, and knew that they were far beyond
the reach of any earthly construction; had the tower
rizen one or two short miles above the surface of the

plain it would have entered a region of air too
rarified to support human nourishment; if this
tremendous irony is forgot, then God's words sound
like the peevish pronuncimentos of a meer absolute
Monarch, who dreads that his people will usurp his
privelege.

14   But the knowledge that the tower would never
reach Heaven belonged to more than God, it belonged to the architect, Nimrod, that valiant warrior
who (Moses tells us) was the first conqueror to
substitute the monarchical yoke for the patriarchal
independancy of the nomadic tribes; for had Nimrod
believed Heaven could really be reached by a tower,
he would have commenced to build, not on a flat
plain, but on the summit of Ararat, or any other
toplofty peak.

15   Like all overweening edifices, the tower was
devized to raize a pack of lords and their followers
above the heads of the commons; who were perswaded to support the superiour stance by the usual
publick lie: that the overexaltation of some would in
time lead to the benefit and happiness of all; but the
building itself was the happiness at which the
imaginations of the builders aimed, for as they
gazed out across the heads of their fellows, they
felt themselves to be gods; and this was the false
heaven, this the bad eminence, which the True God
of Heaven came down to confound, and did so most
mercifully, out of the builders' mouths.

16   For men who overmaster their own kind cannot
long continue to deceive and servilize them without
the cloak of a different language, by the cause that
knowing little about the handling and making of
solid things, and their chiefest concern being management of those who do, their speech becomes a
jargoning about bonds, monopolies, legal niceties,

scholastick abstractions, ostentatious sophistry, flattery, backbiting, gossip about those positioned higher than themselves and contempt of those below.

17 At last they sound so different from the commoners as to be almost unintellegible to them, and vice-versa, and this provokes the just Nemesis of God.

18 For the less they understand the suffering cries from underneath, the harder they press, in their pursuit of wealth and eminence, upon the necks of those who feed, cloath and build for them; till in tame nations an utter civil collapse ensues, and in brave ones, a revolt.

19 The most notorious modern example of Babelonian enterprize (he said) was the newmade mosque of the Bishop of Rome, pretentiously lifted up to the Glory of God, but really to the glory of an immund impanative Papacy, the funds being raized by selling pardons for crimes not yet committed, to the rich and poor sinners of Germany; which act soon split all Christendom into four times as many Christian sects as there are Christian governments.

20 He also predicted, that if the rumour hath substance, that young Lewis the French Autocrat will wall off the discontents of his people by building, outside Paris, the biggest Regal dwelling since Nero's Golden House in Rome, then Lewis will one day perish in the same schismatick cataclysm that befel Nimrod, the Roman Caesars, and the Papal Catholicks.

21 I thank God, he concluded, that the British, at least, have proved they are not tame; and placing a finger on one side of his neck, he drew it rapidly across to the other.

22 I told him that, as a Royalist and a Scottish Knight-Baron, I could not concur in the levelling

tendency of his remarks, but certainly, our habit of cultivating the recognition of our kind by a speech which makes us unintelligible to most of them, is a paradox as notorious as our habit of seeking peace by multiplying the instruments of warfare.

23 Every trade and profession fortifies its power in the state by turning its mastery into a mystery, and cultivating a jargon which is never fully disclosed to the uninitiated.

24 Even under the present Commonwealth the sckolars and grammarians, whose duty it is to increase the national stock of wisdom (that is to say, intelligible thought) so entrench and fortify themselves behind recondite polysyllabilification, that they hardly understand each other, and mean nothing to the soldier who defends them or the ploughman who grows their bread; and some such mystification must, indeed, have undermined Nimrod's Colloseum, and scattered the first nation abroad.

25 But, said I, since that first broadcasting of mankind some 3870 years ago, two events have transformed the faith and renewed the hope of every well-informed soul: Eternal Goodness, incarnate in Christ Jesus, hath promised Heaven to whoever loves Him, and England, by embracing the experimental sciences of Lord Verulam and Galileo, is now foremost navigating nation in the whole aquaterrestrial sphere. (I might also have mentioned the Dutch, but was arguing *ad hominem*.)

26 The first event teaches us, that it is no longer impiety, but our sacred duty, to set our imaginations upon Heaven, and work for it, aye, even here upon this earth, providing we toyl by the light of Christian common sense: the second event makes plain, that the dispersed nations of men are becoming known

to one another again, and in one or two centuries will all know each other completely, if the schisms between our separated tongues be sufficiently healed.

27   This healing can only be worked, by a universal and artificial language capable, by the conciseness and abundance of its expression, of involving the excellencies of every other; for in the passage of more than three millenia each language hath received so distinct a character, from the national genius of the many excellent spirits who have spoken and written therein, that it is now not possible to transliterate a profound truth from one speech to another, without somewhat changing the originarie sense: thus the philosophy of the Greek, which is the clearest language for subtile thought, loses as much by being expressed in Latin, the best language for distinct curt commandments, as in modern Italian, which is best for mellifluent courtierlike urbanity.

28   Only a multiverbal logopandocy can express without distorting the Dialogues of Plato, Laws of Justinian, Romances of Ariosto, and what is still to be retrieved from the languages of East and West Indians, the Civil Aztecs, Toltecs, Japaneses and Chineses.

29   I have devized this new language.

30   If widely adopted it will speed the traffick of human thought as greatly as modern navigation hath speeded traffick in commodities; for like the mercantile fleet which brings the potato, coffee, pepper, ginger, sugar and tobacco from the Americas to Europe and the Orient, and Oriental silks, muslins, tea and opium to the Americas and Europe, and European clocks, printing presses and gunpowder to everywhere, my new speech will carry the

Christian message of salvation with the new European learning into pagan and heathen nations, while instructing us in the arts and sciences whereby these nations have also reconciled themselves to the Loving Wisdom of God and His Mighty Depute, Nature.

31 And truly, it is a harmonious dictat of Jehovus (he bit his lip, God, I swiftly added) that an inhabiter of Brittain should divize this language, for these Islands, which to Greeks were the last land and Ultima Thule before the arctick Pole, and to Romans an unruly colony on the verge of intransitive Ocean, is now the amphitheatrickal centre and meridial point between the cradeling paradise of mankind in the East, and those new Atlantises, some not found or founded yet, which await us in the West.

32 He aroze and paced the chamber before saying, that he himself was too inchanted by exotick learning not to be sympathically stirred by my over-splendid esteem of it, but he must open his heart to me with the words of Ecclesiastes, the preacher: *For in much wisdom is much grief: and he that increaseth knowledge increaseth sorrow.* Which truth is also to be evinced trifold from the oldest book of Holy Writ, from the life of individual men, and from universal history.

33 Genesis shows the Satanic snake flattering our first mother with falsely gorgeous hopes until, by the filching of an apple and breaking of a law, sin, sadness and new knowledge all enter the world together, the fall of man being a fall into knowledge of his own wilful division from Goodness.

34 Individual men are condemned to repeat this tragedy, for when suckling at the breast they will never be so purely happy again, as is testified by their blissful faces and tiny erected penes.

35   Universal history repeats this tragedy: the most
notorious modern instance (which he viewed less
complacently than myself) being Don Conquista-
dore's disclosure that the world held two more
continents than the ancients knew, which uncovery
brought slaughter, slavery and the Spanish inquisi-
tion to several proud nations; and to Europe so much
silver and gold that the common currency hath ever
since lost value, thus placing more and more oeconomies in the hands of usurors, and bringing also to
Europe that disease of the generative root which
makes men rot and bleed at the centre of their most
poignant desires and pleasures.

36   He ended by saying, I am no friend of ignorance, but concur with Christ and Socrates in con-
demning as vainglory all knowledge that does not
encourage right conduct, and since a language is but
an instrument conveying unto us things good to be
known, should a great linguist pride himself to have
all the tongues that Babel cleft the world into, yet if
he have not studied the solid things in them, as well
as the words and lexicons, he is less truly learned
than a yeoman or tradesman competently wise in his
mother dialect only.

37   To this I responded courteously, that what he
said was correct: words are indeed the instruments
by which men denote things, but in being so used
they become also the instruments by which we
discover, and shape, and share our passions.

38   It follows from this, that a bad man cannot
describe his reasons in good language without be-
traying himself.

39   It is inexactness of signification which permits
false rhetoric to confuse causes with effects, acci-
dents with intentions, abstracts with particulars,
thereby provoking (to the corrupt rhetorician's

advantage) misled passions in the heart of the malinformed hearer, who may also pass these wrong passions to others by parroting the ear-catching phrase whereby he first received them.

40 My new speech cannot be abused in this way; liars, using it grammatically, will at once contradict themselves or place within the listener's head ample evidence for their own speedy undoing; the greedy and vicious may not disguise their passions in it, and will be compelled to dissemble their vices under cloud of unsocial dumbness.

41 As for the variedly virtuous, the vocabulary of each will fluctuate to exactly fill the altering bounds of their experiential knowledge, growing more colourful or more austere as their passions wax or wane, but each passion clearly correlated by a thought-word to the unique state and thing which is its cause and aim.

42 Even fools will talk wisely in my new language for they will lack the materials to do otherwise.

43 He stared at me then asked sharply how such a language was devized?

44 By grammatical logarithms, said I, for each letter in my alphabet of twenty-five consonants and ten vowels, hath the value of a number linking it to a class of things (in the case of the consonants) or class of actions (in the case of the vowels).

45 The student of my language is taught very few and simple words, and these as example only, for he is given (to be metaphorickal) the bricks wherewith any word he needs may be builded, besides a grammar by which these words may be swiftly presented to the understanding of an instructed fellow.

46 This allows an educated man to bestow upon anything he encounters in the universe a name

entirely different from any other, yet so intelligible
that a well taught child of ten years can, from that
name alone, even if it signifies a thing of which the
child hath had no previous knowledge, imagine at
once the form, colour, material, weight, bigness,
usefulness or danger of the signified thing, and
conceive it so accurately that, if the thing be
artificial, the child can at once construct an accurate
replica, provided only that he hath possession and
mastery of the requisite tools.

47   This significant nomenclature would hugely
benefit the art of wars; for if (as is the French
custom) a new recruit received a *nom de guerre*,
and it were in my new diction, so short a name as
Kohudlitex or Palipugisk, whispered to a commander at a review of troops, would let him know a
soldier's rank, regiment, age, birthplace, ancestry
and character, and inable him to address that man
with that familiarity which inspireth true loyaltie and
devotion, when manifested by the nobility toward

****

****

****

*******   *HERE A GREAT PART*   *******

*******   *OF THE MANUSCRIPT*   *******

******* *HAS BEEN ATE BY MICE*   *******

****

****

****

uttered in such nonsounding things as silence, or
tears.

83   I asked him for a particular example of what he
meant; he said he would relate a peculiar domestic
circumstance.

84   My wife's family were of the Royal faction
(said he, sighing) which I did not know at first, for

her father owed mine money he was unwilling to
repay, and for fear of a lawsuit (my father was a
scrivener and understood the courts) he conversed
only upon such topicks as did not promote disunion.
85   Indeed, my good wise father, knowing that I
yearned toward matrimony, and that his debtor had
a marriageable daughter, proposed an alliance which
would sink the debt in a marriage settlement, which
proposal was not unwelcome; so I was taken to the
girl, and finding her meek mannered, without apparent defects of face and form (indeed, she was
beautiful) I gladly bestowed myself upon her.
86   I was thirty-five years of age at that time, and
since early youth, when it first dawned upon my
developing soul that God had endowed it with no
ordinary qualities, I had prepared myself to write a
book which the world would not willingly let die,
partly by reading everything great which preceeded
me: yes, but also by the cultivation of fortitude,
sobriety and chastity, for no good thing may emanate
from a bad man.
87   I had conceived an Epic on the story of King
Arthur, and was now sure I needed nothing to begin
it but that well of constant sensible solace which is
owed by a wife to the husband of her body.
88   What my wife brought me was silence; meek
she had seemed and meek her manner remained, as
befitted one not much more than half my age, but
that meekness enclosed a cold sullen obdurate
resistance which granted to my mind, heart and
soul *nothing*.
89   Our conjoyned society was therefor mutual
torture, but my torture was greater, for whether
beside her or apart from her I desired her continually and hopelessly, whereas she found a little
happiness in my occasional absences.

90 After a very few weeks she got a pretext for visiting her family in Oxfordshire, and refused to return from thence, being supported in this rebellion by her Royalist father and brothers (the King had just inaugurated a greater Rebellion by making Oxford his capital city, where his followers gloried in their first slight early triumphs).

91 Did I not find her departure a great relief? Oh no I did not.

92 My publick self did not suffer, I infused new vigour into my service to the Commonwealth, authoring in a brief space no less than four treatises on divorce, and one upon a general reform of education, and one defending the right of all to print what they willed: for the Pressbiters were snarling at my heels – I did but prompt the age to quit their clogs by the known rules of ancient liberty, when straight a barbarous noise environed me of owls and cuckoos, asses, apes and dogs.

93 I also saw off the press a complete collection of my short earlier poems, but this was in some sort a farewell to poesy: for despairing of all lawful domestic solace (for my advocacy of divorce had not perswaded the rational part of parlement to change the laws) I must despair of all honest manhood: so my plan to write a great Protestant Christian Epic which would cleanse the matrix of Civil Liberty and Justice from the obfuscs put upon it by the too voluptuous pens of courtly Ariosto, Spencer and Tasso, had become dross rubbish to me.

94 And I am certain poetry would have remained dead to me, had not my wife's family opened negotiations to return her, for Cromwel was begining to take the helm of state, and clearly the King would not now last long in England; so in tears she returned to me and –

95   He paused, himself overcome by tears.

96   Seeing that his flagon was emptied I refilled it, remarking softly, that I was glad the Royal defeat had brought unity to one family at least.

97   Whatever produced those tears, (he cried suddenly aloud) her repentance, her wish to be one with me was genuine and complete, and these appealing tears, melting my very marrow, made me see that I had erred as greatly as she, for feeling unloved by her, my love of God had become without true content or gratitude: to me the Grandeur of the Creation, the Incarnation, Christ's Loving Mercy, the Resurrection of the Flesh had been meer words, meer empty words without her tearful return.

98   I asked him if he had not placed upon the domestic bond a greater weight than it could bear: he seemed not to hear that question.

99   And now (said he) though I will soon be as stone blind as Homer was, my mind's eye commands so wide a firmament that beneath it the matter of England, great though it be, appears as small a thing as would appear the matter of Troy, Rome and Jerusalem envisioned from the glowing Zenith by the Enthroned First Mover.

100   When time is ripe for it, my verse will do far more than illuminate the best essence of Thomas Malory's text, it will translate, clarify and augment the greatest and most truly Original Book in the Universe.

101   Such (said I) is my aim also, and I am thunderstruck to discover in the Puritan camp one who admires the work of Rabelais as greatly as I do; but speaking as a printed poet myself, I greatly doubt if verse is the fittest craft to convoy into English all the varied and witty exellencies of that

```
************************************************
************************************************
************************************************
************************************************
*******   MORE EXCISIONS HERE   *******
*******      BY TOOTH OF        *******
*******   EDITORIAL RODENTS     *******
************************************************
************************************************
************************************************
************************************************
```

algebra, which cannot yield the longitude; but by travelling the line of latitude, I would inevitably hit it.

144 He agreed that such a discovery must not only utterly transform and glorify myself who made it (if I made it) but equally transform and glorify whoever conversed with me afterward, and whoever afterward conversed with them &cetera, until by meer conversation the whole world was made again in God's image, every man, woman and child becoming (he sank here to a meckanical metaphor) a sounding pipe in the Creator's organ.

145 However (he lowered his voice still further) he knew that the Cabinet Council would by no reason clear my estate of its encumbrances, or finance such an expedition, and he hoped this news did not utterly gravel me, for though he had called here from curiosity rather than kindness, he now knew I was more than a meer madman, and his heart went out to me.

146 I walked to the end of the chamber and looked through the window to hide my face; having mastered myself I then turned, adopted the true stance of the acomplished rhetorician, and answered him in the words of my best epigram.

147   *We weep to breathe, when we to being come,*
      After which Agon, all we gain is gift:
      Air, sunlight, ground to stand on, yeah, disease
      Which turns the soul to all from it bereft
      By Adam's greed, pain showing what was, left.
      Delight *without* disease *would stand us still.*
      Hell *herds us hence to* Heaven: *ill antidotes ill.*

148   He nodded and smiled with one side of his
mouth as if I had uttered a negligible truth, and I
realized that I was again confronted by the jealousy
of a fellow poetizer; but after a pause he said that the
Council of State did not think that I greatly menaced
the Commonwealth, and would soon admit me to
perfect freedom.
149   I answered that such freedom would be worse
than the vilest slavery, for it would leave me free to
do nothing but grappel till death with clusterfist
creditors and esurient Kirkists; I now had a vision of
a nobler sprout than my family tree; if meerly
released I must live to tend the latter with pain,
vexation and ingratitude: it would be better if I could
escape abroad, for in that case I would be at least
welcomed by friends of the Steward in exile, and be
some degrees nearer my Goal.
150   After long silence he said, that shortly, if the
parole which for more than two years has permitted
me to wander wheresoever I list within the liberties
of London, were withdrawn, and Lieutenant Apsley
knew that any omission to lock me in would be set
down to an underling's negligible oversight, then
what thereafter befel would reflect dishonour upon
nobody; but I must know his words were idle,
random, unintended and unlinked to any outcome,
whether speculative or eventual. And he took his
leave absently, as though pondering something.

26 MAY 1660:
IN THE ERSTWHILE SCHISMATIC
PAPAL PALAZZO OF AVIGNON.

Into all lugs is verbal gold poured! The glib tongue
of informed rumour dinneth it abroad that, lacking
their Lord Paramount Protector (his tumble-down
son Dick having proved a dwaibly mainstay) and the
Model Army of the General Monck concurring, (the
synagogical sanhedrins of the regicidal regiments
glowring but holding aloof) the London Lords
and Commons hath done no less a thing than invite
from his den in the Nether Lands, the Eighth Royal
Steward and Second Steward Charlemagnus, to
become this very day Instaurated, Instellarated
and Incoronated upon the throne of the whole
Brittanic League of Kingdoms and Commonweals!
At which bruit fell I into such ecstasy of mirth that I
was like to have departed this life. But my greatest
attempt recalled me.

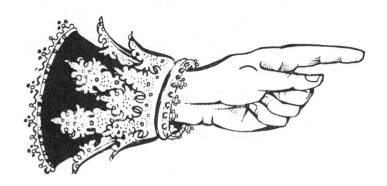

26 JUNE 1660:
IN THE STRADO CURTIZANO, VENICE.
The women of this republick leave a man as they
discover him, but reduced.

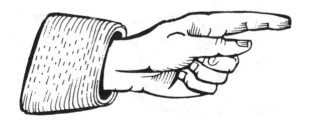

26 JULY 1660:
AT SEA BETWIXT BYZANTIUM
AND CRIM-TARTARY.
A good wind, but misled by light. Cannot account
for this phenomenon.

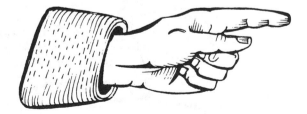

3 AY AE E OE 2 EOE E EIE
EI I-AAY A AAA
ew ie i oo O ae i o oo ae a ie ae ea i e ei ie a aue e oe a
eay a eei oe iaiaio ai uaio a aiio ee u ae a i e e I i ye
aoui o a i eo ee I ae oui

3 DS FTR TH CMT, 2 BFR TH CLPS:
BTWXT CRM-TRTRY ND SMRKND.
N wn s pr. ld wtr s nt gd. Wtr nd wn r qul n th vns.
Whl hlf mtrs th thr hlf dcs. Wht flngs ls mgntn gns.
Sbtrctn nd ddtn kp sch pc tht n th nd fnd mslf
mntng t tht frst zr whr strtd cntng.

MORE THAN A YEAR AFTER THE
FOREGOING: AMONG ROCKS.
My guide has absconded and I am at a loss to comprehend what the last four entries signify, in particular the previous two, which, were they not clearly indited in my own hand, would suggest the gibberish jottings of a dotard, drunkard or dizzard. Can I, in a moment of sublimity (which the Eternal Omniscience may wreak upon whom he listeth) have achieved that logopandocy whose Genesistical root Cromwell's latinist sectary agrees was split at Babelon, and I hold to be the concluding Revelation of the Holy Ghost operant through mankind generally, and myself especially? And have I since, like an overstrained athlete, lapsed so far below my best achievement as to find its memorials incomprehensible? Did I indeed, when fevered with ague on a foggy island in that wide marsh, write dialects of the tongues of the Cherubim and Seraphim? I doubt. I doubt. However cryptogrammed I am certain that a sentence of the archangelic tongue would twang my discernment with some resonance of pluterperfect Pythagorean jubilee, and these syllables, omnivowelant and omniconsonant, evoke a strangely familiar dulness. No water here, but I suck the dew which distillates between the fibrils of my cloak.

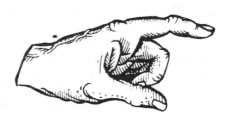

SOME YEARS AFTER THE FOREGOING:
A NAMELESS TOWN.

I can describe this place but have no word for it. The speech of the people is so sing-song-sibilant that my ear cannot divide one syllable from another, nor detect the least root of any tongue, ancient or modern, within the recorded frontiers of Europe, Asia, Africa and those twin Columbias so unjustly cartographed and mappamundified as Amerigo Vespucci-land. Their writing is no aid to understanding them, for it is hieroglyphical. The figure *man* I can easily distinguish, but always with some variant, viz. a hat, or the male member more protruberant, or the leggs a-jigging, or the posture prone, so that when I lay my finger on a figure and tilt my head and raize my eyebrows interrogatively, my host makes a sound which is each time completely novel. Maybe they do not use verb, adjective or adverb forms, but make a different noun for the same thing when it is differently engaged or favoured. We too use different noun-names for a man when he is of social rank, or tumescent, or gymnastickal, or dead. E.g. You are a presiding magistrate, you are a fornicator, you are a comedian, you are a corpse.

If the language of this people is indeed a linking of modified qualified nouns it is closer to my Logopandocy than any I have encountered. Do they speak the language used by Adam and Eve before Babel? No. Or if not no, they speak but a parcel of it, for the omnipotent Power who furnished us with these speech-tools of throat, tongue, roof of mouth, teeth and lips, must naturally have provided a language which, like a mighty choir, used these to the full; and though I could easier convey the jabber of these townsfolk by musical notation than by alphabet, their noise is all in the treble register.

The town covers a space of forty-four square miles, enclosed by a low earth embankment of no defensive value at all, but more of that anon. It is the rich metropolis of no nation, standing in a desert where three trade-routes meet, but industry and irrigation have given it an aspect that would keep me here, did pleasure and not a great enterprize drive me. In the early morning I climb up to the citadel, the only building with stone walls. It contains neither arsenal nor garrison, but is employed as a communal warehouse by the paper manufacturers. From here the town is a mass of trees and gardens with almost no houses to be seen, and I gaze across them at the distant but majestic mountains and wonder which divides me from my goal. As the heat of the day increases the dust of the plain beyond the rampart rizes up in a great cloud like a wall with nothing seen above it but the tips of a few snowy peaks. And then I descend to the town spread cool beneath the trees. But here again the names of things defeat me, for can they be called trees which lack bark, branches, twigs and leaves? The stems, though as tall as great elms, are pale, smooth and nearly translucid. A grove of five or six share the one root, but above ground slant and taper away from each other, each supporting a single great scrolled and ferny frond which casts a mild green shadow. Since it never rains here the groves are refreshed by melted mountain snow, brought hither through an aqueduct branching into slender canals floored with copper, furnished also with sluices which divert pure streams into every grove and garden. I have calculated there are no less than 2,000 places in the stone-paved streets and squares where iced water may be obtained free, sprouting freshly from fountains or served by ladles from earthenware reservoirs. These waterworks also contain bream, trout, eels, crayfish and prawns which are the best of their diet, adding savour to vegetables resembling oak, cedar and pine trees, but only a few inches high, and which must be softened by steaming in goblets of perforated bronze. The main manufactures of the place are saddles, swords, satin, silk, but paper most of all, every texture and thickness of paper from translucent tissue to waterproof-stout. Which brings me to their architecture.

Each building is founded on a well-paved stone platform containing a deep cellar. Above this, on a frame of poles, stands a pavilion with paper walls and roof. The visitor does not perceive their flimsiness at first as the women and children, especially in the poor districts, delight to paint these structures with the patterns of mosaic, and marquetry, and glazed tile inlay, so the town appears the richest in the world, though lacking that regularity and symmetry which exalts the architecture of Europe.

Soon after I arrived here a watcher on the citadel's single tower sounded a great gong which was repeated and re-echoed through every garden and grove. Quickly, but without panic, the squares and streets emptied as the citizens repaired to their homes, where they raized a stone in the foundation, descended to the cellar and sealed themselves in. My host pressed me to join him, but from curiosity I refused and went to my vantage point on the citadel where I sat crosslegged, the only man above ground. Presently, with a thunder of steady hooves, enters a band of tartar cavalry, ferociously visored, armoured and bannered, followed by a tribe of their women and children pushing great carts. The horsemen then ride in circles raizing a great yellyhoo, sounding horns and banging drums while their followers fill the carts with food from the market, goods from the workshops and such furniture and treasures as remain in the houses. The citadel was not attacked, though I was stared upon. My experience of men is, that the worst of them will seldom pester he who remains quiet, unafraid, keeps his weapons hid and offers no violence. When the carts were filled the cavalry set fire to the buildings and departed. The entire metropolis was burned to its foundations in a matter of minutes, after which the plundered citizens emerged and with great stoicism started sweeping away the cinders. I wondered at first why the invaders had not raided the cellars where the rich citizens store the best of their property; but realized this would delay the rebuilding of the city for a long time, giving the tartars less to plunder when they returned, which they do about twice a year. This style of warfare is therefor as civilized as ours. The only folk who lose everything by it are without riches stored below ground, and these folk, who belong to every country, are accustomed to losing. I have now seen the city raided three times, and always by the same tartar tribe. If these predators keep other plundering tribes from the place, then the whole region is more like a European state than the difference of language suggests.

Since the quantifying faculty of numbering and measuring is different from the naming faculty, I hoped that my skill as a geometer might make me useful and admired here, and so it proved. After

witnessing the town's great conflagration I measured
the platform for a house in my host's garden, which
nobody was busy upon, and drew on a great scroll of
good, smooth paper the plans and perspective eleva-
tions of a noble and symmetrical palace in the style
of Whitehall, London, and which, using the local
methods, could be erected in a few hours at the cost
of a few shillings. I offered this to my host, who
received it with expressions of pleasure which I
could not doubt, and when I made designs for
other buildings, drawing upon the memory of my
extensive travels, and presented them to my host's
colleagues and neighbours, they also laughed heartily
and gave me gifts; so that I believed that in a week or
two a nobler style of architecture would prevail, and
the whole city have an aspect combining the best
features of Aberdeen, Oxford, Paris, Florence, Venice and Imperial Rome. I found later, however,
they had no conception of what my outline meant,
for they filled between them with tincts of coloured
water, very skilfully, producing patterns which they
attached to standing screens, frequently upside-
down. I have been here too long, but have yet to
find a suitable guide who can guess where I am
going.

MANY DAYS LATER.
At last I am in the height of the mighty pass, and
indite this hastily before descending to the plain, or
valley, or ocean, which is hid below the bright mist.
My seat is the fallen pillar of a Roman *terminus* or
boundary stone, engrooved (if I misread it not) with
the name and dignities of the Caesar Caligula; but it
may be the prone stalk of a uniquely smooth tree
whose bark hath been disfigured by accidentally
runic crevices, for the mist is so dazzling-white that
I can distinguish a very few inches past the coupled
convergent apertures of my eliptical nose-thirls.
The guide says we will arrive in an hour. She conveys
her meaning by smiles and stroaks of the hand
which I comprehend perfectly (there are waterfalls
all round whose liquid cluckings, gurglings and
yellings drown all words) and it occurs to me that
the first pure language my ancestors shared before
Babylon was not of voice but of exactly these smiles
and stroaks of the hand. I believe I am come
to the edge of the greatest
and happiest discovery
of my life.

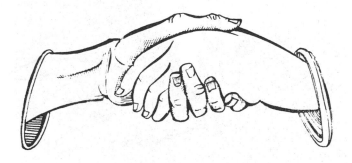

M. POLLARD'S
PROMETHEUS

IT WAS UNKIND OF THE JEWS TO GIVE
the job of building the world to one man for it made
him very lonely. Earlier people saw the creator as a
woman giving birth, which is sore, but not sore on
the head, and fulfils body and soul until the empty
feeling starts. But these wandering shepherds were
so used to featureless plains under a vast sky (not
even the sea is vaster than the sky) that they thrust a
naked man into formless void and left him there
forever with nothing to remember, not even the
sweetness of a mother's breast.

Roman Catholics and the English parliamentary
poet Milton evade the horror of this by placing the
void below a mansion where God lives in luxury
among angelic flunkeys. Satan, his sinister head
waiter, provokes a palace rebellion resulting in a
serious staff-shortage; so God, without leaving his
throne, gives orders which create a breeding and
testing ground (the earth) for a new race of servants
(mankind). This notion is very reassuring to people
with power and to those weaklings and parasites
who admire them. Most citizens with a religion
really do believe that heaven is a large private
property, and that without a boss to command them
they would be nobody. I reject this bourgeois image
of God. If God is the first cause of things then he
started in a vacuum with no support and no ideas
except those arising from his passions. Some com-
mentators present the void as a sort of watery egg on
which God broods like a hen until it hatches. Oh
yes, why not? This sweet notion is easily reconciled
with the splitting of that grand primordial atom
which scientists have made so popular. But I am
better than a scientist. The Jewish Genesis intox-
icates me by attributing all creation to a mind like

mine, so to understand God I need only imagine myself in his situation.

First, then, black void, pure and unflawed by sensations. No heat, no cold, no pressure, no extent. What is there to do? Be. Being is all that can be done. But gradually a sensation does occur, the sensation of duration. We perceive that we have been for a long time, that we will be forever in this darkness unless we do something. The more we endure of our dark self the less we can bear it. We move from boredom to unease and then to panic-horror of an eternity like this. We are in Hell. So the cry "Let there be light" is not an order but a desperate prayer to our own unknown powers. It is also a scream rejecting everything we know by committing us to an unimaginable opposite. And there is *light*. And oh, what appalling vertigo we feel when eternity becomes infinity also and we find ourselves floating beside above beneath that dazzling blank bright breadth, height, depth with no content but ourselves. The light is too much for us, we turn to darkness again. And the evening and the morning are the first day.

Genesis says God saw the light, that it was good, but I cannot imagine him standing happily upon that boundless floor of light before he has peopled it with creatures. His first creature is water, a body compatible with his agitation and as formless as his thinking at this stage. Its sparkling movement reflects and refracts the light into every possible tone and tint, there is a rainbow in each drop of it. With this water he makes the sliding architecture of the sea and the steady, starry flood of the firmament. Unscientific? Good. I would have it so. I will skip most of the other stages. By the sixth day God is almost wholly incarnate. We taste earth and dew through a million roots, our leaves and blossoms sense and scent the air, we graze on our herbs and strike beaks into our squealing flesh while our unutterable doubt of the whole enterprise sneaks searchingly through sunlit grass in the body of the serpent. Our largest intellectual powers are almost (but not quite) realized in Adam, who kneels to study, in a puzzled way, his reflection in a quiet stream. The reflection causes a stiffening in his ureter which has to do with the attached seed-balls, but the stiffening is not sufficient to impregnate the image in the water or the moist gravel under it. What other body do we need? Eve, of course, our last and most intricate creature. So Adam knew Eve, his wife, and she conceived and bare Cain. And Cain knew *his* wife, who conceived and bare Enoch, who builded a city. And after more generations of knowing and conceiving, a Seventh-Day Adventist, Joseph Pollard, cleaved to his far more liberal wife Marie, who conceived and bare myself, the poet. If your education is adequate you already know I have been paraphrasing the start of my *Sacred Sociology*, printed privately at Dijon in 1934.

My infancy resembled that of God, my ancestor. I only dimly recall the dark time before I screamed into light, but I was in that dark, like all of us, and I screamed, and there was light. I may have found the light emptier than most. My mother once told me, in an amused voice, that as a baby I screamed continually until one day they sent for a doctor. He examined me minutely then said, "Madam, what you have here is a screaming baby." Clearly she had never wondered what I was screaming *for*. Herself, probably. But soon my vocal chaos acquired the rhythm and colours of articulate speech and I named and commanded a child's small universe. My command was not absolute. In my tenth year Marie Pollard eloped to Algiers with one of her husband's business acquaintances. I sympathized with at least half the feelings which compelled her. Illness had made Joseph Pollard hard to live with. His fits of blinding rage destroyed a great deal of furniture and did not always spare the human body. But I am grateful to him. Paul Cezanne once said, "My father was the real genius. He left me a million francs." Father Pollard was not such a genius as Father Cezanne, but in my eighteenth year he freed me from himself and the curse of earning my bread by succumbing to cancer of the spleen. The consequent income did not permit me to marry, or support a housekeeper, or to frequent respectable brothels; but I silenced the desperate hunger in my young heart by studying it, and the world containing it, and by learning to read all the great sacred books in their original tongues. And I depressed my professors at the Sorbonne by finally submitting no thesis. A poet need not truck with bureaucrats.

I am shy, fastidious and arrogant. I am unattractive, but do not need friends. I am a close reasoner, and love language. My poetic vision is deep, but lacks breadth. It is the drama of their infancy which makes men poets, but the writers of the greatest divine and human comedies are men of the world, they discover and represent that drama in commonplace streets, bedrooms and battlefields. I can only represent Gods, and lonely intelligences, and multitudes viewed from a very great distance. I will never be popular. To pay the printers of the *Sacred*

Sociology and *Child's Dictionary of Abstractions** I
went shabby and hungry for many days and these
books made no great stir. An early act of folly cured
me of seeking fame in the reviews. I sent Gide the
Sacred Sociology with a letter indicating that his
protestant education had made him capable of
appreciating it. He returned the copy with a se-
ven-word comment: "Literature cannot be founded
on Larousse Encyclopedias." His rage, when his wife
burned all his letters to her, still amuses me extremely. Bravo, Madame Gide! You hoarded these
scribblings as long as you believed he had no other
way of making love, but thrust them in the stove
when you discovered he enjoyed that passion, physically, elsewhere. You refused to be a postbox
through which the great man despatched himself
to posterity, bravissimo. I am the opposite of Gide. I
now address the public in order to be read by one
woman I can reach in no other way. Love drives me
to this. Gide was driven by vanity.

I am as old as my century. In the late sixties the
respectable working men who frequent the café
where I dine began to be ousted by students and
other members of the lower intellectual classes. This
led to an increase of prices and one day I told the
manageress that I could no longer afford to patronize
her establishment. A shade of unease came to her
face and was instantly quelled. After a moment she
indicated that, to a customer of long standing, a
reduction of five per cent was permissible. She was
not being friendly. She had been friendly twenty
years earlier, but I then made certain detailed
proposals which she construed as insults. She is

* M. Pollard clearly wishes to consign to oblivion his translation of Carlyle's
French Revolution into heroic Alexandrines, published privately at Dijon in 1927.

one of those strict atheists who determine themselves
far more completely than a priest determines a good
Catholic. Over the years her splendid body had come
to depend on the corset for its shape but I still found
the sight of it entertaining; she knew this and
cordially detested me. I told her that a fifteen per
cent reduction might ensure my continued custom
and, after quelling a distinct flicker of wrath, she
agreed. I left the café proud to be a Frenchman. The
change in clientele was due to myself. Though
unpopular I had clearly become famous, and where
else in the world would intellectual eminence receive
such tactful regard? I remembered also that my mail
had recently become abundant, though I only open
envelopes from publishers and from the bank which
manages my estate. I decided to give myself a holiday.
I usually study in a small useful library containing no
publications after 1765. Today, in a spirit of sheer
caprice, I visited the Bibliothèque Nationale and
investigated the history of my reputation.

My books had suffered from an absence of agreement upon how to regard them. In the thirties, the
only period when I associated with a political movement, my support of the National Front led the
surrealists and left wing generally to regard the
Sacred Sociology as a satire against religion in the
fashion of Anatole France; but Claudel called it a
grand heresy revealing the truth through the agony of
estrangement, Celine praised it as hilarious anti-
semitic comedy, and Saint-Exupéry noticed that it
did not seek to deface or replace the scriptures, but to
be bound in with them. In the forties the existent-
ialists had just begun to bracket me with Kierkegaard
when I printed *A Child's Plainchant Dictionary of
Abstractions*. This was thought an inept satire against

dictionaries and final proof that I was not a serious
thinker. Twelve years later a disciple of Levi-Strauss
discovered that, though printed as prose, each definition in my dictionary was a pattern of assonance,
dissonance, half-rhyme and alliteration invoking the
emotions upon which words like *truth, greed, government, distaste* and *freedom* depend for their meanings.
My definition of *digestion*, for example, if spoken
aloud, soothes stomachs suffering from indigestion.
This realization brought me the reverence of the
structuralists who now used my dictionary as a text
in three universities. I was often quoted in controver-
sies surrounding the American linguist, Chomsky. It
seemed that among my unopened mail lay an invitation
to join the French Academy and the offer of a Nobel
prize for literature. There was widespread speculation
about my current work. My first two books were of
different kinds and I still pursued the habits of study
which had produced them. It was noted that five years
earlier I had begun subscribing to a journal devoted to
classical Greek researches. All things considered, there
was a chance that, before the century ended my name
might be attached to a metro terminus.

I left the Bibliothèque Nationale knowing a new
epoch was begun. I had become magnetic. In the
café, when I raised a finger to order a Pernod, the
manageress brought it then turned her haunches on
me in a manner less suggestive of the slamming of a
door. The glances of the other customers kept
flickering toward my meagre person in a way which
showed it reassured them. I was filled with social
warmth which I did not need to express, dismissing
importunate journalists and research students with a
blank stare or aloof monosyllable. This procedure
greatly entertained the respectable working men. I

came to notice a nearby face, a well-exercised face of the sort I like. The fine lines between the brows and the corners of the mouth and eyes showed it was accustomed to smiling and scowling and was often near to tears; the main expression was eager and desperate. My own face is too big for my body and bland to the point of dullness. My only lines are some horizontal ones on the brow which show I am sometimes surprised, but not often and not much. I arranged my features to indicate that if I was approached I would not be repellent, and after hesitating a moment she left her table and sat down facing me, vastly disturbing in the circumambient field of attention. We were silent until it settled.

She was in the mid-thirties with long, rather dry, straw-coloured hair topped by a defiant red beret. Her other clothes (baggy sweater, trousers, clogs) had been chosen to muffle rather than display her not very tall figure, which was nonetheless good. My personality is modelled upon August Dupin. I eventually said, "There is a book in your handbag?" She opened the bag and laid a thin pamphlet on the table between us. I could not read the author's name, but it was not by me, so must be her own, or by her lover, or perhaps child. I said, "Poems?" She nodded. I said, "Why do you approach someone so famous for taciturnity as myself? Have you been rejected by the more accessible celebrities?" She said, "In approaching you I have not been guided by reason. You are an almost complete reactionary. I ought to despise you. But when a young girl your dictionary gave me an ineradicable respect for the meanings, the colours, the whole *sense* of our language. If your talent is not dead from disuse, if you are not wholly the dotard you im-

personate, you may help me, perhaps. I so much
want to be a good poet."
I am not accustomed to challenges, my usual habits
prevent them. Her words released into my veins an
utterly intoxicating flood of adrenalin. I gazed on her
with awe and gratitude. She had turned her face
sideways and tears slid down the curve of her cheek.
I lifted the little book and said playfully, "If I dislike
this you will think me a dead man; if I love it there is
hope for me?"
She said coldly, "I am not a fool."
Her proud chin was at an angle as defiant as the
beret, her small nose was as tip-tilted as a sparrow's
beak. The bridge may have been broken. I, who have
never touched a woman tenderly in my life, longed to
lift and cradle her protectingly. So much sudden new
experience could overstrain an old heart. I pocketed
the book, climbed down to the floor and said,
"Madam, my habits are invariable, you may find
me here whenever you please. I will have read your
book in two days."

For the second time in four years I allowed myself
a holiday. On the sunlit pavement I was gripped by a
walking frenzy. She had given me a precious part of
herself (I stroked the book in my pocket) and defied
me, and asked for help, and wept. I loved her, of
course, and did not regret that this state, for me,
would be painful and perhaps impossible. Romeo
and Juliet, Anthony and Cleopatra found love painful and almost impossible. Phaedra and Medea found
it quite impossible, but nobody doubts they were
enhanced by it. I was enhanced by it. I am a wholly
suburban Parisian who distrusts, as much as any
provincial, that collection of stale imperial pie-crusts
calling itself *Paris*. We require it to awe the foreigner

who would otherwise menace our language and culture, but I refuse to be awed. So I was amused to find myself standing on one of the curving benches of the Pont-Neuf, my arms on the parapet, staring downstream at one of our ugliest* buildings with a strong sentiment of admiration and delight. Since I was physically unable to seduce her I must persuade her to seduce me. This required me to remain aloof, while feeding her with increasingly useful parts of my mind, cunningly sauced with flattery to induce addiction. Everything depended on her poems. If they were entirely bad I would lose interest and botch the whole business. I sat down and read.

I was lucky. The person of the book was intelligent, tough, and on the way to being a good writer. She was a feminist, vivisecting her mauled sexual organs to display the damage and making the surgery icily comic by indicating, in a quiet lip-licking way, "It's even more fun when I slice up him." Some poems showed her embracing and embraced by a lover and unable to tell him something essential, either because of his indifference or from her fear that big truths are too destructive to be shared by a society of two. It was entertaining to see a woman in these Byronic postures but she was potentially greater than Byron. Her best work showed respect for human pain at a profounder level than sexual combat. It was spoiled by too many ideas. A good poem is a tautology. It expands one word by adding a number which clarify it, thus making a new word which has never before been spoken. The seed-word is always so ordinary that hardly anyone perceives it. Classical odes grow from *and* or *because*,

* An insult to the home of the Academie Francaise.

romantic lyrics from *but* and *if*. Immature verses
expand a personal pronoun ad nauseam, the greatest
works bring glory to a common verb. Good poems,
therefore, are always close to banality, above which,
however, they tower like precipices. My woman
avoided banality (which has, indeed, swallowed
hordes of us) by turbulent conjunctions. Her book
was filled with centaurs because she had not fully
grasped the complexity of actual people, actual
horses. Her instinct to approach me had been
sound. I could teach her a great deal.

I bought a note pad from a stationer in the Place
Dauphin. It was Sunday. I entered the Louvre and
fought my way through the polyglot mobs to the
Maria de Medici salon where I always feel at
home. The canvases adorning this temple to
female government bubble with enough good-
humoured breasts to suckle a universe. My favourite painting, which always gives me a wicked thrill,
shows the Italian banker's fat daughter handing
over the tiller of state to her son, a boy with the
clothes, rigid stance and far too solemn face of a
very small adult. The ship of state has a mast with
Athene beside it pointing the way, her curves compressed by armour which recalls the corsets of my
manageress. The motive power of the vessel is
provided by lusty women representing Prudence,
Fortitude, etc., who toil at heavy oars with pained,
indignant expressions which suggest that work comes
to them as a horrible surprise. Unluckily there is no
sofa near this painting. I settled before the canvases
which show Maria's coronation inaugurating a new
golden age and there, in the severe language of
literary criticism, wrote the first love-letter of my
life. I was inspired. I filled twenty-four pages with

minute writing before closing time, then walked
home, corrected them in red ink, typed them,
recorrected, retyped, then sealed them in a large
manilla envelope of the sort used for preserving legal
documents. My heart palpitated as I inscribed her
name upon it.

I had said I would read her poems within two
days. For a week I extended my lunch hour beyond
the normal and on the eighth day her shadow fell
across the print of the book I was reading. Without
raising my eyes I placed the letter between us,
saying, "You may wish to digest this in private."
I heard the envelope torn, then looked up. She was
giving the letter an attention which excluded myself
and everything else. She read slowly, and some
passages more than once. An hour elapsed. She
slid the pages into her handbag, gave me a full,
sincere smile and said, "Thanks. You have misun-
derstood my work almost completely, but your
warped picture of it conveys insights which I will
one day find useful. Thanks."
She tapped the tabletop with her fingers, perhaps
preparing to leave. I grew afraid. I said, "Will you
now explain why, in our first encounter, you called
me reactionary?"
"Your work explains that."
"The *Sacred Sociology*?"
"Yes, for the most part."
I sighed and said, "Madam, it is not my custom to
justify myself or criticize others. Both practices
indicate insufficiency. But to you I surrender. Your
poems suggest you love freedom, and want a just
communism to release human souls from the bankvaults of the West, the labour camps of the East."
"And from the hospitals and asylums!" she cried

ardently. "And from the armies, churches and bad marriages!"

"Good. You desire a world-wide anarchic commonwealth where government may be safely left to a committee of retired housekeepers chosen by lot, like a jury."

She smiled and nodded. I said, "Madam, I wish that also. For centuries men have been misled by words like God, fate, nature, necessity, world, time, civilization and history: words which hide from us our cause and condition. The bourgeois say that because of these things our state can change very little, except for the worse. But these words are nothing but names for *people*. *We* are our God, fate, nature, necessity, world, time, civilization and history. Common people achieved these limbs, this brain, the emotions and the skills and the languages which share them. We have made every blessing we enjoy, including sunlight, for the sun would be a meaner thing without our eyes to reflect it. The fact that man is infinitely valuable – that man is essentially God – underlies every sacred code. And when I say *man is God* I refer least of all to God the landlord, God the director, God the ruler with power to crush a majority for the good of the rest. To hell with these overpaid demiurges! My gratitude is to God the migrant labourer, the collectivized peasant, the slave of Rio Tinto Zinc and the American Fruit Company. *He* is the heavenly host whose body is broken day after day to nourish smart people like you and me. The *Sacred Sociology* tried to make news of this ancient truth. Did it fail?"

"Yes!" she said. "It failed. The good wine of truth cannot be poured out of filthy old bottles. I will quote something. *Our largest intellectual powers are almost realized in Adam who kneels to study, in a puzzled way, his reflection in a quiet stream. It causes a stiffening in his ureter which has to do with the attached seedballs, but the stiffening is not sufficient to impregnate the image in the water or the moist gravel under it. What other body does he need? Eve, of course, our last and most intricate creation.* Ha! You have done nothing but reaffirm the old lie that a big man made the world, then created a small man to take charge of it, then begot a woman on him to mass-produce replicas of himself. What could be more perverse? You have been deceived, Mr. Pollard. There is a great garden in your brain which is in total darkness. You have been taken in by the status-quo of men and women and what sex is about, much as people were taken in by the Empire and the Church. You don't know *how* you have been oppressed because you have a penis."

I was silent for a while then said, "Correct. You have put your finger exactly upon my weakness, which is sexual. Speak of work which does not refer to the sexes. Speak of my dictionary."

She said, "It liberated me. My education was thoroughly religious in the worst sense but a cousin lent me de Beauvoir's memoirs and your dictionary and they liberated me. At university you were my special study. Do you know how the professors use you? Not to free, but to bind. You are understood to support their systems. The students study commentaries on your book, not the book itself. I defended your assertion of the radical, sensual monosyllable. I was not allowed to complete the course."

I nodded sadly and said, "Yes. I support common sense with uncommon intelligence so the bourgeois have appropriated me, as they appropriate all splendid things. But my book is called *A Child's Plainchant*

Dictionary of Abstractions. I wanted it set to music
and sung in primary schools throughout France.
Impossible, for I have no friends in high places.
But if children sang my definitions with the voices
of thrushes, larks and little owls they would get them
by heart and easily detect fools and rascals who use
words to bind and blind us. The revolution we
require would be many days nearer." "A dictator!"
she cried scornfully. "You! A dwarf! Would dictate
language to the children of a nation!" I laughed aloud.
It is a rare relief when an interlocutor refers to my
stature. She blushed at her audacity, then laughed
also and said, "Intellectually you are a giant, of
course, but you do not live like one. You live like
the English authors who all believe the highest civic
virtue is passivity under laws which money-owners
can manipulate to their own advantage. The second
Charlemagne* has made our country a near dictator-
ship. In Algeria, Hungary, Vietnam and Ireland
governments are employing torturers to reinforce
racial, social and sexual oppression. The intelligent
young hate all this and are looking for allies. And you,
whose words would be eagerly studied by every
intelligence in Europe, say nothing."
I said, "I have no wish to be the mundane con-
science of my tribe. Our Sartre can do that for us."
I was sublimely happy. She saw me as a position to
be captured. I longed for captivity; and if I was
mistaken, and she only saw me as a barricade to be
crossed, might she not, in crossing, be physically
astride me for a few moments? My reference to
Sartre was making her regard me with complete
disdain. I raised an imploring hand and said, "Par-
don me! I have no talent for immediate events. My art

* Charles de Gaulle, with no declared political programme, was ruler of
France.

is solving injustice through historical metaphor and even there I may be defeated."
"Explain that."
I looked directly into her eyes. I had expected sharp blue ones, but they were mild golden-brown and went well with the straw-coloured hair. I said, "You asked for my help to become a better poet. I need yours to finish my last and greatest work. I lack the knowledge to complete it myself."
She whispered, "What work?"
"*Prometheus Unbound.*"

I hoped this conversation would be the first of a series lasting the rest of my life. Her curt, impetuous words, together with a haunted look, as if she must shortly run away, had led me to speak of Prometheus at least a year before I intended, but it was now too late to speak of less important things. I asked her to be patient if I told her a story she perhaps knew already. She glanced at her wristwatch then nodded.

The early Greeks (I said) believed the earth was a woman who, heated by his lightningstrokes, fertilized by his rain, undulated beneath her first offspring, the sky. She gave birth to herbs, trees, beasts and titans. The titans can be named but never clearly defined. There is Atlas the maker of space, and Cronos whom Aristotle identifies with time. There is also Prometheus, whose name means *foresight* and *torch*. He was a craftsman, and moulded men from the dust of his mother's body. The multiplying children of earth could not leave her. She tired of her husband's lust, needing room for her family, room to think. She persuaded Cronos to castrate his dad with a stone

sickle. The sky recoiled from her and *time* became
master of the universe. When people came to live in
cities they looked back on the reign of Cronos as a
golden age, for in those days we were mainly
shepherds and food-gatherers and shared the goods
of the earth equally, without much warfare. But we
had cyclops too, great men who worked in metal.
Cronos feared those and locked them in hell, a place
as far below the earth as the sky is above her. And
when Cronos mated with his sister Rhea he became
a cruel husband. He knew how dangerous a man's
children can be and swallowed his own as soon as
they were born. The earth disliked that. She
advised Rhea to give her man a stone when the
next child came. Time, who has no organs of taste,
swallowed this stone thinking it was yet another
son. The boy's mother called him Zeus and had him
privately educated. When he was old enough to
fight his father for the government of the universe
he tricked the old man into drinking emetic wine
and vomiting up the other children he had swallowed. These were the gods, and Zeus became their
leader. The gods were more cunning than the titans,
but less strong, and only Prometheus saw that
cunning would replace strength as master of the
universe. He tried to reconcile the two sides. When
this proved impossible he joined the rebels.

The war which followed lasted ten years. Prometheus advised Zeus to release the cyclops from
hell and when this was done they equipped the gods
with helmet, trident and thunderbolt. Zeus won, of
course, being supported by his brothers, by the
earthmother, by the cyclops, by Prometheus and
by men. What followed? The new boss of the
universe confirmed his power by threatening man-

kind with death. Prometheus saved us by giving us
hope (which allows us to despise death) and fire
(which the gods wanted to keep to themselves). So
Zeus punished Prometheus by crucifying him on a
granite cliff. But Prometheus is Immortal. He
writhes there to the present day.

"Madam," I asked my woman, "do these matters
seem savage and remote from you? This oppressed
mother always plotting with a son or daughter
against a husband or father, yet breeding nothing
but a new generation of oppressors? This new
administration crushing a clumsy old one with the
help of the skilled workers, common people and a
radical intellectual, and then taking control with the
old threats of prison and bloody punishment."
She nodded seriously and said, "It is savage, but not
remote."
I said, "Exactly. Our political theatres keep changing
but the management always presents the tragedy of
Prometheus or *foresight abused*. The ancient titans
are the natural elements which shape and govern us
when we live in small tribes. Foresight helps us build
cities which give protection from the revolving
seasons and erratic crops. Unluckily these states
are also formed through warfare. They are managed
by winners who enrich themselves at the expense of
the rest and pretend their advantages are as natural
as the seasons, their mismanagement as inevitable as
bad weather. In these states the fate of Prometheus
warns clear-sighted people not to help the commoners against their bosses. But wherever we notice
that poverty is not natural, but created by some of us
unfairly distributing what the rest have made,
democracy is conceived. The iron wedges nailing
Prometheus to his rock begin to loosen. This is why

the poem which presents Prometheus as a hero was written for the world's first and greatest democratic state. I mean Athens, of course."

"Ancient Athens," said my woman firmly, "oppressed women, kept slaves, and fought unjust wars for gain."

"Yes!" I cried. "And in that it was like every other state in the history of mankind. But what made Athens different was the unusual freedom enjoyed by most men in it. When these men compared themselves with the inhabiters of the great surrounding empires (military Persia, priestridden Egypt, Carthage with its huge navy and stock-exchange) they were astonished by their freedom."

She said, "Define freedom."

I said, "It is the experience of active people who live by work they do best, are at ease with their neighbours, and responsible for their government."

She said, "You have just admitted that your free, active Athenians oppressed their neighbours and more than half their own people."

I said, "Yes, and to that extent they were not free, and knew it. Their popular drama, the first plays which the common memory of mankind has seen fit to preserve, shows that warfare and slavery – especially sexual slavery – are horrible things, and at last destroy the winners and the empires who use them."

"Which means," cried my woman, looking more like a tragic heroine with every utterance, "that the Athenians were like our educated bourgeois of Western Europe and North America, who draw unearned income from the poor of their own and other countries, yet feel superior to the equivalent class in Russia, because we applaud writers who tell us we are corrupt."

After a silence I said, "Correct, madam. But do not be offended if I draw a little comfort from just one Athenian achievement: the tragic poem *Prometheus Bound* which was written by Aeschylus and is the world's second oldest play. It shows Prometheus, creative foresight, being crucified and buried by the cunning lords of this world after they have seized power. But Prometheus prophesies that one day he will be released, and tyranny cast down, and men will see their future clear. Aeschylus wrote a sequel, *Prometheus Unbound*, describing that event. It was lost, and I can tell you why.

"The democracy of Athens, great as it was, flawed as it was, tried to become an empire, was defeated, and finally failed. All the great states which followed it were oligarchies. Some, like Florence and Holland, claimed to be republics, but all were oligarchies in which poets and dramatists were so attached to the prosperous classes that they came to despise, yes really despise, the commoners. They saw them as incurably inferior, deserving a tear and a charitable breadcrust in bad times, but potentially dangerous and at best merely comic, like the grave-diggers in *Hamlet*. No doubt the rulers of states thought *Prometheus Unbound* was seditious, but it must also have annoyed educated people by showing how slavish their best hopes had become. They could no longer imagine a good state where intelligence served everyone equally. In twenty-three centuries of human endurance and pain only one hero, Jesus of Nazareth, declared that a common man was the maker of all earthly good, and that by loving and sharing with him we would build the classless kingdom of heaven. And, madam," I told her, "you know what the churches have made of *that*

message. How cunning the winners are! How
horrible!"
And I, who had not wept since I was a baby, shed
passionate tears. I felt her grip my hand across the
tabletop and though I had never before felt such
pure grief for abused humanity, I have never felt
such happiness and peace. It was a while before I
could continue.

"But one day France, madam, yes our own France
declared that democracy must return; that liberty,
equality, fraternity are indivisible; that what the
Athenians started, we will achieve. We have not
achieved it yet, but the world will never know peace
until we have done so. The main task of poetry today
is to show the modern state the way to liberty and
peace by remaking the lost verse-drama, *Prometheus
Unbound*. I have completed half of it."
She stared at me. I hoped she was fascinated. I
described my play.

It starts with the supreme God (spelt with a
capital G to separate him from lesser gods) standing
on a mountaintop after the defeat of the titans. The
sky behind him is a deep dark blue, his face and
physique are as Michelangelo painted him, only
younger – he looks about thirty. Round his feet
flows a milky cloud and under the cloud, on a
curving ridge, stands the committee of Olympus:
Juno, Mars, Venus etcetera. These are the chorus.
On two hills lower down sit Pan and Bacchus among
the small agents of fertility and harvest: nymphs,
fauns, satyrs and bacchantes with fiddles, drums,
bagpipes and flutes. This orchestra makes music for
the scene-changes. A dark vertical cleft divides the
two hills. At the base of it is spread out a great tribe
of common people who may as well be played by the

audience. Their task is to enhance the play with their attention and applause until, at the end, the release of Prometheus releases them too. But at the start God's gravely jubilant voice addresses the universe while the sky grows light behind him.

He speaks like any politician who has just come to power after a struggle. Together (he tells us) we have destroyed chaos and oppression. Prosperity and peace are dawning under new rules which will make everybody happy. Even the wildest districts are now well-governed. My brother Neptune commands the sea, storms and earthquake. My brother Pluto rules the dead. Let us praise the cyclops! The powers of reason would have been defeated without the weapons they made. They have been sent back to hell, but to an improved, useful hell managed by my son Vulcan. He is employing them to make the thunderbolts I need to coerce law-breakers. For alas, law-breakers exist, hot-heads who protest because my new state is not equally good to everyone. It is true that, just now, some must have very little so that, eventually, everyone has more; but those who rage at this are prolonging sufferings which I can only cure with the help of time . . . God is interrupted here by a voice from the ridge below him. Minerva-Athene, his minister of education, or else Cupid his popular clown, point out that the recent war was fought to destroy old time yet now God says he needs time to let him do good. Yes! (cries God) for time is no longer your tyrant, he is my slave. Time will eventually show how kind I am, how good my laws are, how well I have made everything.

Throughout this speech God's nature is clearly changing. From sounding like the spokesman of a

renewed people he has used the language of a
lawmaker, dictator, and finally creator. At his last
words the cloud under him divides and floats left and
right uncovering the shining black face of the earthmother. It is calm and unlined, with slanting eyes
under arched brows like a Buddha, and flat negro
lips like the Sphinx. The white cloud is her hair, the
ridge where the gods stand is her collarbone, the
orchestra sits on her breasts, the audience in her lap.
God, erect on top of her head, with one foot slightly
advanced and arms firmly folded, looks slightly
ridiculous but perfectly at home. When she parts
her lips a soft voice fills the air with melodious
grumbling. She knows that God's claim to be a
creator is false but she is endlessly tolerant and
merely complains instead of shaking him off. Her
grammar is difficult. She is twisting a huge statement into a question and does not divide what she
knows into separate sentences and tenses.

EARTH
Who was before I am dark
without limbs, dancing, spinning
space without heat who
was before I am alight
without body, blazing, dividing
continents on rocking mud who
was before I am breathing
without eyes, floating, rooted
bloody with outcry who
was before I am a singing
ground, wormy-dark, alight
aloud with leaves, eyes and
gardeners, the last plants I grew who
uplifted you who
was before I am?

GOD
Who is before you now!
I grasp all ground, mother.
The gardeners you grew were common men,
    a brood
too silly and shapeless to be any good
outside my state, which has made them new.
They cannot remember being born by you.
They are my image now. I am who
they all want to obey, or if not obey, be.

EARTH
Not Prometheus.

GOD
Yes, Prometheus! Punishment is changing him
into a cracked mirror of me.

There is a sudden terrible cry of pain. Two great
birds with dripping beaks fly out of the cleft between
the earth's breasts. Light enters it and shows the
crucified Prometheus, a strong man of middle age
with a bleeding wound in his side. Though smaller
than his mother he is a giant to the God who stands
high above him and declares that this is the end of
the titan who made men, and made them hard to
govern, by giving them hope of better life. The great
mother, with a touch of passion, tells God that
though he is supreme he is also very new, and his
state will perish one day, like all states, and only
Prometheus knows how. God does not deny this. He
says he has a lot of work to do and will reconsider the
case of Prometheus when he has more time. He turns
and goes down behind the earth's head. The cloud
closes over her. Prometheus, twisting his face up,
asks the gods on the ridge to tell him the present
state of mankind. They sing a chorus describing the

passage of over two thousand years. Men combine into rich empires by many submitting to a few. They discover the world is vaster than they thought, and add new realms to tyranny. Liberators are born who create new religions and states, and the rulers of the world take these over and continue to tighten their grip. At last human cunning grasps, not just the world but the moon and the adjacent planets, yet half mankind dies young from bad feeding, and young courage and talent is still warped and killed by warfare. The controllers of the world fear the people under them as much as each other, and are prepared to defend their position by destroying mankind and the earth which bore them. This is the final state to which we have been brought by cunning without foresight. Prometheus cries out, "This cannot last!" From the middle of her cloud this cry is repeated by the great mother, then by the chorus and orchestra, and then (the cloud clearing) by God himself, who stands on the height with his arms flung sideways in a gesture which resembles the crucified Prometheus. God is also now a middle-aged man. He walks down from the height, sits on the edge of the cleft and tries to engage Prometheus in friendly conversation. He is sorry he punished Prometheus so harshly and promises not to set vultures on him again. When he came to power he had to be harsh, to keep control. People needed strong government, in those days, to drag them out of the idiocy of rural life. But the whole world now belongs to the city states. He is sure Prometheus knows that neither of them is completely good or completely bad, and have a lot to give each other. If they cooperate they can save mankind. He asks Prometheus for the secret of the force which will destroy him. Prometheus asks to be released first.

God is sorry, but he cannot release Prometheus. If
he did Prometheus would seize power.

GOD
I am not the stark power who chained you here.
I am softened by what you endured, while my
    laws
have made you a hard reflection of the tyrant I
    once was.
It cannot be right to enthrone
a killing revenge the world should have outgrown,
or if right, then right will make greater wrong.

PROMETHEUS
It is right to give back what you stole – liberty.
You see me as I am. You cannot see
who I will become when I am free.
Why do you think I will kill?

GOD
Your every glance threatens me terrible ill.

PROMETHEUS
I am in pain! My illness, the illness you dread,
is yours, is you!

GOD
Then endure my terrible nature!
I must endure it too.

(God has lost his temper. Prometheus laughs bitterly.)

PROMETHEUS
At last you unmask, old man
and show what you are again:
the ruler of a kingdom kept by pain.
All history has added nothing to you
but a mad wish to be pitied for what you do.

I paused. My woman said, "What happens then?"
I said, "I cannot imagine."
She started laughing. I said, "To end happily my
play needs a new character, someone we have already
seen, without much interest, in the chorus, or even
audience. The action until now is between a man, a
big woman, and another man. To strike a balance the
fourth character must be a woman. She is a new
wisdom who will unite our imprisoned intelligence
with the productive earth, reducing government
from a form of mastery to a form of service. She
is sensuous, for both governments and rebels keep
asking us to crush our senses in order to gain an
ultimate victory which never arrives. But she is not
disorderly, not a beatnik, not careless. She is living
proof that when our senses are freed from fear our
main desire is to make the world a good home for
everyone. I cannot conceive such a heroine. Can you
conceive her? Could we conceive her together?"
My woman looked thoughtful then said slowly, "I
am qualified to assist you. I have been a daughter
and a mother, a victim and a tyrant. I saw my father
torment his wife into her grave. I have driven a man
to suicide, or very nearly. I know how love heats and
warps us, but I feel there is still hope for me, and the
world."
I said, "That indicates a kind of balance."
"I have climbed mountains in Scotland and Germany. I have swum underground rivers in the
Auvergne."
I said, "That also indicates balance, but a balance of
extremes. The tension you feel must be nearly
unbearable. We must connect the extremes where
you squander so much energy with the centre where
my knowledge lies chained and stagnant."
Her mouth and eyes opened wide, she raised her

chin and gazed upward like the Pythoness on the
tripod when Apollo enters her. For nearly a minute
she became pure priestess. Then her gaze shrank,
descended and focussed on the table where my great,
droll, attentive head rested sideways on my folded
arms. A look of incredulity came upon her face. I
had never before seemed to her so improbably
grotesque. She pretended to glance at her wristwatch, saying, "Excuse me, I must go."
"May I write to you, madam? A literary collabora-
tion is perhaps best prosecuted by letter."
"Yes."
"Your address?"
"I don't know – I am moving elsewhere, I don't
know where yet. I have many arrangements to make.
Leave your letters with the management here. I will
find a way to collect them."
I said, "Good," and achieved a smile. She arose,
came to my side and hesitated. I signalled by a small
headshake that condescension would be unwelcome.
She turned and hurried out. I sat perfectly still,
attending to the beaks of the vultures tearing at my
liver. They had never felt so sharp. The manageress
came over and asked if I felt well? I grinned at her
and nodded repeatedly until she went away.

After that I waited. I could do almost nothing
else. Study was impossible, sleep difficult. I
addressed to her a parcel of worknotes for *Prometheus
Unbound* and it lay on the zinc beside the till, but I
was always sitting nearby for I wanted not to leave
the only place where I might see her again. I waited
a day, a week, three weeks. I was dozing over my
book and glass one afternoon when I grew conscious
of her talking to the manageress. She seemed to
have been doing it for some time. They frowned,

nodded, glanced towards me, shrugged and smiled. I
was very confused and prayed God that when she sat
facing me I would be calm and firm. She patted the
manageress's arm and walked straight out through
the door. I screamed her name, scrambled down
from the chair, charged into the crowded street and
ran screaming to the right, banging against knees,
treading on feet and sometimes trodden on. Not
seeing her I turned and ran to the left. As I passed
the café door I was seized and lifted, yes, lifted up by
one who held her face to mine so that our noses
touched, and whispered, "Mister Pollard, this conduct does you no good. I have a letter."
I became very icy and hissed, "Put me down,
madam."
I should have asked to be taken home. I could
suddenly hardly walk. I got to my table and opened
the letter, noticing that my parcel lay uncollected
beside the till.

My dear friend,
   *I no longer wish to be a poet. It requires an obsessional
balancing of tiny phrases and meanings, an immersion in
language which seems to me a kind of cowardice. As a
man and poet I can respect you but only because you are
also a dwarf. For people of ordinary health and height,
with a clear view of the world and a wish to do well, it is a
waste of time making signboards pointing to the good and
bad things in life. If we do not personally struggle towards
good and fight the bad, people will merely praise or
denounce our signs and go on living as usual. I must
make my own life the book where people read what I
believe. I decided this years ago when I became a socialist, but
I still grasped, like a cuddly toy, my wish to be a poet. That
wish came from the dwarfish part of me, the frightened lonely
child who hoped that a DECLARATION would bring*

the love of mother earth, the respect of daddy god, the admiration of the million sisters and brothers who normally do not care if I live or die. Your critical letter had an effect you did not intend. It showed me that my declarations are futile. It has taken a while for the message to sink in. I am grateful to you, but also very bitter. I cannot be completely logical.

My sweet, you are the cleverest, most deluded man I ever met. Rewriting PROMETHEUS UNBOUND is like rewriting GENESIS, it can be done but who needs it? It is just another effort to put good wine in a filthy old bottle. I was touched when you poured over me your adolescent enthusiasm for ancient Athens but I also wanted to laugh or vomit. I am educated. I have been to Greece. I have stood on the Acropolis facing the Erichtheon and can tell you that Greece represents:

men against women

war	*,,*	*peace*
business	*,,*	*play*
intellect	*,,*	*emotions*
authority	*,,*	*anarchy*
hierarchy	*,,*	*equality*
discipline	*,,*	*sensuality*
property-inheritance	*,,*	*sexuality*
patriarchy	*,,*	*everything*

Yet you see civilization as an unfinished story the Athenians started and which a few well-chosen words will help to a satisfactory finish! You are wrong. The best state in the world was that primitive matriarchy which the Athenians were foremost in dismantling. Men were happy and peaceful when women ruled them, but so naturally wicked that they turned our greatest strength (motherhood) into weakness by taking advantage of it and enslaving us. Men have made hell of the world ever since and are now prepared to destroy all life in it rather than admit they are wrong. Masculine foresight cannot help our civilization because it is travelling backward. Even our enemies realize this. In the last fifty years they have driven us to the brink of the dark age. The rational Greek foundation of things has been unbuilt, unlearned. And you did not notice! My poor dwarf, you are the last nineteenth-century romantic liberal. That is why a corrupt government wishes to make you a national institution.

Which brings me, beloved, to what you really *want from me: cunt. In your eyes it probably looks like an entrance to the human race. Believe me, you are human enough without. No good was ever done by those who thought sexual pleasure a goal in life. I speak from experience. I divorced a perfectly nice husband who could only give me that stultifying happiness, that delicious security which leads to nothing but more of itself. But if you require that delight you can have it by merely relaxing. As a national institution – a blend of tribal totempole and pampered baby – you are ringed by admirers you have so far had the sense and courage to ignore. Weaken, enjoy your fame and get all the breasts you want: except mine. When I first spoke to you I accused you of impersonating a dead man. That was jealousy speaking. I admired you then and I regret I unhinged you so easily. I did not want to do that. I love you, but in a way you cannot perceive and I cannot enjoy. So I also hate you.*

I am a monster. The cutting words I write cut my heart too. I am under unusual strain. I am about to do something difficult and big which, if discovered, will end my freedom forever. My friends will think me insane, an unstable element, a traitor if they learn I have told you this. But you love me and deserve to know what I am leaving you for, and I do trust you, my teacher, my liberator.

Adieu.

Is printing the above letter for the world to read a betrayal of her trust? Is a secret police computer, as a result of this story, stamping the card of every female, blonde, brown-eyed, snub-nosed poet with a number which means *suspect political crime investigate*? No. This story is a poem, a wordgame. I am not a highly literate French dwarf, my lost woman is not a revolutionary writer manqué, my details are fictions, only my meaning is true and I must make that meaning clear by playing the wordgame to the bitter end.

Having read the letter I sat holding it, feeling paralysed, staring at the words until they seemed dark stains on a white surface like THIS one, like THIS one. I was broken. She had made me unable to bear loneliness. And though we had only met twice I had shown the world that women could approach me. I sat at the table, drinking, I suppose, and in the evening a girl sat opposite and asked what I thought of de Gaulle's latest speech? I asked her to inform me of it. Later we were joined by another girl and a young man, students, all of them. It seemed we were on the brink of revolution. I ordered wine. Said the young man, "Tomorrow we will not protest, we will occupy!"
"You must come with us, Mister Pollard!" cried the girls, who were very excited. I agreed and laughed and bought more wine, then grew enraged and changed my position. I quoted Marx to support de Gaulle and Lenin to condemn the students. The uselessness of discourse became so evident that at last I merely howled like a dog and grew unconscious. And awoke with a bad headache, in darkness, beside a great soft cleft cliff: the bum of my manageress. I had been conveyed into her bed. I was almost glad.

In the morning she said, "Mister Pollard, you
know I have been a widow for seven months."
I said nothing. She said, "Some years ago you made
to me certain detailed proposals which, as a respectable, newly-married, very young woman I could not
entertain. What you suggested then is now perfectly
possible. Of course, we must first marry."

Lucie, you have made me need you, or if not you,
someone. Lucie, if you do not return I must fall
forever into her abyss. Lucie, she makes me completely happy, but only in the dark. Oh Lucie Lucie
Lucie save me from her. The one word this poem
exists to clarify is *lonely*. I am Prometheus.
I am lonely.

THE END OF
THE AXLETREE

The emperor died, and his tomb was built in the centre of the capital city, then enlarged to enclose everything he had wanted. His suggestions for the name were also adopted. The inhabiters called it *the work*, outsiders called it *the axletree*. People travelling there saw it for a fortnight before arriving and I speak of the work itself, not the pillar of cloud overhead, creamy-gold on bright days, thunder-black on dull ones, and flickering with reflected orange light in the hours of darkness. As the traveller drew near, the huge solitary bulk so filled his mind that sometimes he grew frightened and turned back before seeing the canals and merchant navies entering the artificial sea around the foundation. The roads bridged this by viaducts sloping up to market-gallery-level, a full mile above sea-level, yet rising

so easily that blind travellers thought they were flat.
It was a safe structure in those days and foreign
kings bought shares in it as a way of banking their
wealth. The construction company became the
government of the empire – our emperors dropped
their ancient title and were known as company
chairmen. The first of these was a man of simple
tastes who had a farm near the top of the work where
he grew his own vegetables. He liked to feel he did
not need the earth below, but everyone else in the
axletree was fed off that. People in the nearest
provinces usually looked thin and glum. It must
also have been very depressing to live where half the
world bent up to shut you out. Dwellers in remoter
provinces saw us as a steep-sided mountain on the
horizon, but to insiders we were not one thing but
many: our living rooms and the rooms of friends,
some connecting galleries lined with shops and
parkland, the offices where we calculated or the
scaffolding where we laboured. The simplest thing
we knew was the world spread below like a map.
Merchants, soldiers and tax-collectors had to visit
that. Most of us were luckier.

Not everyone inside the great work was happy
there. When the structure was repaired the masons
found odd cavernous spaces full of mummified
bodies. These had been slaves who died while putting the building up. They were buried this way
because it did not interrupt the labour, and because
the founding emperor wanted everyone who worked
on his tomb to end up inside. But the re-opened
crypts held signs of life: rough tables with winestains
and cheap candlesticks on them, and there were
gaps in the surrounding stonework just big enough
to admit people on their hands and knees. The

police discovered that these crypts were used by a society of slaves, labourers and women who met there once a week to exchange subversive gossip. The society was co-operative. Members paid small sums to an agent who cooked them a communal meal and guarded their articles of association. These articles set out the wildest hopes of uneducated people in the language of company law. They said:

1. God had designed the axletree as a home for all who worked on it.
2. The construction company had stolen it and was building for private profit.
3. When the top touched heaven the divine architect would come down and lock up the directors and shareholders in their treasure vaults.
4. And give members of the co-operative society an eternally happy home.

Members sometimes disagreed about whether they would occupy the finished work as ghosts or bodies, or use it as a stair to enter heaven. Their disputes were settled by the works foreman, the society's chief agent. He was supposed to know far more about building than the company chairman, though he was elected for his ability as a caterer.

The company chairman thought this society would start a rebellion among his labour force. It was banned and the police killed many of its agents, including the first two foremen. Yet it gained members and grew, for it helped the worst-paid people believe that their enslavement to the axletree would eventually do them good.

One day the rim of the empire was penetrated by a fast-moving barbarian horde. They came so near the axletree that distant shareholders grew afraid of losing touch with their wealth and started drawing it from the company vaults. This had a bad effect on trade, and discontented provinces demanded independence. Building came to a halt. In the resulting unemployment it was clear that the co-operative society was giving ordinary folk courage and hope which cost the construction company nothing. The company chairman sought an interview with the works foreman and afterwards they announced that:

1. The entire work belonged to God now, and everyone in it was his servant.
2. The co-operative was now a legal building society. The company chairman had joined it, so had the major shareholders, and God would welcome them into heaven when the work was done.
3. The foreman of the work, in God's name, had taken over the summit of the work, and was now in charge of the building, which would be paid for out of co-operative funds.
4. The construction company would hold onto the treasure-vaults, the markets and government offices, in order to guard the foundation and maintain the fabric.

The news made many people happy. We thought rich and poor would unite to defend the empire and complete the building.

But the empire was being attacked on every side and there was no labour to spare for the building. The construction company kept an appearance of order by bribing enemies to stay away. Our market shrank, the canals silted up and the pillar of cloud, which was mainly produced by body-heat, gradually dissolved. Then an army of barbarians too large to bribe marched inside and plundered as they pleased. The scale of the work so daunted them that they could not plunder everything, but when they finally left we found that the last of the company chairmen had absconded with the last of the company's gold. The vaults of the work became the lair of bats and foxes. The population dwindled to a few farmers grazing their herds on the dry bed of the ancient sea. The only government left was the works foreman. Once a week he served meals to his followers on the great floor surrounding the founder's sarcophagus, and once a year he supervised the shifting of a stone from the foundation to the summit where it was cemented firmly into place. This was the end of the first big building-boom.

Meanwhile the separate provinces fought the invaders and lost touch with each other until the biggest unit of government was a war-lord with a troop of horsemen and a fort on a hill. Language dissolved into a babble of barbaric new dialects. But agents of the building society travelled around the continent opening branch-offices shaped like the work at the centre. Members used these offices as holiday homes, schools and hospitals. Since there was no currency they paid their contributions in gifts of food and labour, and the agents served everyone with regular meals as a foretaste of the day when all good people would live together in God's eternal house. Society business was conducted in the language of the old construction company, the only language which could be written and read, so the local rulers needed the help of an agent before they could send a letter or inscribe a law. When at last, under threat of new invasions from the rim, the warlords united into dukedoms and kingdoms, the building society provided them with a civil service. The new kingdoms did not exactly correspond to the ancient provinces. They fitted together like the wedges of a cut cake, the thin edges touching the axletree at the centre. Trade revived, gold flowed into the foreman's vaults, the work was gradually re-peopled and repaired. Then building resumed. The work arose in arching buttresses and glittering pinnacles until it vanished into the bright cloud which reappeared above it. The work now went ahead as in the days of the old construction company, but with a different aim. The old company had been making a safe home for shareholders and their servants in the present. The new building society offered a safe home to everybody in the future.

When the great work entered the cloud many of us thought heaven had been reached and our foreman was talking to the divine architect. Everyone with spare money travelled to see him and tried to eat a meal in the works canteen. This led to over-crowding, so a foreman was elected who promised to enlarge the canteen and decorate it more lavishly than before. But finding himself short of cash he raised it by issuing a block of shares and auctioning them round the continent. These promised the buyers priority over other members when God came to allocate comfortable apartments in the finished work. Unluckily, however, the building society was still nominally a co-operative, and its advertisements still promised the best apartments to the poorest members, partly to compensate them for the living conditions they endured while the work was being built, partly because their labour was more important to it than gold. An angry agent working at ground level in a northern kingdom nailed up a list of objections:
1. The great work belonged to God, so nobody could buy

or sell a place in it, and the foreman's shares were useless paper.

2. The new canteen was a waste of money and labour. The first and best foremen had been rough labourers who served humble meals in dark cellars.
3. Corrupt agents inside the axletree had brought real building to a halt. In recent years the only work on the summit had turned it into a pleasure-park for the amusement of the foreman and his friends.

The foreman replied that:

1. The work certainly belonged to God, who had decided to sell some of it and had told the foreman to act as his broker.
2. The canteen was the most essential part of the axletree, for nobody would work on it without regular meals. The earliest foremen had indeed been poor cooks by modern standards but only because the laws of the time stopped them using a decent kitchen.
3. Building had not come to a halt. More people laboured on the work than ever before. There was no amusement park on the summit, just a good hotel for important visitors.

The protesting agent responded by calling on kings and people everywhere to seize the axletree and restore it to co-operative management. So great armies assembled, some to defend the work and some to seize it, for many were jealous of the wealth it contained.

Before the fighting began one of the architects employed on the fabric made a surprising suggestion. He said the building had run into financial trouble because it was conical – every three feet on the height required an addition of two to the entire circumference. This ensured stability, but unless the workforce continually increased it also ensured that the growth of the building became imperceptible, as was the present case. Since steady growth was financially impossible the work was therefore condemned by its shape to a history of booms and slumps. The last slump had destroyed the old construction company. The next would break up the building society, unless it used a cheaper method of working. He suggested that if the axletree were built on a framework of iron beams and hoops it could rise from the present summit in a straight, safe, and surprisingly cheap shaft. Even if heaven were twice the height of the present structure he would undertake to reach it in fifty years. Our foreman and the protesting agent found the idea so ludicrous that they hardly even denounced it, for both thought the shape of the axletree was as much God's gift as its purpose, and to doubt one was to doubt the other. So armies marched inside and warfare spread along every gallery from base to summit.

At first the foreman's people held the high places and the attackers tried to starve them by intercepting food supplies from the base, but the base was vast, and when the attackers got onto higher platforms they lost control of it. Soon both sides held vertical sections converging at the top and separated by uncertain people in the middle. The contestants paused to gather more wealth and weapons from their supporters on the ground, and during this pause leaders on both sides started squabbling – each was a king in his own lands and disliked sharing his gains with the rest. So by mutual agreement, by force or by fraud the great work was split into as many sections as the surrounding nations, and this arrangement was also unstable. Many had fought

for their king because he had promised to share out
the profits locked in the axletree. They now found
they had given him extra power to tax them and
were not even getting the social benefits granted by
the building society. Revolts broke out at ground
level, kings fought their own people and did not
always win. Many new sorts of government got into
the axletree but all looked rather like the old
construction company. We had monarchies ruled
by a company chairman, and plutocracies with a
strong board of directors, and republics with a
parliament of shareholders; yet all got their food,
fuel and raw material from poorly paid people on
the ground outside. Half these companies acknowledged the works foreman and ate food cooked by
his agents, but they did not pay him enough money
to go on building. His hotel on the old summit was
now ringed by a crown of separate summits, for
each national company had begun building on the
highest part of its own side, using the methods of the
discredited architect. Iron frames were common but
conservative companies built as much as possible
with stone, so their summits tended to top-heaviness.
Very competitive companies over-awed their rivals
with grandiose summits of bravely painted plaster,
for the highest had reached a level of calm air high
above the cloud and winds which soaked and buf-
feted the building lower down. And all these summits
were bright with flags and glittering weapons, though
fear of warfare at that height prevented fighting
from rising far above ground level. It was a long time
before the strength of the super-structures was
tested. The managers in them were much closer to
each other than to their employees lower down, so
the summits were linked by bridges which provided
reinforcement, though each bridge had a section

which could be pulled back when neighbours quarrelled. And the word *tower* was never spoken, because towers were still notorious for sometimes falling down.

Now that a dozen competing companies owned the axletree it grew so fast that the continent below could no longer supply enough material. Our merchants crossed oceans, deserts and mountains to tell remote people of God's great unfinished house in the middle of the world, and to persuade them to contribute to its enlargement. They were being honest when they spoke like this, for from a distance the axletree was clearly a single work. Some foreigners tried to resist us but they could not withstand the tools and weapons we had devised to elevate our axletree. The best produce of every sea and continent on the globe was brought by ship and carriage into our insatiable market. The food was eventually excreted in rivers of sewage which streamed for leagues across the surrounding country and fuel was turned into mountains of cinders which kept light from the inhabiters of the lowest galleries. Smoke poured down from vents in the national towers, staining the clouds and discolouring everything below them.

And then the national companies found the material of the whole world was not enough for them and began fighting for it in the biggest wars the world has ever seen. Armies fired on each other from ground level up to the axletree's highest platforms. Summits crumbled and toppled through clouds in avalanches of soldiers, flags and weapons which crushed whole populations on the lower levels, sweeping them down to the ashes and excrement of the land beneath. The axletree seemed to be reducing itself to a heap of ruin, but when the smoke cleared most of it was intact and only very old-fashioned parts were badly damaged. One superstructure was so top-heavy that all the directors and shareholders went down in the first shock of war, and the remaining managers were labour-leaders who tried to organize their people into a co-operative building society. Critics say they eventually failed in this, and the workers were as ill-treated as in the worst construction companies. Even so, the new co-operative worked until its summit was one of the biggest, and other summits were repaired just as quickly. The death of millions delayed the building by only a few years, for the strength of the work was not in armies and leaders, but in the central markets and bankvaults which companies shared while their employees murdered each other in the sunlight. Some historians suggested that great wars were the axletree's way of shedding obsolete structures and superfluous populations, and described the great work as a growing creature with its own intelligence. Others said that a growth which shed old branches by burning off its healthiest leaves and fruit did not show intelligence of a high kind.

An uneasy time began. The managers of the largest summits tried to keep their fights for material to remote lands producing it, while secretly preparing for a war vast enough to kill everyone in the world. Construction companies tried to raise their profits by pressing down the wages of the work-force, and labour leaders fought back by organizing strikes and threatening to turn their companies into co-operatives. Some of the worst-run companies did turn co-operative, and signed treaties with the first co-operative, which wanted allies. And whether they headed construction companies or co-operatives, very few directors in the high summits trusted their employees, but spent more and more money on spies and policemen. And the summits went on rising until one day, among rumours of revolt and corruption and increasing poverty and accumulating weapons, we came to the sky.

A college of investigators had been founded to protect summits from lightning, to study and stabilize the weather, and to maintain ventilation. This college employed clever people from most companies in the work, for no single company could control the climate alone, and although each company liked to keep knowledge to itself they noticed that knowledge grew faster among people who shared it. I was a secretary in that college, recording its achievements and reporting them to the directors of the highest summit of all, for I had been born there.

One evening I sat beside the professor of air, checking rockets at a table on the balcony of our office. This was in a low part of the work above a gate where the coalfleets sailed in, for one of our jobs was to superintend the nearby smoke station. We had found that smoke, enclosed in bags, could lift large weights, and had used this discovery to create a new transport system. My chief was testing the powder which made the rockets fly, I tested the fuses. Without raising my eyes I could see fat black ships wallowing up the shining creek from a distant ocean. They docked directly under us but it would be a week before they unloaded. This was mid-summer and a general holiday. All building had stopped, most fires were damped, the college had made a gale the night before and swept the sky clear and blue. The cries of children and picnickers came tiny and shrill, like birdnotes, from the green hills and valleys beside the creek. These smooth slopes had been made by giving ashbings a coat of soil and turf, and the lowest people liked to holiday on them. Even I had happy memories of playing there as a child. But the companies had started turning the old ashes into brick, and already half the green park had been scraped flat. The diggers had uncovered a viaduct of arches built two thousand years before by the old imperial construction company. The sight might have given me a melancholy sense of the booms and slumps of history but I was too excited. I was going to visit the height of the axletree.

The chief packed his rockets in a slingbag. I shouldered a light launching tube. We walked through our offices in the thickness of the outer wall and down some steps to the smokestation.

A two-seater lift was locked to our platform. We climbed in and arranged cushions round us while the bag filled up. It was a light blue bag with the college sign on the side: a yellow silk flame with an eye in the centre. The chief unlocked us and we swung into the hot oblique updraught used by very important people. We crossed the docks, the retorts and crucibles of the furnacemen and a crowded circus cheering a ball-game. We passed through the grate of an ancient portcullis, ascended a canyon between sewage cylinders with cedar forests on top, then swooped through a ventilator in the first ceiling. Within an hour we had pierced ceilings which separated six national companies, the customs officers leaping up to salute us on the lip of the ventilators as soon as they recognized the college

colours. In solemn music we crossed the great
canteen, rising into the dome as the foreman of
the work, like a bright white bee, served the sacred
food to a swarm of faithful on the floor below. The
ventilator in the dome opened into a windcave where
an international orchestra was distilling rain with
bright instruments into an aquarium that was the
head water of three national rivers. We lost the hot
updraught here but the chief steered us into a
current flowing up a slide of rubble where an
ancient summit had been shaken down by earthquakes during the first big slump. It was landscaped
with heather, gorse and hunting lodges. Above that
we entered the base of the tallest summit of all,
ascending vertically through floors which were all
familiar to me: hospitals, nurseries, schools, empor-
iums, casinos, banks, courts and boardrooms. Here
we were stopped at a ventilator for the first time,
since the highest inhabited parts of the tower
belonged to the military. The chief spent a long
time proving that his rockets were not weapons but
tools for testing the upper air, and even so he was
only allowed through when I showed the examining
colonel, by a secret sign, that I was not only a
member of the college but an agent of his company. So we were allowed to rise up the glass funnel
to the scaffolding. On every side we saw officers in
neat identical clothes tending the huge steel catapults
and firing pans poised to pour down thunderbolts
and lightning on the other parts of the work,
especially toward towers with co-operative connec-
tions. We passed through a builders' village, deserted
except for its watchmen, then nothing surrounded
us but a frame of slender rods and the deep blue
blue blue of the gloaming sky. The thin cold air
began to hurt my lungs. We stopped when our bag

touched the highest platform. The chief slung the rockets from his shoulder and climbed a ladder to the very top. I followed him.

I had never known such space. The pure dark blueness was unstained by the faintest wisp of cloud. I lay flat on the planks with my head over the platform edge, trying to see the sunset on the horizon, but the golden shine of it was cut small by the web of bridges linking the summits lower down. I felt like a fly clinging to the tip of an arrow, the first of a flight of them soaring through infinite air. Lights were blinking on the tips of summits below. These were the signals of college men who would observe our experiments with lens and theodolite. The chief signalled back at them with a handlamp. He even blinked at the spiky summit of the great co-operative, which was nearest. This was a joke, because the co-operative pretended to ignore the work of our college, while watching it very closely.

The chief set the tube to launch a rocket vertically for a quarter of a mile: the colour and length of the fiery tail would show the nature of the air it travelled through. All being ready, he told me to start the water clock, then lit the short fuse. My eyes, of course, were on the clock, which ticked off only four drops before I heard an explosion. Looking up I saw a great shower of sparks. Our rocket had broken at a height of sixty feet. "A dud," said the chief, and fired another, which also broke up too soon. "Sir!" I said, staring at the clock. "It has exploded at exactly the same height."
"Coincidence!" grunted the chief, but checked the third rocket very carefully before firing, and that also broke at the same height. I trembled and the chief was sweating. With great precision he angled

the tube and fired the fourth rocket upward along
the diagonal of a square. It exploded six drops later.
We fired the remaining rockets at the same angle in
twenty different directions with the same result.
Which showed there was a very wide obstruction
sixty feet above our heads.

You cannot understand our feelings unless you
realize that for several centuries men had stopped
believing that the world hung like a yolk inside an
eggshell of sky. Holy people still thought the sky was
God's home, and in wartime the heads of most big
companies declared their tower was closest to God's
original plan and would reach heaven first. But
clearly the various companies were not building to
reach anywhere but to surpass each other for financial and military reasons. So educated men regarded
the universe as an infinite space only measurable by
the distance between the bodies it contained. We
thought we could go on building for ever.

The chief and I stared upward. It was hard to
believe that these starry globes we had studied from
infancy (some shining with reflected light, some
composed of it) were on the far side of a barrier.
We were roused by a breath of breeze. Lights on the
lower summits were blinking frantic questions at us.
The chief took his lamp and signalled that he would
confer on the matter soon, then led me down the
ladder to the lift. He said, "I believe you spy for the
directors of this tower. How can I obtain an immediate interview with its president?" I told him the
president could be most quickly contacted through
his generals. We descended to the military level
where the officer in charge let the chief write this
note, and took us into custody while it was delivered.

Sir: Shortly before midnight I conducted tests which show there is a vast obstruction sixty feet above the top platform of your tower. This is either a zone of intense heat or the under-surface of that great transparent ceiling our ancestors called *the sky*. Please allow me to supervise the final stage of your building and test the nature of the barrier it will strike. As professor of air, director of international climate and inventor of the smokelift I am clearly qualified to do this.

We were taken to the president's office soon after dawn. He sat at the head of a long table with directors and generals down each side, and we stood at the foot of it, but were not greatly impressed. This was the most powerful committee in the world but it had the exhausted, unshaven look of men who had been arguing all night, and compared with his official portraits the president seemed small and furtive. Without raising his eyes from a paper on the table he read these words in a quick monotone.

"By virtue of the powers invested in me by this great Company I grant your request to supervise the final stage of the work. You are allocated a director's salary, office, and apartments at the highest executive level of our summit, and your employment commences upon signing your agreement of the following conditions.
FIRSTLY Your superior in this project is the commander of the armed forces. All requests for materials and assistance, all orders and all communications with the world below will pass through his office.
SECONDLY You will create as soon as possible a thick cloud to hide our building operation from other summits, and will give scientific reasons for

this which raise no political, financial or religious speculations in the management of other summits or in the general public.

THIRDLY On reaching the sky you will conduct tests for the purpose of answering these questions: How thick is it?

Can it be penetrated?

Is the substance of it commercially useful?

Does the upper surface support life?

If so, is that life intelligent and/or belligerent and/or commercially useful?

Can the upper surface support men?

Is it strong enough to support big buildings?

LASTLY All your activities, and the reasons for them, and any discoveries you make, are official secrets, and from the present moment in time any failure to fulfil these conditions is a treasonable act punishable by life imprisonment or death without public trial as stipulated in the Company Laws Employees Protection Section paragraph 73 clause 19."

The president raised his eyes and we all looked at the chief, who nodded thoughtfully then said, "I am grateful for the trust you have placed in me, sir, and will try to deserve it. But secrecy is impossible. My tests last night were observed by experts on all the adjacent summits. Several hours have passed since then, and although this is a holiday I see that our neighbour in the east is already shifting large amounts of building material onto his upper platform."

One wall of the room was a single sheet of glass and the directors and generals sprang up and crowded to it. The co-operative summit had become very dark and distinct against the brightness of the ascending sun and there was spiderlike activity

among the bristling cranes at the top. The commander of the armed forces punched one hand with the
other and cried, "If they want to make a race of it
they haven't a hope in hell! We've sixty feet to go,
they've six hundred. Professor, I'll see you later."
He strode from the room. After a variety of exclamations the rest of the company stared at the
president who had sunk into his chair looking very
tired and cross. At last he sighed and said, "Well, if
other governments know the facts already we can
show we have nothing to hide by announcing them
publicly. But God knows how the stock exchange
will react. On second thoughts, no public announcements. I bind everyone here to the strictest secrecy. I
will pass the information to other heads of state in a
private memorandum. I'm sure that even old – " (he
named the chairman of the co-operative) "– will see
the value of keeping his people ignorant. So sign the
agreement, professor, and get on with the job."

Three days later I stood with the chief on top of a
strong, prefabricated silver pylon, and the sky was a
few inches above my upturned face. It was too
transparent to be seen directly, but glanced at
sideways the lucid blue was rippled by rainbow
glimmerings like those golden lines cast by sunlight
on sand under shallow water. The ripples came from
the point in the sky where the sun's rays pierced
most directly, and their speed and tints changed
throughout the day. At dawn they were slow and
tinted with saffron, quickening toward noon with
glints of gold, green and crimson, then gradually
toward purple-blue in the gloaming. It took a while
to recognize this. The summit was swaying through
a wide circle, so the ripples crossed our vision in a
cataract of broken dazzlings until the pylon started

travelling in the same direction, and then they only
became clear for five minutes. At these times I did
not feel I was looking up. The whole axletree seemed
a long rope tied to my heels. I felt I was hanging
above a heavenly floor from a world as remote as the
moon. Yet I was not dizzy. I liked this immensity. I
wanted the axletree to break and let me fall into it.
As gently as possible I stretched out my hand and
touched. The sky was cool and silken-smooth with
an underlying softness and warmth. I felt it with my
whole body. The feeling was not sexual, for it excited
no part more than the rest, not even the fingertips
touching the slender rippling rainbows. The sway of
the tower began diverging from the flow of the
ripples, which took on a broken look. Fearing that
the loveliness was escaping, my hand pressed instinctively harder and a tide of blood flowed down
from the fingertips, staining the arm to the elbow. I
stared at it, still pressing hard and feeling no pain
until the chief struck my arm down and I fainted.

I woke with a bandaged hand and four fingers
shortened by the length of the nails. It was late
afternoon and the chief was poking the sky with little
rods. He stopped when he saw I was conscious,
asked about my exact sensations before fainting,
wrote them down, then pointed east and said,
"We are no longer alone."
Several towers had sprouted surprisingly in the last
three days. One of them, by employing acrobats as
construction workers, had gained a mile-high
superstructure of bamboo canes. But the big co-
operative summit, though still the second highest,
had grown very little in spite of its early start. And
now the vastest smokelift I have ever seen was
tethered to the top of that summit by many cables.

The bag was shaped like an upside-down pyramid. The top surface was level with our platform, and in the centre a crouching figure handled something which flared and sparkled. We heard a brief humming of almost painful intensity and above the lift appeared a white mark which sped across the sky and curved down into a cloud which hid the horizon. The chief said, "He's started testing it with fire. I'm leaving that till last."

Next day the company's directors came up to the platform and stared at the sky with all the expressions of men faced by a beautiful woman. The eyes and mouths of many gaped very wide and a few were moved to tears. The president kept sighing and nodding as if the sky was defeating him in a crucial argument. The commander of the armed forces frowned and fidgeted as if it was wasting his time; he was more interested in the co-operative lift, on which a group of men like our own had gathered. Only the chief looked eager and happy. He grinned determinedly upward as if saying, "Yes, sky, you dazzle and baffle other men, but not me. You won't be able to keep anything from me."
We went down to the president's office, sat round the table, and the chief read out this report.

"Gentlemen, you have just seen a transparent surface which encloses the earthly globe at an altitude of 22 parasangs, or 572 stadia, or 62,920 fathoms. Although this surface is in rapid movement it feels beguilingly smooth, soft and lukewarm if touched gently, but repels anything solid which presses hard, dissolving flesh, crumbling bone and wood to powder, and making stones, metal and crystals explode with a violence growing greater with the density of the mineral and the force driving

it into contact. These explosions exert downward
with no effect upon the heavenly surface, a fact with
political consequences. Less advanced summits are
building catapults at their tops with the clear
intention of testing the sky from a distance by
throwing things at it. This will cause blasts big
enough to damage the advanced summits. We
should make it plain that we will regard such tests
as acts of war. When jets of water, ink, acid, mercury
and molten metal strike the surface it absorbs them
without stain or alteration, but a strong flame leaves
a white scar which allows us to observe and measure
the surface movement. Above our summit the
heavenly continent is turning westward at 7¾ parasangs per hour. The play of prismatic colours across
the surface is an effect of the sunlight, and quite
unrelated to the real movement of the heavenly
sphere, which is regular, continuous, and takes
27⅓ days to turn round the earthly sphere. In other
words, it rotates with the moon.

"You have asked me questions about the heavenly
continent: how thick, if pierceable etcetera. At least
one more test is needed before I can answer accurately, but I can now tell you what is imaginable and
what is likely.

"Classical astronomy would regard the heavenly
firmament as the inner surface of a glassy shell
carrying the moon. But a rigid shell would be
shattered by the speed of its rotation and our air
would not stop a liquid shell falling to the earth
below. The classical model only holds good if the sky
is made of transparent vapour, at once lighter than
air and as dense as molten metal. Such a vapour is
impossible.

"So let us imagine there is a dense, transparent
fluid filling the entire universe. Our earth occupies a

bubble of air in this fluid, a bubble at the centre of a whirlpool. The heavenly bodies are floating round us in different currents at different speeds, the nearest current carrying the moon. This idea is both attractive and convincing: until we remember that the light of the farthest and steadiest stars would be reaching us through fluid moving in different speeds and directions. This would give the highest heavens a warped and shifting aspect they do not possess.

"I offer you a third model. You perhaps know that all water has a skin protecting it from air. This skin is invisible to the human eye, impalpable to human touch, yet tough enough for small insects to hang from, walk across, and build upon. Imagine, then, that there is a light vapour which lies upon air as air lies upon water, and reacts with air to create a tense surface, perhaps only a few atoms thick. This surface has properties which human insects cannot understand before they have sampled the vapour on the far side, but it moves with the moon because the moon pulls it along as it pulls the oceans of the world below. The greater speed is explained by the absence of shores and a solid bottom.

"This is the likeliest model of the world we occupy, and I ask leave to test it by the following means.

"Only flame impresses the heavenly surface, so let us build in our summit a furnace with a ring of burners, and let us direct against the sky a circle of flame five feet in diameter. If this does not cut a hole into the upper universe let us keep the furnace burning for a lunar month of 28 days. This should engrave a fault-line round the inside of the cosmic egg-shell, perhaps splitting it open long enough for us to grab a sample of what lies beyond.

"This test should endanger nobody, unless, perhaps, those beside the burners, foremost of whom will be myself. The sky will suffer no great injury. Flames mark it, yes, but since the start of the world it has been pierced from above, every night, by jagged meteorites of white-hot stone and iron. The heavenly surface would be scarred all over if these had done lasting damage. You can authorize my test in the knowledge that the natural forces maintaining the sky will start repairing it as soon as we relax our efforts. Man can no more destroy the sky than he can destroy the ocean."

The chief laid his paper on the table. The president muttered, "You shouldn't have mentioned the ocean. The excrement from our factories and refineries has poisoned most of it."

The chief seemed not to hear. He folded his arms, leaned back in his chair and remarked conversationally, "Our utmost skill, of course, may fail to pierce this barrier. In which case your great summit will soon be equalled by all the others in the work."

There was a long silence. The eyes of nearly everyone round the table seemed to be staring inside themselves. Then a director spoke in a low voice which gradually grew very loud.

"I am a religious man. That sky we gazed upon less than an hour ago – that moving sea of heavenly blossom – was the loveliest work of God's hand I have ever beheld. I am certain that this sky, like everything else men have not corrupted, exists for a great good reason. Humanity has lived beneath this dome, been sheltered by this dome from the dawn of creation. And you, professor, ask us to rip it open tomorrow like a can of beans? You have given us three little toy pictures of the universe, and told us to believe in the safest one, and asked permission to test it. The fact that you need to test it shows your ignorance. Your test may destroy something essential and beautiful which you did not make and cannot replace. Mankind has taken the whole of human history to reach this height. Why should we not pause for a couple of years and consider the situation carefully?"

"Because of the co-ops!" cried the commander of the armed forces. "And because of our so-called allies. Believe me, that sky is going to be shafted by someone sooner or later, and whoever reaches the far side first will have a *colossal* military advantage. Just now the advantage is ours. The co-ops know everything we know, but they can't float a furnace on a smoke-filled envelope. Give them a month or two, though, and they'll carve their way through and claim the upper surface for themselves. We've got to get there first and claim it for free people everywhere. Then we can hold it against all comers."

"Gentlemen," said the president, "I do not wholly agree with my military adviser. The sky is not a territory we should defend against other summits – that would unite the whole world against us. But the sky *must* be pierced, not to give us advantages in a future war but to prevent war beginning here and now. Our entire structure is committed to growth. All wealth which does not go into building goes into weaponry. If we do not expand upward we must do it sideways, which means absorbing the bases of the neighbouring summits. In a quiet way our company is doing that already, but at least we have the excuse of needing the extra ground to build higher. Without that excuse our enlargement will be an obvious act of naked aggression. Professor, make this burner of yours as big as you can. Employ all the skill and manpower you can, use more than you need, build

several damned furnaces in case one of them goes
wrong. Blast a hole the entire axletree can use. And
maybe we'll be able to maintain a stable state for
another twenty years. By that time the world will
have run out of building materials. But it won't be
our problem."

There was a director who served on an international committee which attended to plumbing in the
axletree's basement. He compensated for this squalid
work by writing wildly hopeful poetry about the
future of mankind. He said, "Mr. President, your
description of our unhealthy state is accurate, but
you suggest no cure. It is clear that for many years
continuous expansion has done us great harm. The
highest summits in the work contain the greatest
extremes of wealth and poverty, the greatest expenditure on soldiers and policemen, and the greatest
fears for the future, as your speech has demonstrated. The safest summits are a few low ones
whose tops can still be seen by people on the ground
outside, structures whose comforts and opportunities
are shared by a whole community. I realize we
cannot halt the whole great work by simply refusing
to build, so let us announce, today, that we will leave
the sky intact and build no higher if other companies
and societies will stop building too. And let us call
for the formation of an international parliament to
rule the heavens, and let us give our highest platforms to that parliament. Then the sky can be tested,
not rashly and rapidly, but carefully, over a period of
years."
"You have not understood me," said the president.
"If I even hint at halting our building programme the
shareholders will withdraw their money from
the constructive side of the work and invest it in

the destructive side, the military side, which con-
sumes nearly half our revenue already. Then allies
and enemies will think we are about to make war, and
will over-arm themselves too. In a matter of weeks
this will lead to the catastrophic battle everyone
dreads, the battle which destroys the whole axletree."
"But we are the most powerful company in the
world!" said the poet. "Let us make our shareholders invest in things which do people good!
Directly or indirectly we control the world's labour
force, yet most labourers live very poorly. Mountains
of grain rot in our warehouses while thousands of
families die by famine in the lands outside."
"There is no profit in feeding poor people," said the
financial secretary, "except on rare occasions when it
will prevent a revolt. Believe me, I know people on
the ground outside. They are lazy, ignorant, selfish
and greedy. Give them a taste of wealth and security
and they'll demand more of it. They'll refuse to obey
us. They'll drag us down to their own sordid level.
Not even the co-operatives are crazy enough to trust
their surplus to the folk who produce it."
"But we are using our surplus to organize disasters!"
said the poet. "If those who have grabbed more food
and space and material than they need would share
it, instead of bribing and threatening the rest with it,
the world could become a splendid garden where
many plants will grow beside this damned, prickly,
many-headed, bloodstained cactus of a poisoned and
poisoning TOWER."
"Strike that word from the minutes!" said the
president swiftly.

Directors had jumped to their feet, one hid his
face in his hands, the rest stared haggardly before
them. The poet looked defiant. The chief seemed

amused. The president said quietly, "Sit down, gentlemen. Our colleague is over-excited because his work at the lowest level of government has given him exaggerated notions of what can be done at the highest. We do as things do with us, and the biggest thing we know is the axletree."

The poet said, "It is not bigger than the earth below."

The president said, "But it has cut us off from the earth below. On the common earth men can save nothing, and their highest ambition is to die in one of our works hospitals. But the axletree is full of comfortable, well-meaning people who expect to rise to a higher position before they die and who mean to pass on their advantages to their children. They can only do this in a structure which keeps getting larger. They cannot see they are dealing out crime, famine and war to the earth below, because the axletree shelters them from these things. If we oppose the unspoken wishes of the people in the axletree – unspoken because everybody shares them – we will be called levellers, and in two days our closest supporters will have replaced us."

There was silence, then the religious director said sadly, "I used to wish I lived in the age of faith when our great work was a shining structure with a single summit revered by the whole continent. I now suspect it only did good during the slump when it was a crumbling ruin whose servants fed hungry people upon ordinary ground. Until recently I still believed the axletree was planned by God to maintain art, knowledge and happiness. I now fear it is a gigantic dead end, that human history is an enormous joke."

"The fact remains," said the commander of the armed forces, "that we can only prevent an overall catastrophe by preparing what may become an overall catastrophe. People who can't face that fact have no place in politics."

"I disagree once more with my military adviser," said the president. "There is always a place for the idealist in politics. Our poet has given us a wonderful idea. He suggests we form an international parliament to rule the heavens. We certainly will! Our allies will like us for it, our competitors will think they can use it to delay us. Loud-mouthed statesmen everywhere will feel important because they are members of it, which will reduce the risk of war. I hope, sir" – he addressed the poet – "I hope you will represent us in this parliament. The whole conception is yours. You will be inaugurating a new era."

The poet blushed and looked pleased.

"Meanwhile," said the president, "since the formation of this parliament may take years, mankind will advance to its destiny in the sky. Science will open a gateway into a universal store-house of empty space, remote minerals, and unbreathable gas."

My chief and the army commander worked hard in the following days and all the people of the summit were drawn into money-making activity. Low-level fuel-bunkers and furnaces were built beneath crucibles from which pipes ran up the central lift-shaft. Lifts with clamps fixed to them now slid up cables attached to the axletree's outer wall. The top pylon sprouted three huge burners, each differently shaped, with spire-like drills in the centres and domes beneath to shield the operators. Meanwhile, foreign statesmen met the poet in a steering committee to draw up an agenda for an international legal committee which would write a constitution for an international parliament which would govern the heavens. The steering committee's first meetings were inconclusive. And then the first big test was held.

It lasted six seconds, made a mark on the sky like a twisted stocking, and produced a sound which paralysed the nearest operators and put observers on other summits into a coma lasting several hours. The sound was less concentrated at ground level, where the irritation it caused did not result in unconsciousness. And inside the axletree nobody heard it at all, or experienced it only as a pang of inexplicable unease: the outer shape of the building baffled the vibration. The chief announced to the directors that the test had been successful. He said, "We now know that our machines work perfectly. We now know, and can guard against, their effect on human beings. My technicians and all foreign observers are being issued with padded helmets which make the wearers deaf to exterior vibration. People on ground level can protect themselves by plugging their ears with twists of cloth or withered grass, though small lumps of rubber would be more suitable. We will start the main test in two days' time."

"You intend to deafen half the dwellers on the continent for a whole *month*?" said the president. "Listen, I don't like groundlings more than anybody else here. But I need their support. So does the axletree. So do you."

"We have enough resources to do without their support for at least four weeks," said the director of food and fuel.

"But that din causes headaches and vomiting," said the president. "If twisted grass is not one hundred per cent effective the outsiders will swarm into the axletree and swamp us. The axletree will be the only place they can hear themselves think."

"All immigration into the axletree was banned the day before yesterday," said the director of public security. "The police are armed and alert."

"But here is a protest signed by many great scientists," said the president, waving a paper. "Most of them work for the professor's college. They say the tests have been planned on a too-ambitious scale, and the effect on world climate could be disastrous."

"Our new wave of prosperity will collapse if tests are curtailed," said the financial secretary. "Even outsiders get employment through that. They should be prepared to suffer some inconveniences."

"The scientists who signed that paper are crypto-cooperators," said the army commander.

The president got up and walked round the room. He pointed to his chair and said, "Would anyone like to take my place? Whoever sits there will go down in history as a weakling or a coward, no matter what he decides to do."

Several directors eyed the chair thoughtfully, but nobody moved. "Right," said the president. "Let all outsiders on the earth below be supplied with ear-plugs and sleeping-pills. I authorize a test lasting one whole night, starting at sunset and ending at dawn. The public reaction will decide what we do after that. They may want us to hand over the whole works to our scribbler's heavenly parliament. The steering committee has agreed on an agenda now. I promoted that crazy scheme to distract attention from our activities, but I fear it will soon be my only hope of shedding *unbearable* responsibility. So now get out, all of you. Leave me alone."

Preparations for the big test were organized very quickly, and security precautions on our summit were so increased that movement there became very difficult. Machinery was being installed which only the army chief and the leading industrialists understood. The president seemed unwell and I was employed to guard and help him. He announced that he would pass the night of the test on the ground outside, using nothing but the protection supplied to ordinary people, and this was such good publicity that the other directors allowed it. So he and I travelled west to a mild brown land where low hills were clothed with vines and olives. We waited for sunset on the terrace of a villa. The president removed his shoes and walked barefoot on the warm soil. He said, "I like the feel of this. It's nourishing." He lay down with his head in a bush of sweet-smelling herb. Bees walked across his face. "You can see they aren't afraid of me," he muttered through rigid lips. He sat up and pointed to the axletree, saying, "Everybody in there is crazy. I wonder what keeps it up?"
The sky overhead was clear and smooth but beyond a range of blue mountains lay a vaster range of turbulent clouds. These hid the axletree base so that the rest did, indeed, seem built on cloud.

The air grew cold, the sun set and the land was dark, but above the clouds the axletree was still sunlit. No separate summits were distinct, it looked like a golden tusk flushing to pinkness above the dark advancing up it from the base. Inside that dark the tiny lights of many windows defined the axletree against the large, accidental, irregular stars. My eye fixed on the top which flushed pink, then dimmed, and a white spark appeared where it had been, and the spark widened into a little white fan.

The noise hit us soon after that. We thrust rubber plugs into our ears, and that reduced it, but it was still unbearable. We would certainly have swallowed the sleeping-pills (which caused instant stupor) had I not produced helmets and clapped them on our heads. The relief was so profound that we both felt, I know, that absolute silence was the loveliest thing in the world. We were sitting on chairs now, and the moon was up, and the earth at our feet began gleaming moistly with worms. All creatures living in the earth or on solid bodies were struggling into the air. Ants, caterpillars and centipedes crawled up trees and clung in bunches to the extreme tips of twigs. Animals went to the tops of hills and crouched side by side, predators and victims, quite uninterested in feeding, but eventually clawing and biting to get on top of each other's backs. Birds tried to escape the air they usually felt at home in. Robins, partridges and finches packed themselves densely into the empty rabbit-holes. Winged insects fled to openings and clefts in animal bodies, which gave the best insulation from the sound. The president and I leapt to our feet, scratching and slapping ourselves in a cloud of midges, moths and mosquitoes. We ran to our cars, followed by the armed guards who came floundering out of the shrubberies.

The journey back was the most fearful in my life, far worse than what came after, because that was so unexpected that I had no time to fear it. On the moonlit road we passed pedestrians without pills who stumbled along retching with hands clapped to their ears. The air above was full of gulls, geese and migratory fowl who had sensed the zone of silence in

the axletree. A parasang from the base I removed my
helmet and found the noise had dwindled to the
intensity of a toothache. The president huddled in
the car corner muttering, "Oh no. Oh no. Oh no."
He took off his helmet when he saw me without mine
and said, "The sun rose two hours ago."
I nodded. He said, "They're still burning the sky."
From the summit a white scrolling line like an
unbroken thread of smoke undulated toward the
western horizon. I told him that the pills eaten by
the populace would keep them unconscious for
another five or six hours. He said, "Can very small
babies go so long without food?"
His maudlin tone annoyed me and I answered
briskly that babies were tougher than we knew.

The entrance was heavily barricaded and we
would not have got in if the soldiers of our guard
had not fired their weapons and roused comradely
feelings among the soldiers inside. At the office of
the weather-college the president was surrounded by
officials who shouted and complained. An influx of
rodents was making the lower dwellings unhabitable.
The president kept whispering, "I'll try. Oh I'll
try." We were lifted to the base of the great summit
and found it as stoutly barricaded as the entrance.
The guards were surprised to see us and took a long
time to let us through. It was late evening when we
reached the presidential office. The president said,
"They're still doing it."
He uncorked a speaking tube which ran to the
control room under the burners. A hideous droning
came out. He screamed and corked it up and
whispered, "How can I talk to them?"
I said I would carry a note for him.

Here is the text of notes which passed between the president and the control room in the next three days.

President to control: STOP. STOP. YOU ARE KILLING PEOPLE. WHEN WILL YOU STOP.

Control to president: WE EXPECT A MAJOR BREAKTHROUGH IN THE NEAR FUTURE.

President to control: MASS SUICIDES ON GROUND BELOW. THOUGH SPRING, TREES, CROPS WITHER. RAT INVASION THREATENS AXLETREE BASE WITH BUBONIC PLAGUE. WHAT *GOOD* ARE YOU DOING?

Control to president: REGRET EXTREME MEASURES NECESSARY TO MAINTAIN STABLE ECONOMY.

President to control: CO-OPERATIVE ULTIMATUM DECLARES TOTAL WAR IF YOU DON'T STOP IN TWENTY-FOUR HOURS.

Control to president: WE'RE READY FOR THEM.

President to control: RAPIDLY CONVENED HEAVENLY PARLIAMENT ORDERS YOU TO STOP. FOREMAN OF WORK DECLARES GOD WANTS YOU TO STOP. EVERYONE ON EARTH BEGS YOU TO STOP. PLEASE STOP. NOBODY SUPPORTS YOU EXCEPT SHAREHOLDERS, A CORRUPTED TRADE UNION, THE ARMY, AND MAD EXPERIMENTERS WITHOUT RESPECT FOR HUMAN LIFE.

Control to president: SUPPORT SUFFICIENT. THE SPIRIT OF MAN IS TOO GREAT TO BE CONFINED BY A PHYSICAL BOUNDARY.

The control room was always a comforting place after the hysteria below. In complete silence (everyone wore helmets) the chief, the army commander and the financial secretary sat round a triangular table controlling the industrial process which produced the flame. Their faces showed the stern jubilation of masterly men who understand exactly what they are doing. Dials and graphs indicated the current bank-rate, stock exchange index, food and fuel reserves, activity of stokers at furnaces, position of soldiers guarding them, flow of chemicals to the crucibles, flow of gas to the burners, and the heat and width of the flame. A needle would flicker, then a hand would change the angle of a lever, or write and despatch an order. Between these times the triumvirate played knockout whist.

I was taking the final note down in the lift when I sensed a silence. Shielding my eyes I leaned out, looked up and saw the blue heaven opening and coming down to us. A lovely white flower bloomed whose hundred petals and stamens reached down and embraced us all. I was suddenly in white mist beside a white wall. The cable holding the lift must have snapped. I was spinning (I now know) downward through drenching whiteness, but I thought I was going up. Until I glimpsed collapsing pinnacles with whiteness gushing round them, water of course. I spun in drenching whiteness down cataracts of drenching whiteness flecked with rubble, bodies or furniture. And then I was in sunshine a few yards above plunging water and, ah, great waves. I went beyond these waves. I saw an edge of foaming water racing across fields, islanding woods and villages. Tiny figures waded, gesticulating from doors, then a huge wave engulfed them. A few floated up, some clinging to each other, then a vaster wave smashed down on them and nothing floated after that. The wind which carried the lift took me skyward and then back toward that white pillar, that waterfall from the sky beneath which the work of two thousand years was melting like a sandcastle. I grinned as I flew toward that dazzling pillar but I did not strike it, the lift went down again and out with the waves again to that foamy edge racing across the ordinary green and brown earth. Later I lost sight of the pillar. Either the heavenly continent had healed up or dissolved completely into water. The sky has been a lighter shade of blue ever since.

I must have managed the lift intelligently for I came down in shallow water near a ridge of rocks, a shore of the new sea. I sat a long time on those rocks, sometimes howling, sometimes weeping, always staring at the waves which drowned everything I knew and will drown it forever. I tried to think of a reason for living and failed, but life is too strong to need reasons. Next day two quite new sensations, hunger and loneliness, made me walk until I met a tribe of nomads. They have strange notions of hygiene but are otherwise tolerant and generous. When I had learned their language they valued my ability to exactly weigh, measure and record their herds and produce. I now have sons who are keen to learn arithmetic but refuse to learn, and will certainly never read, the language of the axletree. The older tribesmen know something about the axletree but the knowledge confuses them. They prefer to forget it. Yet I am the man who touched the sky! And when I try explaining this to my boys, because sons should admire fathers, the younger nudges the elder who says, "Did you visit the sun too? Did you stand on it, Dad? Was it hot?"

A week ago we pitched tents below a rocky cliff. Broken columns stood before the entrance to a ravine, which I explored. It led to a marble block carved with these words in the language of the old empire:

OZYMANDIAS
3D EMPEROR OF THE GREAT WHEEL
RECEIVED
FROM
GOD
IN
THE CAVERN
BEHIND
THIS STONE
THE
PLAN
OF THE
AXLETREE
LOOK ON HIS WORK YE MIGHTY
AND DESPAIR

The block has a crack the width of my finger between the top edge and the granite rock above. Tests with a stick show that the sheepskin on which I write this account can be slid through to fall in the cave behind. The marble is too vast to be moved by any but administrative people commanding a large labour-force to satisfy idle curiosity, so unless there is a shattering earthquake my history will not be found till the next world empire is established. Many centuries will pass before that happens, because tribes dispersed round a central sea will take longer to unify. But mere love-making and house-keeping, mere increase of men will bring us all together again one day, though I suppose ruling castes will speed the business by organising invasion and plunder. So when unity is achieved the accumulation of capital which created the first great tower will lead to another, or to something very similar.

But men are not completely sheeplike. Their vanity ensures that they never exactly repeat the past, if they know what it is. So if you have understood this story you had better tell it to others.

A UNIQUE CASE

The Reverend Dr Phelim MacLeod is a healthy, boyish-looking bachelor who has outlived all his relations except a distant cousin in Canada. Though unsurpassed in his knowledge of Latin, Hebrew and Greek his main reading since retirement has been detective stories, but he can still beat me at the game of chess we play at least once a fortnight. I tell you this to indicate his apparent normality before the accident last year. A badly driven, badly stacked glazier's van crashed beside his garden gate as he walked out of it, and a fragment of glass sheered off a section of skull with his right ear on it. I am his closest friend. At the Royal Infirmary I heard that no visitors could be allowed to see him in his present state, but I would be called if it changed.

I was called a week later. The brain surgeon in charge of him said, 'Dr MacLeod has regained consciousness. We are providing him with peace, privacy and a well-balanced diet. His unique constitution makes it impossible for us to do more.'
"But is he recovering?"
"I think so. Judge for yourself. And please tell him nothing about his appearance that would needlessly disturb him."

In a small ward of his own I found Dr MacLeod propped up in bed reading one of his detective thrillers. He greeted me with his usual calm, self-satisfied smile. I asked how he felt.

"Very well," he said. "You are interested in my wound, I see. How does it look? The staff here are less than informative."

In war films I had seen many buildings with an outer wall missing and the side of my friend's head resembled one. Through a big opening I saw tiny rooms with doors, light fittings and wall sockets, all empty of furniture but with signs of hasty evacuation. There was also scaffolding and heaps of building material suggesting that repair was in progress. I said hesitantly, "You seem to be mending quite well."

Dr MacLeod smiled complacently and pointed out that he would be seventy-six on his next birthday. I asked if he had any pain.

"No pain but a deal of inconvenience. I am forbidden to move my head and am sometimes wakened at night by hammering noises inside it. I sleep best during the day."

After chatting with him about the weather and our acquaintances I returned to the surgeon's office. I told him that my friend seemed surprisingly fit for a man in his condition and asked who was responsible for the improvement.

"Agents," said the surgeon slowly, "who seem to inhabit the undamaged parts of his anatomy, only emerging to operate on him when nobody is looking – nobody like us, I mean. I am carefully keeping students and younger doctors away from this case. Mere curiosity might lead them to kill your friend by delving into what they understand as little as I do."

"There are obviously more things in heaven and earth," I said, "than are dreamed of in your . . ."

The surgeon interrupted testily, saying every experienced medical practitioner knew that better than

Shakespeare. A year seldom passed without them encountering at least one inexplicable case. A hospital he would not name recently treated a woman, otherwise normal, for panic attacks caused by her certainty that a sudden shock would crack her into a million pieces. When every other therapy had failed a psychiatrist, thinking a practical demonstration might work, suddenly tripped her so that she fell on a padded surface which could not have injured a child, and she had cracked into a million pieces.

"With tact," said the surgeon, "your friend's case may have a happier conclusion."

It did. A month later the wound had been closed. Skin grew over it, a new ear, also a few strands of the white hair which elsewhere surrounds Dr Mac-Leod's bald pink dome. He returned home and we meet once more for regular chess games. His character seems in no way changed by the accident. I am sometimes tempted to tell him that he is worked from inside by smaller people and always refrain in case it spoils his play. But maybe it would have no effect at all. Like many Christians he believes that a healthy body is a gift from God, no matter how it works. And like most men he has always thought himself unique.

INCHES IN A COLUMN

I read this story many years ago in a newspaper. It had no big headline and filled very few inches but I cannot forget it.

A London lawcourt sentenced a man to several years' imprisonment because, not for the first time, he had been found guilty of getting money by false pretences. Handcuffed to a policeman he was driven to the yard of a London gaol; there the cuff round the policeman's wrist was unlocked before being attached to a warder's. At that moment our man broke free and ran through the yard gateway which was still open. In the road outside a taxi stood at traffic lights which were about to change. Our man leapt in giving the name of an expensive hotel. The cab accelerated. He was free.

Though the paper did not say so I suspect this sequence took less than a minute and he entered the taxi with pursuers close behind. If they saw the taxi drive off the story is certainly from days before taxis had radios. Not till later that afternoon had the driver reason to think anything was wrong.

Our man's position was this: he was penniless with the police in pursuit of him and a right hand he must keep in his pocket to hide the handcuffs locked to its wrist. He was being driven without luggage to the Ritz or Dorchester or Royal Hilton by someone who would expect payment. If he jumped out at lights before reaching the hotel the driver also would start chasing him. His only advantage was a voice and manner which persuaded folk he was rich.

On the way to the hotel he asked if the driver had other business that day. The driver said no. Our man said, good, in that case he would hire the cab for the afternoon, but first they must have lunch. They entered the hotel where our man told the cabby (who probably wore the peaked cap worn by most London cabbies and chauffeurs in those days) to sit down in the foyer lounge. He then went to the reception counter, gave a false but impressive name, booked a room for the week and explained that his luggage would arrive from abroad later that afternoon. He was very particular in ordering a room facing the quiet side of the hotel and in arranging that a hot-water bottle be put in his bed at 11.30 exactly, since he would soon be going out and might return late. Meanwhile he ordered for himself and his driver a snack lunch of sandwiches and champagne to be served in the foyer lounge, also a racing newspaper. The waiter who served the champagne would also naturally pour the first glass so our man was able to eat and drink with his left hand only. He asked the cabby to look through the paper and tell him what races were on that afternoon. The fact that he asked others to do everything for him must have made him a more convincing member of the British officer class. He decided to be driven to Epsom or Ascot or Goodwood – I cannot remember the racecourse, perhaps the report I read failed to mention it. On the journey there he borrowed money from the driver, saying he would cash a cheque later, and in the crowd at the races he managed to lose the driver in a way that seemed accidental.

But the police knew his methods of work and had phoned hotels until they found the one where he had booked a room. His order of a racing paper gave a clue to his destination. When two plain-clothes policemen suddenly grabbed him in the crowd he played his last trick. Pulling his right hand from his pocket he waved the cuff locked to his wrist in the air by its chain and in commanding tones shouted to everyone around, "I am a police officer! Help! Help me arrest these criminals!"

The trick did not work. Our man was again brought to court where a judge added more time to his first jail sentence. The taxi driver, appearing as witness, said his day with the swindler had been one of the pleasantest in his life.

Were I writing this story as fiction I might imagine the driver saying that but would leave it out. Such details are too sentimental for convincing fiction.

The whole incident tells a lot about the British class system but hints at something greater. Sooner or later most of us find life a desperate effort to postpone meeting the foe who will one day catch and shut us up forever. I prefer the reckless and witty hero of this short story to more famous confidence men who are sometimes praised, sometimes blamed but always celebrated in longer newspaper articles, and official biographies, and history books.

I hope he thoroughly enjoyed his last taste of champagne.

A LIKELY STORY OUTSIDE A DOMESTIC SETTING

"Listen, you owe me an explanation. We've had such great times together – you're beautiful – you know I love you – and now you don't want to see me again. Why? Why?"
"Jings, you take everything very seriously."

A LIKELY STORY WITHIN A DOMESTIC SETTING

"Fuck who you like but the rent is overdue and the electricity is going to be cut off and we've no food and the baby is hungry."
"Our love once meant much more to me than money so I'm not giving you any."

ACKNOWLEDGEMENTS

Dr Philip Hobsbaum helped write the poem near the end of *Five Letters From An Eastern Empire*. A third of *Logopandocy* is edited from pamphlets Sir Thomas Urquhart published when imprisoned in the Tower of London, with additional phrases from the Earl of Clarendon, John Milton, Edward Philips, John Aubrey and Malcolm Hood; also some Greek neologisms devised by Janet Sisson. Tina Reid let parts of her letters be used in *Prometheus*. *A Likely Story Outside A Domestic Setting* is from a reminiscence by Jim Hutcheson, and half of the story within one from a poem by Fred Humble. Both the *Axletree* stories and *Five Letters* are decorative expansions of what Kafka outlined perfectly in *The City Coat of Arms* and *The Great Wall of China*.

Illustrations in this book are drawn from work by Paul Klee, Michelangelo, Raphael, Piranesi, G. Glover, W. Blake, E. H. Shepherd and a Japanese artist whose name has no agreed phonetic equivalent in Roman type. Doreen and Russel Logan kindly allowed their portraits to be used in the scurrilous context of the last two likely stories.

The complicated parts of the book were made possible by the exact typing of Donald Goodbrand Saunders and Scott Pearson, by the free use of John McInespie's photocopying machine, by the bibliographic skill of Jim Hutcheson, and the patience of John Hewer, the typesetter.

Author's Postscript Completed
by Douglas Gifford

The notion of writing a story book struck me at the age of nine or maybe earlier because for what seemed a long time I meant to astonish the reading public by getting it published before I was twelve. Unluckily everything I wrote before the age of sixteen was obviously the work of a child or pretentious adolescent. I knew this by comparing it with Hans Andersen's tales. These were as fantastic as I wanted my own to be, but contained pains and losses too strong to be doubted. 'The Star' was my first story which did not seem silly when compared with (for instance) Andersen's 'Drop of Ditchwater'.

It was also the first story written in a gust of what felt like inspiration. The critic Leavis suggests that inspiration is unconscious memory – that well-made writing only comes without effort when authors instinctively adapt work by earlier writers. Two decades passed before I noticed 'The Star' had been inspired by H. G. Wells's story 'The Crystal Egg', in which the henpecked owner of a seedy little curio shop finds consolation in a lens which allows glimpses of life on another planet. He dies while hiding it from potential purchasers and his rapacious wife. My (unconscious) imagination easily turned this poor man into a lonely child in a bleak Glasgow tenement, his wife into a teacher. I then lived in what I thought was a middle-class tenement and had mainly friendly teachers, but felt a more painful life than mine more likely to interest readers. One advantage 'The Star' has over 'The Crystal Egg' is terseness. My tale of an obscure hero trying to keep a magic gift was hardly two pages; Wells used about a dozen. I did not know how my tale would end before describing the teacher demand the magic gift. It resembled one of those coloured glass balls Scots children call bools or jinkies, English children call marbles. Had I made the teacher treat it as that the reader might suppose all the magic was in the boy's imagination and therefore unreal. Since every human invention, religion and institution was first imagined I disliked stories that reduced imagination to delusion so was pleased and astonished to find three last sentences that left the star as real as the teacher. I suspect they were inspired by the endings of 'The Little Match Girl' and 'The Little Mermaid'.

My plan to publish at the age of twelve was the first of many failed literary plans. A later one led to the title of this collection.

In 1981 I was forty-six years old. My first novel had been published by Canongate of Edinburgh. I was finishing a book for the same firm to be called *Unlikely Stories, Mostly*. It would contain (I thought) all the short narratives I had ever written in the order of writing them and use every known literary form: tales of mystery and imagination, love stories, comic lectures, diary, film-script, autobiography. But fantasies would outnumber the other sorts, hence the title. This plan was upset because one of the most realistic stories (a monologue by a middle-aged alcoholic electrician) expanded into an unintended second novel called *1982 Janine*. At my publisher's suggestion the remaining probable stories were also omitted for use in yet another book. They became the nucleus of *Lean Tales*, a collection eventually shared with James Kelman and Agnes Owens. But being fond of the title *Unlikely Stories, Mostly* I forged an excuse for the third word by inserting, at the last possible moment, two nasty wee likely tales about the course of a love affair. And thus the collection was printed and reprinted for fourteen years until this Canongate Classics edition.

To boost it I have inserted two stories more: 'A Unique Case' and 'Inches in a Column'. The first was written in 1954 or '55 for *Cleg*, a Glasgow art student magazine of one number edited by James Spence. Printed by a stencil process on flimsy paper, all copies seemed to have vanished until a friend of mine found one in a second-hand bookshop a few months ago. It is printed here with a few improvements suggested by the passage of forty and more years. 'Inches in a Column' was written in

1994. It seem highly unlikely but is true to a factual newspaper report on which I based it.

From 'The Star' to 'Inches in a Column' I see all my writing is about personal imagination and social power, or (to put it more crudely) freedom and government. Variety comes from neither side being simply right or wrong. Both are essential. This is as true of 'The Problem', 'The Comedy of the White Dog' and 'Prometheus', in which freedom and control are swapped between two individuals.

But self-love stops authors from impartially judging their work in detail so –

At this point Alasdair Gray broke off to ask me, Douglas Gifford, to end his essay because he was falling behind with his *Anthology of Prefaces*, and because he considered that a professional teacher and critic "could give information more briskly than a fiction writer". Knowing well that a major and satirical theme of Gray's work expresses fundamental suspicion of the repressive role of institutional organisation and indoctrination, I suspected a trap; after all, given the information above concerning the genesis of 'Five Letters from an Eastern Empire', and given that I teach at that very institution which Gray suggests as a model for his spiritually and creatively claustrophobic city, was my aid not being solicited in a fiendishly clever and ironic fashion so that I would act as limiting and pedantic commentator on the collection in the manner of one of his Chinese Headmasters of Literature, thus illustrating his point that Promethean creativity is inevitably cabined and confined by dismantling criticism?

I believe this to be the case; but part of Gray's cleverness lies in his acute diagnosis that, having perceived his trap, I would yet be too much flattered by being even a minuscule part of his achievement to resist.

So I give in, hoping to turn his manipulation into a warning to the reader to read behind the apparent transparency of his elegant and classical style to perceive allegories and trickeries which sustain a unified pair of themes. These are, I believe, to be found throughout his work (the chronology of writing of which is notoriously difficult to work out), and they are on the one hand a surface, but very powerful and Swiftian satire on the injustice and lack of empathetic imagination of the ruling organisations of Western (and all?) human society; and on the other, an underlying admission, expressed through many protagonists and situations, of a deep personal loneliness and a disarming admission of inadequacy in matters of love and art.

Gray has admitted (*Glasgow Herald*, December 6, 1986) that he (and his close friend, the artist Alan Fletcher, who was killed while young) is a recurrent protagonist in his fictions; and *Lanark* (1981), his colossal blend of fantasy, science fiction, *Bildungsroman* and social satire, bears this out with its barely concealed clues that Duncan Thaw, the "real" identity behind all the other versions in nightmare or limbo, has much in common in his Glasgow upbringing and emotional, intellectual and artistic development with the Gray who likewise grew up in years of wartime austerity and family suffering. The other great novels which juxtapose fantasy and satire, *1982, Janine* (1984) and *Poor Things* (1992) also play with this blend of personal and perhaps therapeutic exploration and impersonal commentary on repressive and excessive social authority. An essential shyness causes Gray to simultaneously reveal and conceal himself in his novels and stories, using deception and sleight of hand to tantalise the reader who is continually invited close, then distanced through false voices, withdrawal, and retreat to literary allusion and trickery.

Unlikely Stories, Mostly shows Gray at his elusive best, from its initial bibliographical and typographical trickery to its deepest layers of personal concealment and revelation. On first publication, *Unlikely Stories* had an erratum slip which mocked pedantic correction in its ingenuous 'This erratum slip has been inserted by mistake', and the dust jacket lampooned the ineffectuality of brief authorial biography while allowing Gray as author to slip away:

He was
            and educated
        and became
                        residing
        and remaining
                    and intending
        then on
            became   in
                    and again

But alongside this refusal to fill in the personal gaps ran a more positive social message urging the reader to radical national and personal reconsideration: handsomely printed in gold on its royal blue hard binding, the first edition bore emblematic thistles, with the exhortation:

WORK AS IF YOU WERE
LIVING IN THE EARLY DAYS
OF A BETTER NATION
SCOTLAND   1983

Gray has always enjoyed such antithetical deceptions, exploiting a vast range of literary precedents ranging from the native tradition of James Hogg to that of international modernists like Kurt Vonnegut. As the 'Index to Plagiarisms' of *Lanark* abundantly shows, private creativity works in tension with very public identification of models, from Bunyan and Cervantes to Stevenson and Kafka. But the reader should be aware that behind all the superficial trickery and literary camouflage lies a deeply serious, if paradoxical, agenda: the fundamental questioning of his own unstable position in an unstable world, along with a very Scottish yearning, doomed to almost complete disappointment, for spiritual value and authority.

Many of the stories in *Unlikely Stories* appeared before 1960, and most were written before 1980. Some stories, like 'The Comedy of the White Dog' or 'The Cause of Some Recent Changes', show a love of surrealism and fantasy and the absurdly comic, but without much attempt to explore the relationship of a sick self to a sick society. That said, Gray's enduring love of human metamorphosis on physical and spiritual levels is well seen throughout the early stories. A man splits in two, becoming two identical men; a dog metamorphoses into a sinister and bestial lover, in an urban and modern version of Leda and the Swan, with a disturbingly nasty psychological symbolism; a boy becomes a star; an art school becomes a gateway to an underground world, causing changes in clock speeds and earthquakes which disintegrate the planet. But with 'The Crank that Made the Revolution' and 'The Great Bear Cult' Gray began to move into new territory, 'The Crank' introducing the first of a series of Scottish and other eccentrics who would recur in this volume, and would be writ large in *Lanark* and *Poor Things*, and 'The Bear Cult' opening up Gray's series of social satires. Self and society emerge here as Gray's two main preoccupations, a movement from fantasy and grotesque surrealism for its own sake towards a much more ambitious reconciliation of the autobiographical and personally therapeutic with the socially and politically satirical, of the private with the public. And five stories from the volume seem to me to be amongst his very best work, and to belong to the same period as *Lanark*. These deeply serious satirical allegories in the second half of the book form a five-part sequence, with a recognisably different orientation from the previous tales. Now the narrator announces that he writes 'for those who know my language', signalling a new desire to communicate with readers who have taken the trouble to "tune in", to read between the stories to see the deepening seriousness of this new Scottish blend of myth and satirical allegory.

In 'The Start of the Axletree', the axletree is Gray's powerful symbol for the manipulation of religion and social class for its own selfish ends by centralised imperial power. The dubious achievement of the Emperor is to transform the hub of his "last and greatest world empire" into this axletree, creating a monstrous and vertical Holy City. By giving them the task of endlessly building their city ever higher, in the impossible aim of reaching the sky, he motivates his followers and descendants for all time. To what extent does Gray mean us to recognise British Imperialism in his allegory? Is he creating a timeless story-myth of all the world's capitalism and empire-building? It is the mark of Gray's development as a major writer that he is able to leave his allegory open-ended, signifying so many possible readings.

When Gray turns from social satire in these stories to focus on a central protagonist, there's a curious ambivalence in his recurrent treatment of the figure which can be found throughout his fiction, from Kelvin Walker to Lanark and Jock McLeish. The figures are wise and foolish, flawed human beings and conscientious citizens, Holy Fools of a kind found frequently in Scottish fiction, from Galt's *Sir Andrew Wylie* through MacDonald's *Sir Gibbie* to modern versions in Iain Crichton Smith's fiction and the later work of Robin Jenkins. This Holy Fool, with his confused and ambiguous feelings about the nature of secular and religious Grace, illustrates a deep unease on the part of these Scottish authors towards their society's moral standards and religious heritage. In Gray's presentation, the significance of the figure lies in two directions, in being implicitly auto-biographical; and in the way the biography is handled. Three of the five later stories here illustrate this.

'Five Letters from an Eastern Empire' is one of Gray's most polished satirical allegories. Bohu is the tragic poet of the empire. Tohu is his much smaller, meaner comic counterpart. In an unplaced, timeless, vaguely Chinese background, with an apparently benign Emperor organising a rigidly demarcated society of palaces, gardens, lakes, walls, and humble dwellings, organised on a chequer-board pattern, Bohu moves on huge clogs, pampered, wooden, priggish, yet naively honest, to his destiny; which is to be gulled by the Emperor into writing the shortest of tragic poems – which the Emperor then deploys to justify genocide.

The parallels here with *Lanark* are clear, even in the relationship of Bohu to his parents. There is the same well-meaning concern on their part, the same sense of alienation and sad love, and in both cases the parents seem pathetically small

figures, victims of a system they haven't remotely compre-
hended. Bohu is "honoured" and invested with his orders, just
as Lanark becomes a doctor (and as Duncan Thaw became an
art student). Bohu's weird robes and rituals are his society's
way of placing him above the common herd; Lanark has the
institutional bruise-mark upon his brow. All this fits the theme
of the five-story sequence, that of the misuse of power –
centralisation, privilege and snobbery: "Were you born outside the rim?" is the question asked by those who live inside the
great wheel. Just so Bohu condescends to Tohu, his servants
and lesser mortals. Is all this a mythic statement concerning the
inevitable exploitation of the artist by his society, and, more
locally, the Scottish artist's essentially irrelevant role in his
community? Or is Gray representing the role of the creative
artists in modern capitalist society, seeing them exploited and
becoming, as Althusser described them, "state reinforcing
apparatuses"? And looking more closely at Bohu, one dis-
covers a familiar figure, camouflaged by his unfamiliar territory, but in the end not unlike Kelvin Walker, the innocent and
wise fool, or, even more, Lanark, self-important as ambassador
of Unthank to Provan and the Council, but in fact a laughing
stock who is being used by more worldly operators for their
own ends, exactly as the emperor uses Bohu. A debilitating
sense of the futility of personal belief and action runs throughout these fables.

And nowhere does the ambivalent Holy Fool appear more
eccentric than in 'Logopandocy', the study of one of Scotland's
most endearing eccentrics, Sir Thomas Urquhart of Cromarty,
"the mirror of perfection", as he sees himself, in knightly
attainment of the seventeenth century. Gray's scholastic wit
revels in this presentation of 'The Secret and Apocryphal
Diurnal'. It would be easy to miss the concealed identification
with Urquhart that lies behind this charming, sad, bizarre
account of the progress of a Wise Fool; easy, too, to miss the
amount of Scottish satire, the detailed (but ultimately hopelessly confused) self-assessment by Thomas in the uproarious
'Pro Me/Contra Me' inventory of his assets. Here, for the first
time, a Fool and his foolish countrymen are fully seen,

squandering their talents abroad, fighting for opposite sides
and causes, wilfully wasting themselves. Urquhart's Logopandocy outlandishly applies Napier's logarithms "to the grammar
of an Asiatick people, thought to be the lost tribe of Israel,
whose language predates the Babylonic cataclysm" with the
end of "rationally reintegering God's gift of tongues to Adam".
It is the pursuit of the goal of Alchemy in language, a linguistic
Fool's Gold, and on this and such quests the noble Urquhart
destroys himself.

Or does he? A question arises now that was hinted at in
Bohu's final useless act of integrity, his brief tragic poem – and
one which arises concerning Lanark's final achievement, and
Jock McLeish's hard decisions in *Janine*. Is there, for all his
posturing irrelevance, a point of self-recognition, of socially
useless yet personally valid choice, which, in its final statement
of truth, is the only significant possibility in a lunatic- and
power-distorted world? Thomas disintegrates in a mental
breakdown which can be compared with those of Thaw and
McLeish. Gray apparently redeems Thomas's tragi-comedy by
saving him from his historical death and allowing him to find
love in a strange land. But don't be misled. The journey of
these five stories is not over. The non-literary material, the
illustrations between stories, now reveal their thematic func-
tion, which is to link the apparently disparate narratives,
making them parts of a bigger and concealed story about a
meta-protagonist, shadowy behind unlikely stories, telling
indirectly of his background quest for meaning and love. On
the flyleaf, an eccentric looking knight sails in a silly boat,
blown by a zephyr; then, sword extended, perches precariously
but defiantly, at its prow as the book opens. An inscrutable
wizened Emperor-face (Gray? The saint of 'The Start of the
Axletree'? Emblem of the centralised power Gray so hates?)
broods over all, watching the audacious human voyager; the
voyager decays (note the richly-cuffed knightly hand becoming
impoverished, gnarled, enclosed by a hand of love). But, while
that is the last we hear in the story of Thomas Urquhart,
seventeenth-century Scot, in fact his journey isn't over. The
drawings which began in the fly-leaf continue, Thomas's boat

is blown on, and, transmogrified, reappears in the next story 'Prometheus', in the twin guises of Prometheus and modern French thinker and poet Monsieur Pollard, "shy, fastidious, and arrogant". Thomas had thought himself "come to the edge of the greatest and happiest discovery of my life" at the end of his account; Pollard thinks that he has just encountered a lady who can be sexual partner and witness to his elevated thought and life.

Nothing could seem less personal than these stories, grotesque and distant from the world of a Glasgow Art College student of the 1950s. But the Nastler-Creator of *Lanark* is a wilful and wayward conjuror, and in fact Parisian intellectual Pollard is yet another version of Duncan Thaw, Bohu, Kelvin Walker, McLeish, Lanark, Thomas Urquhart. Pollard's "I can only represent Gods, and lonely intelligences, and multitudes viewed from a very great distance . . . To pay the printers . . . I went shabby and hungry . . ." surely recalls the similar complaints of Lanark, Thaw and Nastler? Even closer to home and to Duncan Thaw is Pollard's student career; "I depressed my professors at the Sorbonne by finally submitting no thesis. A poet need not truck with bureaucrats." But a new and yet more striking identification also enters here. Gray has Pollard explicitly link his loneliness with that of God, and his proud intellectual separation from humanity with God's. "My infancy resembled that of God, my ancestor", he tells us. Behind this "joke" of Pollard lies a strange metaphysic of Gray's, which will extend itself in the Gray-Nastler-Lanark-Thaw manipulations of the novel and become most sophisticated in Jock McLeish's recognition of God within himself, the inner voice which stops his suicide in *Janine*. This story marks the introduction of this final, spiritually enigmatic theme, which enables Gray to envisage a possible and positive ending to his Urquhart-like quest.

Pollard's story doesn't reach the qualified optimism of passages of *Lanark* or the stern acceptance of self in *Janine*. Pollard (the name suiting his human insufficiency, his blighted growth) fails in his attempt to find love, since Lucie will not

accept his estimate of himself as mirrored in the myth of
Prometheus, nor will she surrender to the intolerable self-
ishness which will use her as supporting *anima*. She tells him
that he is "the cleverest, most deluded man I have ever met.
Rewriting *Prometheus Unbound* is like rewriting *Genesis*, it can
be done but who needs it? It is just another effort to put good
wine in a filthy old bottle." Both Pollard and Lucie recognise
the sham of his "divine" vocation, his noble destiny. She
reduces his grandiose self-projections to what could be seen
as their only reality:

> My poor dwarf, you are the last nineteenth-century
> romantic liberal. That is why corrupt government wishes
> to make you a national institution. Which brings me,
> beloved, to what you REALLY want from me: cunt. In
> your eyes it probably looks like an entrance to the human
> race . . .

The Holy Fool is often reduced in Gray's work by the
ferocious female. What emerges is a profoundly personal
statement of despair about the mismatch of human needs
and longings. Beautiful girls love worthless men; the central
figure finds increasingly that talent and intelligence are no
guarantee of success in sexual and emotional relations. Thus
the identification with God is both admission of failure (who
wants a relationship with something so inhuman?) and consolation for that failure. The story ends with a howl of anguish
– trapped by the earthy manageress, his unloved mistress, he
cries out:

> Lucie, if you do not return I must fall forever into her abyss
> . . . Oh Lucie Lucie Lucie save me from her. The one word
> this poem exists to clarify is lonely. I am Prometheus. I am
> lonely . . .

And Gray's carefully arranged illustrations and emblems
now begin to tail off, till, after the drawing of Prometheus,
naked, arms outstretched, falling, we are left with final drawings of the voyaging knight, now an old man, sailing on stoically
till – watch the endpapers – he's last seen edging past Arran,
past Ailsa Craig which carries a sign (his destination?)

"Glasgow 78 miles". Thus Gray slyly connects his allegories to home. 'Prometheus' was even more revealing of this connection. While Lucie had read through Pollard's version of the myth of Prometheus, recognising his distortion of the myth for his own sexual and emotional needs, Pollard had waited, vultures tearing at his liver, for her response – which was rejection. "Pollard" then makes his final revelation.

> This story is a poem, a wordgame. I am not a highly literate French dwarf, my lost woman is not a revolutionary writer manqué, my details are fictions, only my meaning is true and I must make that meaning clear by playing the wordgame to the bitter end.

Who is speaking? It must be the author behind Pollard. Who is that? We can't simply say 'Gray' – for *Lanark* shows us there can be authors behind authors behind authors. Gray's allegories express yet conceal their continual agonising over a basic human situation in which a highly talented but socially eccentric and physically unattractive protagonist has to realise that his idealistic Promethean aspiration after truth and justice and beauty may finally be seen as self-interested sexual desire dressed up to look good.

There's even further satire on Gray's part, in that Pollard's great project, the completion of Aeschylus's lost *Prometheus Unbound*, isn't even original. Gray knows of Shelley's 1820 version, of course, and how Shelley's sentiments anticipate Pollard's. Clearly Pollard is being shown as a derivative egotist rather than an original genius. When one places this alongside Gray's mockery of his own literary creativity (and of course, his mockery of literary criticism) in his "Index of Plagiarisms" in *Lanark*, the full paradox of Gray's literary achievement can be recognised. It is an achievement which rests on Gray's perception of his own creativity which constantly questions the validity of that creativity, and questions the emotional and sexual motivation behind it, firstly in relation to himself, and thereafter in relation to writers and artists at large.

'Prometheus' is thus an important personal statement,

expressing succinctly Gray's private world of self-doubt and anxiety, and yet marvellously creating literature while anatomising what lies behind the act. The final story, 'The End of the Axletree', moves from personal analysis to public satire, completing Gray's essential dualism of theme throughout the volume. Taking up where the Emperor left off, the fable tells how the great vertical city finally reached the sky, which is found to be tangible, a great canopy enclosing the world. Men, of course, can't leave it alone, and (in a marvellous allegory for human greed and destructiveness from the beginning of property-holding to wars and space programmes and their place in political economy) they tear it open, drowning the world in a new Flood. Thus the overall story of the volume is ended; as in *Lanark* and *Janine*, "man is the pie that bakes and eats itself, and the recipe is separation". We war with ourselves, with our society; full of sound and fury, we signify very little, as individuals, artists, societies. We are right to mock our pretensions, destroying ourselves and the earth we live on. And yet, and yet . . . something in the all too tragi-comic lives of Bohu, Urquhart, Pollard – and Lanark, and Kelvin Walker, and Jock McLeish – remains to suggest a glimmer of the transcendental, allowing God, just for the moment to be forgiven, as in the fleeting epiphany given to Lanark as he watches his son climb Ben Rua in sunlight. At the end of *Unlikely Stories, Mostly* it's typical of Gray to leave a benign sting in the tale, lying just beyond literature. The survivor of the volume, the archetypal quixotic Scot, Sir Thomas Urquhart, sails on through time, his little boat moving out over the endpapers, a glimmer of hope in a grotesque world.

Douglas Gifford

WORK AS IF YOU LIVE IN THE EARLY DAYS OF A BETTER NATION 1997

James Bliss
drew this
picture of
Alasdair Gray
9 August 1981

GOODBYE